Love Shouldn't Hurt 4

Lock Down Publications and Ca$h
Presents
Love Shouldn't Hurt 4
A Novel by *Meesha*

Lock Down Publications
P.O. Box 870494
Mesquite, Tx 75187

Visit our website @
www.lockdownpublications.com

Lock Down Publications
Like our page on Facebook: Lock Down Publications @
www.facebook.com/lockdownpublications.ldp
Cover design and layout by: **Dynasty Cover Me**
Book interior design by: **Shawn Walker**
Edited by: **Tisha Andrews**

Stay Connected with Us!

Text **LOCKDOWN** to 22828 to stay up-to-date with new releases, sneak peaks, contests and more…

Thank you.

Submission Guideline.

Submit the first three chapters of your completed manuscript to ldpsubmissions@gmail.com, subject line: Your book's title. The manuscript must be in a .doc file and sent as an attachment. Document should be in Times New Roman, double spaced and in size 12 font. Also, provide your synopsis and full contact information. If sending multiple submissions, they must each be in a separate email.

Have a story but no way to send it electronically? You can still submit to LDP/Ca$h Presents. Send in the first three chapters, written or typed, of your completed manuscript to:

LDP: Submissions Dept
Po Box 870494
Mesquite, Tx 75187

DO NOT send original manuscript. Must be a duplicate.

Provide your synopsis and a cover letter containing your full contact information.

Thanks for considering LDP and Ca$h Presents.

Meesha

Chapter 1

Montez

"Code blue! Code blue! Dr. Brim, we're losing her!"

I'm not an expert in the medical field, but I knew what that term meant. Something was definitely wrong. How did I go from hearing my baby girl let out her first cry, to machines beeping uncontrollably because my wife had flatlined on the delivery table? Racing to Poetry's side, one of the nurses grabbed my arm and pushed me toward the door.

"What are you doing? I have to check on my wife!" I yelled, yanking away from her.

"Sir, in order for us to help her, I need you to step out of the room so we can do our job! Please, do *that* for your wife," the nurse said with fear in her eyes.

I didn't want to leave, but I didn't have a choice. Glancing back at Poetry, tears clouded my vision as I stepped out of the room. Before the door closed, a team of nurses rolled my daughter out of the room and I looked down at her. She was the spitting image of her mother but had my caramel complexion. She was so beautiful. Her doe shaped eyes held a sense of sadness as if she knew something was wrong. I bent down and kissed her forehead and a tear fell on her little cheek.

"I love you, baby," I choked out before they rushed her to the nursery.

The shades were drawn inside the delivery room and I couldn't see shit. My nerves were at an all time high because of my fear of losing Poetry after everything we had endured and it was killing me. The last couple of months we had, danced vividly in my mind and I tried to shake them away. I didn't want memories. I wanted my wife.

I could hear the doctor and nurses scrambling about inside the room and I had no idea what was going on. A group of doctors in scrubs raced down the hall with a defibrillator machine and my heart fell to my feet. That was a sign that Poetry still wasn't breathing. As the group entered the room, I peeked inside and Dr. Brim was administering compressions to Poetry's chest. She was lying lifeless as the machines continued to scream. Entering the room, I couldn't take my eyes off her.

"I'm here, baby! Hold on for me, Poe! I love you!" I screamed as a nurse pushed back into the hall.

"Mr. Williams! I need you to go tell your family what's going on," the nurse said solemnly.

"What the fuck am I supposed to tell them, huh? I don't know what's going on!" I yelled. "That's my soulmate in there fighting for her fuckin' life!" I fell to my knees and let out a cry I'd never heard before. My heart felt as if it was being ripped from my chest.

The nurse placed her hand on my shoulder. "Your wife's heart stopped, but we are doing everything we can to stabilize her. She flatlined three times, but we got her back and that was from chest compressions. We have the defibrillator and pray it keeps her heart going. We won't give up, Mr. Williams," the nurse explained. "Deliver that news to your family and Dr. Brim will be out as soon as she can to give you an update."

The nurse went back into the room and I closed my eyes, letting the tears roll freely down my face. I wasn't a praying nigga, but I needed a higher power at that moment. There was no other place to go at that point but to God. I was afraid Poetry wasn't going to make it, but it was out of my hands. In the middle of the corridor on my knees, I prayed like never before.

"Please, Lord. Save my wife. We have so much to accomplish together and our daughter needs her mama. I know the life I've lived wasn't right, but I'm done with all that, I promise. It's all behind me and I'm ready to be the best husband and father I can be. I'm begging you to place life back into Poetry and let her live.

There's so much she has to experience on earth, Lord. It may be selfish, but I don't want her to leave me. It's too soon. We haven't had the chance to be happy as husband and wife. You have to give me the chance to make things right with her! Lord, we need you now. If anyone can change the direction of this day, I know you can. Amen."

I cried until my face felt like I had a facial mask on. Getting up off the floor, I walked and placed my hand on the window before I made my way to the waiting room to deliver the news to everyone. Moving my feet was a hard task at that moment. All the energy I had going into the delivery room was gone as I left. My heart was so heavy. I didn't know how I was going to tell Mrs. Chris and Stan that their daughter was fighting for her life.

Pushing the doors open, I walked slowly into the room and everyone was there. Kaymee was the first to notice me coming out. She stood and all eyes were trained in my direction. My throat felt like it was closing up and I was struggling to breathe. Mrs. Chris rose from her seat with tears in her eyes. Her hands were pressed together tightly in front of her face as she walked toward me.

"Monty, what's wrong? Did Poetry have the baby?" she asked in a shaky voice.

I couldn't do anything other than shake my head up and down, taking a deep breath. "She had a beautiful baby girl that looks just like her," I croaked. "Poetry isn't doing too good," I said as tears fell from my eyes.

"What do you mean she's not doing good? Where's my baby, Monty!" Mrs. Chris cried out.

"They had to do an emergency cesarean and when my baby girl was delivered, Poetry—Poetry—the machines started beeping as soon as the baby cried. Dr. Brim started chest compressions and they pushed me out the room. I can't lose her man," I cried as I fell against the door.

"What are you trying to say, Monty? Chest compressions? What happened in there?" Poetry's mother screamed as she wrapped her arms around me.

I knew I had to get myself together because Kaymee was crying and Stan, Poetry's dad, had a grim look on his face. Jonathan and Katrina walked up, as well as G, Scony, and the rest of the clan. Los hugged Kaymee and she turned and cried in his chest.

Everyone was waiting for me to tell them what was going on with my wife. Clearing my throat, I wiped my nose on my arm and stared Mrs. Chris in her eyes.

"Poetry flatlined three times and they brought her back," I choked out.

"Oh my God!" Mrs. Chris screamed as she started crying harder. "The doctors were still working on her when I came out here to tell you guys. It's not looking good, but we will not give up on her. She's a fighter and she will be alright. I know because she didn't marry me to leave me alone. We have a baby to raise," I said in between sobs.

"I need to see her, Stan!" her mama cried.

"Chris, if they put Monty out, there's no way we will be able to see her until they come out to get us. I want you to prepare yourself for whatever they say when they come out here. We won't question anything God has planned," Stan said, closing his eyes. His mouth moved rapidly and I could tell he was silently praying.

Glancing to my left, Kaymee was crying her heart out. I knew her pain oh so well. I walked over to her and held her tightly. I felt her tears soaking my shirt, but I didn't care. Poetry was her best friend and I knew she was hurting. Kaymee's body went limp and I was glad I was holding her. Jonathan ran to my side and we carried her to the sofa that was by the window.

"Go get a cold towel and some water from somewhere!" Jonathan barked. "Kaymee, baby," he said, tapping her cheek lightly.

Her eyes were rolling behind her eyelids, but they didn't open. Nova came back with a handful of wet paper towels and used them to wipe her face and neck. Kaymee's eyes fluttered open and she looked around in a daze.

"I'm okay," she said, trying to sit up.

"Lay back, Kaymee," Jonathan said calmly. "You fainted and I want you to relax."

"I need to check on Poetry," she said with tears in her eyes.

"We have to wait for the doctor to come out and let us know what's going on," Mrs. Chris said, sitting next to her on the couch.

10

"I don't want you to get sick on us, baby. This is hard for all of us and it's in God's hands at this point. She turned back to me and forced a smile. "Monty, tell us about the baby. How much does she weigh?"

"I don't know. I was only able to see her for a few seconds before they took her to the nursery. I've heard so many happy birth stories from some of the homies and none of them were ever like this. Poetry heard the baby cry and it seemed like she waited to make sure baby girl was good before she flatlined," I said with fresh tears forming in my eyes. "I didn't know if I should go to the baby or to my wife, so I chose my wife, but was turned away. The image of her lying on that bed is still etched in my mind. I felt so helpless because there was nothing I could do to make her better," I openly cried.

"Brah, don't beat yourself up," Los said, standing in front of me. "Like you said, Poetry is strong and she is a fighter. We are here to get you through this, but you have to keep faith."

"I'm with Los on this one, Monty. Poetry may not be my blood relative, but she has a place in my heart. The bond that she and Kaymee have, has automatically secured her a spot in my life. I'm here for you too," Jonathan said, giving me a brotherly hug. Everyone found a seat and all we could do was wait for someone to come out and give whatever news they had for us.

***

About an hour later, I was lying on three chairs I had put together to make a cot. I was expecting everyone to be gone, but the room was still packed with bodies sprawled wherever they landed. Kaymee had fallen asleep on the couch, Mrs. Chris was sitting with her head on Stan's shoulder, and Jonathan was standing up, looking out the window. Katrina was sleeping in a chair looking uncomfortable as hell while G was hugging his wife as she slept on his lap. Monica was sleeping in another chair with Jade next to her. Scony was doing something on his phone and Los was pacing back and forth.

Glancing down at my watch, it was one in the morning and the doctors still hadn't been out. I stood and walked toward the doors. "Monty, where are you going?" Jonathan asked.

"I need to check on my wife. It's been too long and nobody has been out to tell us anything," I said without looking back.

"That's a good sign, man. If anything happened, they would've come out and said something by now. Come sit down," he said, walking across the room.

"I should at least be able to go see my baby," I said, trying to find any excuse to leave the waiting room.

"Okay, I'll go with you," Jonathan said.

We walked down the hall and the door to the room Poetry had the baby in was opened. Peeking inside, it was cleaned and empty. My heart started beating fast as I rushed to the nurse's station. There were a couple of nurses sitting behind the counter either writing or tapping away at a computer. When I walked up, one of the nurses raised her head and waited for me to get closer.

"Mr. Williams, how may I help you?"

"I was trying to get an update on my wife. No one came out to tell me anything and I was worried," I said as calmly as I could.

"She's still in surgery—"

"Surgery! What happened?"

"I don't have any information for you, but as soon as I do, you and your family will be updated," the nurse said nicely.

"It would've been nice to know that she was having the surgery. Don't y'all need permission to do something like this?" I was pissed and I didn't try to hide it.

"Mr. Williams, your wife was rushed off as soon as she stabilized. There was no time to spare. It was a matter of life and death. The doctor will be able to answer all of your questions once she's finished in the operating room. In the meantime, let's go see your beautiful baby girl," she said, standing from the chair she was sitting in.

Leading us down the hall, she entered the nursery and allowed both Jonathan and myself to follow her. "Both of you scrub up and put on a gown," she said, rolling the baby across the room. We washed our hands and put on the gowns that were folded on the counter. I went over to the little bed and looked down at my sleeping beauty. She didn't have a worry in the world and she was so pretty.

"Damn, you didn't have nothing to do with that, fam. She looks just like Poetry with your bright ass skin," Jonathan said, laughing. "That will be short-lived too because look at the tip of her ears. They are dark. You are going to have two chocolate kisses in your household. They are going to be prejudice against yo' white ass."

We both laughed and the baby started moving around irritably. Before long, she was fussing. "Dad, you are right on time. You want to feed her?" the nurse asked.

I was scared because she was so small. I'd never handled a baby that size before, but there was no better time to learn than the present. Sitting in the recliner that sat beside the bed, I sat nervously watching the nurse reach in to pick her up.

"Here you go. Make sure you support her head at all times. Her neck isn't strong enough to do it on her own yet," she explained.

Cradling my daughter in my arms was the best feeling I ever had. While waiting for the nurse to bring me the bottle, I couldn't take my eyes off my little angel. She was still fussing and I had no idea how to make her stop. I started rocking her gently, hoping that would calm her, but it seemed to only make her cry louder.

"Hey, you too cute to be making all that noise," I spoke to her softly. "You gon' wake the other babies and daddy is gon' have to beat some ass up in here," I said with a laugh.

She stopped crying and looked up at me with those pretty doe eyes and smirked at me. I was falling in love with her with every second that went by. Bringing her to my face to give her a kiss, she placed her hand on my nose.

"We are starting her with four ounces of milk, but she may only drink two or three," the nurse said, walking over and handing me the tiny bottle.

Barely getting the nipple in her mouth, my baby started suck-ling on it right away. The nurse didn't know what the hell she was talking about because the baby I held in my arms was going to have an appetite just like her daddy. She was fucking that milk up and I was going to let her eat as much as she wanted. Jonathan looked on as I bonded with my first born.

"Monty, she is so beautiful. Have you thought of a name yet?" he asked as we continued to watch her eat.

"Poetry picked the name Aria and I agreed. We didn't come up with a middle name, but I think Aria Renee Williams will be her name."

"That's what's up, fam. I think that is a great idea to give Po-etry's middle name as her own. Look at how she's hanging on to your every word like she knows you're talking about her. I remember when Kaymee was that size. I always had her in my arms until Dot's ass started acting crazy," he said, shaking his head.

"Speaking of Dot, have you heard anything about her nutty ass?" I asked.

"Nah, the last time I heard anything was when Kaymee told me she called for some money. Supposedly, she needed it because she was getting evicted from her apartment and needed nine hundred dollars. Dot put her foot in her mouth and started talking shit, so Kaymee hung up on her after telling her ass off."

"Dot ain't never gon' be right, man. Tell Mee to stop answer-ing the phone for her ignorant ass, man," I said, glancing down at Aria. She had finished all the milk and fell asleep. "Excuse me," I said lowly to the nurse. She walked over after changing one of the other babies and I handed her the bottle.

"She did good! You have to burp her now. Do you know how to do that?" she asked.

I had never done it myself, but I'd seen it done. Placing Aria on the blanket, the nurse draped over my shoulder. I patted her on the back a few times before she burped loudly. She snuggled under my chin and I inhaled her scent, never wanting to let her go.

"I'll change her diaper and lay her back down, unless you just want to sit here with her," the nurse said.

"Go ahead and do yo' thang. I'll take a couple pictures of her to show my family back in the waiting room."

It didn't take long for the nurse to get Aria cleaned up and I took a thousand pictures of her sleeping before a text came through on my phone. Poetry's mom said Dr. Brim was out there giving an update. I snapped a few more pictures before I bent down and kissed my baby on the cheek.

"Keep an eye on my baby. I have to go back to the waiting room. Dr. Brim is out to let us know what's going on with my wife," I said, heading to the door.

"Mr. Williams," the nurse called out my name. "I need to put this on your wrist because it will be the only way you can get in to see the baby. She will be here a couple days to make sure everything is okay with her. So far, she's doing really good," she said, walking over to me.

Attaching a band to my wrist, I automatically read what was printed on it. Baby Williams is what the band read and I knew I needed to change that. Her name was Aria Renee Williams.

"She won't be referred to as Baby Williams anymore. When I come back, I would like to fill out the paperwork to make her name official. Her name is Aria. Take good care of her for me," I said, rushing out of the nursery with Jonathan on my heels.

As we got closer to the waiting room, I started to get hot. My heart was beating fast in my chest and I was nervous about what Dr. Brim had to say. Pushing the door open, everyone was sitting with worried looks on their faces. Mrs. Chris looked up as I walked in.

"I was waiting on you to get back before I started, Mr. Williams," Dr. Brim spoke lowly.

"How is she?" I asked nervously. "Give me good news, doc," I pleaded.

"The surgery was extensive, but we got through it. Let me start off by saying it took a lot for us to get her stabilized before we left the delivery room. As you already know, she flatlined three times, but your wife's a fighter. Once we had her stabilized, I remembered Poetry had been complaining about headaches.

So I decided to do a CT scan on her head. It was something we couldn't do while she was pregnant. What I found was disturbing. Poetry has been suffering from an aneurysm in her brain," Dr. Brim explained.

Mrs. Chris started crying and Stan held on to her tightly. "There was no time to come out to consult with you because I was worried about what I saw. It was a life or death situation, so I acted accordingly. I called for a neurologist we have here in the hospital for these types of emergencies and we went to work. We conducted a procedure called surgical clipping. The surgery was performed under general anesthesia.

An opening was cut in the skull called a craniotomy. We retracted the brain gently so the artery with the aneurysm could be located. A small clip made of titanium was placed across the neck of the aneurysm to block the normal blood flow from entering the aneurysm. The clip is permanent and recovery time typically is four to six weeks."

"Ya'll had to cut her head open?" Stan screamed.

"Unfortunately, we did. The aneurysm was growing before our eyes and that was the only choice we had. Poetry is a young woman that has her entire life ahead of her and I wanted to give her the opportunity to live. She deserves a chance to care for her baby. We had to place her on a ventilator because her body is very weak.

Without the machine, she will flatline again. That's something we don't want. Dr. Wong, the neurologist, believes it's best for her body to rest. At this point, it's up to her how she pulls through this."

Hearing Dr. Brim explain Poetry's prognosis weighed down on my soul. But there was a light at the end of the tunnel because she was still here with us. My emotions were all over the place. I didn't know if I wanted to be happy or sad.

"Can we see her?" I asked.

"I will allow two people in to see her. She is no longer on this floor. She is in the Intensive Care Unit upstairs because her condition is critical right now. She will be monitored closely because the first twenty-four hours are the toughest. Who are the two going to go see her?" Dr. Brim asked.

Turning to Poetry's parents, as much as I wanted to see her, this was not about me. I'd only been her boyfriend for four years and her husband for a month. They have been her parents all her life. There was no way I was going to step on their toes about this.

"I think you two should go. I'll wait until visiting hours to see her,"

"Monty, thank you. Go home and get some sleep. I'll call you if anything changes because I'm not leaving my baby," Mrs. Chris choked.

"We don't usually let anyone stay in the room in the Intensive Care Unit, but I will make an exception for you guys," Dr. Brim said.

"Thank you," I said to Dr. Brim as I opened my arms to hug Poetry's mama. "She is going to be alright. God ain't ready for her yet. I will send pictures of the baby to your phone. It will give you something to smile about," I said, kissing her cheek.

"What did you name her, Monty?" she asked.

"Aria Renee Williams," I responded with my chest out.

"That is a beautiful name and I love it. I can't wait to see her," she said, grabbing my hand and squeezing it before she and Stan followed Dr. Brim out of the room.

I sat in the nearest chair, placed my head in my hands and cried like a baby. Everyone crowded around me and we all shared one big hug. Having a support system like the one I had was something I was grateful for. Without it, I would've fallen apart.

Meesha

Chapter 2

Dot

Dirty had been coming through to check on me as well as keeping a roof over my head and food in my stomach. He bought me clothes and a pair of shoes. One thing he hadn't done was put money in my hand. His young ass was all good until he started telling me what I had to do.

Dirty wanted me to stop doing drugs. The last time I checked, I was over grown and couldn't nobody tell me shit. Smoking crack wasn't something I wanted to do. It was forced on me. I couldn't just wake up one day and say I'm done. It seemed like my body needed it to function.

The money I stole from Dirty was low as hell. I had to travel to the southside to buy drugs because he stopped providing me with it. High as a kite, I was sprawled on the bed in nothing but the skin I was born in. Raising my head was a task I couldn't perform for shit. My body felt like cement was weighing it down. Struggling to sit up, the only thing I needed to do in my mind was take another hit.

Dirty probably wasn't coming to my room anytime soon, so I wasn't worried about him seeing me in this state. He told me if he saw any signs of me getting high, he was going to stop paying for the room. I had to be careful. Mustering up the strength, I grabbed the rock I purchased from a guy I met coming out of the gas station. I knew smoking it wasn't going to get me where I wanted to be, so I prepared it so I could shoot up.

Shooting up was new to me, but I caught on fast and fell in love. Dirty couldn't detect the smell and the needles were easy to hide. Placing the rock in the spoon, I added a little water and grabbed my lighter to cook the dope in the spoon I stole from the diner I went to the other day. My mouth watered as the rock dissolved into liquid. When it was ready, I put the spoon on the dresser so I could get every drop into the needle.

I didn't want to have ugly track marks on my arms, so I started shooting up between my toes. As I inserted the liquid crack, the feeling I got was different for some reason. It didn't stop me from pushing the drug into my body. Before I could finish, my body started shaking uncontrollably and my mouth went dry. Falling back on the bed, my heart felt like it was about to explode in my chest. I couldn't breathe and my eyes rolled in my head. I heard the door opening, but I couldn't speak.

"Dot, what the hell!" I heard Dirty scream. "What the fuck did you do?" he asked in a panicky voice.

Shaking me ferociously by the shoulders, Dirty was doing everything he could to get a response. I tried to open my eyes, but the muscles weren't working in my favor. My teeth sunk into my tongue and I couldn't even scream out in pain.

"Fuck! You bet not die on me, bitch!" he barked, rolling me on my side while trying to get his fingers in my mouth.

I didn't have any control over my body and my eyes were rolling to the back of my head. My body was jerking about like a fish out of water and there was nothing I could do about it. A foamy substance slid out the corner of my mouth and onto the sheets.

Dirty snatched his fingers out of my mouth and a few seconds later, I felt a piece of cloth being inserted inside. I felt my teeth separate from my tongue and I heard Dirty talking. "Yeah, I need an ambulance at the Winterville motel, room one zero seven! I think she is overdosing! Hurry up and send somebody! Hold on, let me check."

I felt his hand on my wrist and then he shouted frantically, "She has a faint pulse, but I don't know how long that will last! Is someone on the way? She has a pulse. Why do I have to do CPR?" he asked out loud. "She got white shit coming out of her mouth! Get somebody to this muthafucka, now!" I could hear him breathing loud and fast as he listened to the person on the other end of the phone. "No, her eyes are rolling around behind the lids. I hear sirens. I have to leave her to escort the paramedics in," he said, removing his clothed hand from my mouth.

20

I heard the door open and Dirty screamed, "Over here!" The voices were muffled and it sounded like I was under water. My body started shaking again and a tear rolled out my left eye. The way my body felt, the first thing that came to my mind was death.

"She's on the bed," I heard Dirty say before my body went limp.

***

Without opening my eyes, I knew I was in the hospital. I said a silent prayer to God for allowing me to live another day. The only thing I remembered was sticking the needle between my toes and hearing Dirty's voice. He saved my life because if he hadn't shown up, I would've died in that hotel room.

A phone ringing made me turn my head to the left and Dirty was sitting in a chair sleeping. His phone was going off back to back and he still didn't budge. Dirty was knocked out and I had questions. Looking at my hand, there was an IV inserted in the back of it. My mind automatically went to a hit when the needle and drugs should've been the last thing on my mind.

"Dirty," I croaked. My throat was raw, sore, and not to mention, dry as cotton. "Dirty," I said again just above a whisper. He still didn't wake up.

Trying to turn on my side was painful. It felt like I had broken ribs or something. As I grabbed the bar on the bed and rolled over, the pain shot up my back. I groaned loudly and buried my face in the pillow. The sound of my pain should've been loud enough for Dirty to wake up, it wasn't.

I reached out and tapped him on the head until he woke up. Dirty's eyes snapped opened quickly. In an instant, he grasped my hand tightly. Wincing in pain, I groaned because the hold he had on my hand put pressure on the needle.

"Why would you hit me like that?" he asked sternly as he released my hand.

"I was calling your name, but you didn't hear me. I did what I could to get your attention. You were sleeping hard. How long have I been here?"

Dirty glared at me for a few seconds before he responded. "How long don't matter. Let's talk about why you're in this muthafucka. Dot, I thought we had an agreement. You were supposed to stopped getting' high in exchange for the room!"

"I did stop getting high, Dirty!" I whined.

"Lie one mo' time and I'll put so much air in that damn IV tube that it will burst a blood vessel!"

The look in his eyes told me he would make good on his threat. I hesitated answering his question because I was trying to come up with another lie to tell. Glancing down at my hands, he snatched me by the chin and turned my head back in his direction.

"Answer the muthafuckin' question! How long have you been back on that shit?" he growled.

"I'm not—"

"Bitch, what did I just say to yo' ass? I already know you on the shit because you had a muthafuckin' needle stickin' out yo' foot! If I hadn't come to the room, you would be in the County morgue! Now, stop fuckin' lyin'!" he said, hitting the railing of the bed. His actions startled me and I started crying.

"It's too late for you to start crying. Yo' ass almost died and you still won't own up to what you were doing! What's it gon' take for you to quit this shit, Dot? I was the only muthafucka out here trying to help you! It's impossible if you don't want to help yourself!

The first step is admitting that you have a problem, man. Do you know I would've been fucked up if you died on me? I didn't know what to do when I saw you seizing on that bed. God was on your side when the paramedics got there in a matter of minutes. That shit don't happen often. The doctor said the drugs you took were bad. Where did you get it from?" he asked.

"You stopped giving me drugs, so I had to go elsewhere to get what I needed so I wouldn't be sick."

"That's not what I asked you, Dot. Where did you get the drugs from?" he asked louder.

"I got it from a dude on the southside."

"A dude? You mean to tell me you went and copped some shit from a nigga you knew nothing about? That was stupid as fuck!"

"I didn't have a choice! You told everybody but Dee not to sell to me. I didn't have a choice!"

"Oh, you had a choice, I gave you one. I told you I would be there to help you get clean and you said you were ready! But I see you only agreed so you wouldn't be out on the streets. I sat here for the past four days off and on making sure you were good. Asking myself the whole time why are you doing so much for her?

You have so much to live for, Dot. Before this shit took over your life, you were beautiful. You didn't do right by your daughter or your life, but it's never too late. There's so much potential inside of you and I want to be the person to bring it back out.

This isn't the life you want. There's nothing good at the end of the road you're traveling. If you continue going down this path, you're going to self-destruct. I want better for you, ma."

It's been a long time since anyone gave a fuck about me. The words Dirty spoke touched a place in my soul that I thought died years ago. My mama used to tell me things like that, but I didn't listen. All I wanted to do was run the streets. Shit, I did what I had to do for me without thinking of anybody else, including my daughter.

Kaymee hated me and she had every right to feel that way. I didn't show her any kind of love and it wasn't right. Dirty had me thinking about a lot of shit I did in my life, and it was hurting me to reflect on those things.

"I signed you up to go to rehab, Dot. You will be leaving this hospital in two days. That don't mean get scared and sign yourself out. Yep, I put that little bug in ya ear because if you do leave, I'll find you and kill you myself. That would tell me that you've chosen drugs over your life and you don't value it.

I'm going to press this button so the nurse can bring in the papers for you to sign. If you refuse, I'll walk out. The next time I see you, there won't be any talking," he said, pushing the button.

"What can I help you with?" a nurse said over the intercom.

"Ms. Morrison is awake. Would you bring her some water and the papers she needs to sign, please?"

"That is great! I'll be right in. I have to check her vitals anyway," she said, ending the conversation.

Lying back on the pillows, tears flowed down my face. I didn't know if I was ready to stop doing drugs. Honestly, it took my mind off everything I was enduring in my life and I didn't really want to face reality. It seemed like I didn't have a choice in the matter. I would either wait to die slowly or die by the gun because Dirty wasn't playing.

The nurse came in the room with the items Dirty requested. I took the papers and pen and without hesitation, I signed myself into the treatment center.

Chapter 3

Kaymee

It's been four days and Poetry hadn't opened her eyes. She gets excited when she hears Monty's voice so I know she's trying to fight her way back. There hadn't been a day that went gone by that I hadn't been by her side. The situation has been hard for all of us but especially hard for Monty. Everyone was still in town to be in his corner during this time.

I was feeding baby Aria while Monty sat rubbing Poetry's hand. The baby has been his light through the struggle. She looked more like her mama as the days went by. Bro made sure to have Aria in the room with him instead of in the nursery. He even placed her on Poetry's chest so she could have a sense of closeness with her mama.

"Have the doctors decided when Aria can go home?" I asked Monty. He looked over at his daughter and smiled.

"Nah, but we are here with her mama and that's all that matters right now. I don't want to go back to my apartment without my family being complete," he said, running his thumb back and forth across the back of Poe's hand.

"All I want is for her to open her eyes and tell me she loves me, sis. I miss her voice. The doctor says her vitals are strong, so I don't know why she hasn't opened her eyes yet. You've witnessed her reaction to my voice. She is trying and I love her for that."

"I know, bro. Give it a little more time and she will utter those words to you. She's responding and that's a great thing. Bringing the baby in let's her know she has so much to live for. She's fighting for both of y'all and for herself as well."

Aria started whining because the milk was gone. I placed the blanket on my shoulder to burp her and she started wailing loudly. At that precise moment, Poetry's heart machine started beeping, which only made the baby cry louder.

"Hand her to me, sis," Monty said, holding out his arm.

Meesha

He released Poetry's hand as I handed the baby to him. Lying Aria on Poetry's chest, the machine slowly started beeping normally. Monty patted the baby on her back and she belched while snuggling deeper into her mama. The sight before me was beautiful because I was witnessing the bond between a mother and child in a way I'd never seen before.

"I think putting her on Poe's chest has spoiled her. It's the only way she will sleep now," Monty said, without taking his eyes off the two women in his life. "I love you, Poetry Renee Williams. We need you, baby. Come back to us," he said sadly.

Seeing Monty like this was tearing me apart, but I was ready to help him any way possible. The longing in his eyes as he stared sadly at Poe and the baby, had me praying she would stir a little bit and smile. I knew it wasn't going to happen, but wishful thinking worked sometimes.

"What's up with you and Los?" Monty asked.

"Nothing. We are getting to know each other, but that's about all. I'm just trying to get to know him and enjoy the friendship."

"I'm not telling you to fall head over hills for him, Mee. Give him a chance. He's a good dude." I gave his ass the side eye because his homeboy recommendations hadn't sat well with me thus far. "Why are you looking at me like that?" he asked.

"Monty, I'm through with your friends. Look what happened with Dray! I'm good on that shit, bro," I said, laughing.

"Nope, you not about to blame that nigga's actions on me. If I would've known he was going to put you through the shit he did, I wouldn't have introduced y'all. Dray was a stand up nigga and I trusted him. Did I know he was fuckin' wit females here? Yep, I did. But I told him to dead that shit when I saw y'all getting closer.

I told him if he wasn't gon' do right, leave you alone. Dray decided to wrong you and put fear in your heart. I whooped that nigga's ass and now, whenever I see him again, he will die. Dray didn't come off as being the kind of dude I saw when I read those messages. The drug use surprised me, too. I didn't know."

"I didn't see any of this coming either. Dray was an entirely different person in Chicago. The true Drayton Montgomery

26

showed up in Atlanta. Monty, I wanted to tell y'all what was happening, but I love you and my daddy and need y'all out in these streets with me."

"Don't worry about the small shit, sis. If anybody is mistreating you in any way, I want to know about it. Leave the other shit to me and Jonathan. You didn't come here to watch your back. You're here to get that degree and make something out of yourself. It's time for you to have fun and get your life together.

The things you've went through is behind you now. Life's too short for any of us to take for granted. I want to thank you for being here with me and Poetry, too."

"No thanks needed, bro. We are family and this is what family do for one another," I said sincerely.

My phone rang and I reached into my purse, pulling it out. "You talked your boy up," I said, laughing before I answered the phone. "Hello."

"Hey, cutie. What you got going on?" Los asked.

"I'm at the hospital with Monty."

"How's Poetry?"

"She's the same. The only change is she's reacting to the baby's cries and Monty's voice. The machines start going crazy when she hears them. She still hasn't opened her eyes yet," I explained.

"In due time, beautiful. In due time. I wanted to know if you wanted to go out to eat with the kid."

"Los, I would love to go but—"

"What time, homie? Pick her up from here. You're on the list."

"Monty, I'm staying here with y'all."

"We just talked about this, Mee. Go out and enjoy yourself. Everything is good here. If there are any changes, I'll call you. I promise."

"I'm on my way, Kaymee. See you in a bit," Los said.

"Wait. I'm—" he hung up before I could tell him not to come. Monty was smiling at me and I wanted to cuss his ass out.

"Don't fight it, man. I'll be good here with my favorite girls. Plus, Chris and Stan are coming in a few hours. You have nothing to worry about," Monty said, turning his attention back to the bed. "Has Dray's pussy ass tried to contact you?"

"Not since the day he thought I was trying to set him up. I don't want to talk about him. He's the last person I need you to talk up," I said, standing up.

"Where you going?" Monty asked, staring at me.

"To the bathroom to make sure my makeup is good since you're kicking me out," I said and laughed.

"Whatever, man. You need to laugh a little to take your mind off what's going on. Shit, one of us need to get out and do something."

"You should meet up with us when Mama Chris and Stan get here. The air will be good for you, too. School starts back next week. Are you going back?"

"Yeah, Poetry's parents are going to help with Aria while I'm in class. They're staying here until Poe is able to move around on her own. It's a good thing because I don't think I'd be able to handle a baby and everything else on my own."

"You wouldn't be on your own. I'm here."

"I know, but you have school, too. We would be gone about the same time, so we still would need someone else to care for Aria. She's my responsibility and I will be there every day of her life."

"You could've called my daddy and Katrina. They won't mind helping out, too. Shit, the entire Goon Squad is still here and are willing to help. Bro, you have all the help in the world. Utilize that shit before you burn yourself out. We're here for you."

"I know, but I want to be here if anything happens. Get yourself together because you're getting out when Los comes," he said, grinning.

"Yeah, yeah, yeah," I said, walking into the bathroom.

As soon as I stepped into the bathroom, a call came through messenger. It was Dray. Ignoring the call, I was pissed because Monty's ass always spoke shit into existence. Opening my purse after placing my phone on the counter, my phone chimed with a message. I opened the messenger app and, of course, it was him.

Drayton Montgomery: I see you still mad at me. It don't matter, though. You still belong to me. Ignoring me wouldn't be a wise thing for you to do. I know where you are. Do you know where I am? LOL.

Sassylocs: Dray, leave me alone, okay? If you're not going to show your face, keep your threats to yourself. I'm over your bullshit and I'm not worried about you. I have moved on with my life. Find something else to do.

I wasn't in the mood for his shenanigans. Dray could kiss my ass. Peeking my head out of the door, I called out to Monty. "Hey, bro. Dray just messaged me talking shit again. Talking about me ignoring him and saying I still belong to him."

"Let him keep talking. He will eventually slip up and tell you his whereabouts and dig himself into a deeper hole," he called back.

My phone chimed again and I knew it was him. I touched up my makeup before I picked up my phone. Reading his message, I laughed lowly because Dray sounded miserable as fuck.

Drayton Montgomery: Moved on with yo' life? What you mean by that? It bet not be another nigga you're referring to.

I didn't respond and my phone started ringing. I declined the messenger call and put my phone back in my purse. As I walked out of the bathroom, I heard Los' voice and I got all giddy inside. I liked him, but I was afraid to open up to him. Dray really messed me up mentally and the wall I had up was solid.

"There she goes," Los said, walking over to me. He pulled me into a hug and whispered in my ear, "You look, beautiful."

My cheeks instantly became warm and I stepped out of his embrace. "Thank you. Where are we heading?"

"Wherever you want to go, we're there."

"Take her nerdy ass to the Martin Luther King Jr. National Historical Park," Monty said.

"Shut up, Monty! I'm not a nerd even though I've been waiting to check that out," I shot back.

"If he leaves shit up to you, y'all will go around the block and back," he said, laughing.

"Shid, I like my women intelligent. There's nothing wrong with beauty and brains," Los said, giving my body a once over.

My lady parts started humming because I hadn't had sex since I was back home in Chicago. It was the last thing on my mind until now. Los had on a pair of black jeans, a white tee with a black leather bomber jacket and a black fitted cap turned to the back. The white and black Nike sneakers he had on complemented his outfit well.

Los didn't take his eyes off me and I continued to blush. I looked good in my white tee that had the logo of my favorite author, Meesha, on the front. The jeans I had on fit like a glove and my green short leather jacket matched the color in my shirt. My locs were fresh, hanging down my back loosely.

"Are y'all gon' stand there lusting over each other or are y'all going out?" Monty asked, chuckling.

I didn't realize I was gazing until he said something. Reaching over, I smacked him upside his head. Aria took that moment to start fussing. Monty got up and picked her up off Poe's chest, checking her diaper.

"Damn, Aria. You know I don't like cleaning boo boo," he said, scrunching his nose.

"That's my cue to leave," I said and laughed. "Have fun with that, daddy," I said, walking to the door.

"Come on, Mee. Change her before you leave."

"You need to get your practice on. Make sure you clean her good now. I'll be back soon, brother," I said, walking over to kiss his cheek.

"You ain't shit! Where's the love?"

"You know I got nothing but love for ya, but I have a friendly outing to attend," I said, leaving out of the door.

***

Los and I spent a couple hours walking around the grounds of the park and I was glad I decided to go. We took lots of memorable pictures alone and many together. The picture of the two of us standing in front of Dr. King's and Coretta's tombs was my screen saver. I hated to admit, but we looked good together. I was hungry and ready to grab something to eat.

"Where are we going to eat?" Los asked as we climbed in his Jeep Cherokee.

"You're reading my mind. I was thinking the same thing a second ago. I have a taste for some buffalo wings. Let's hit Buffalo Wild Wings."

"We can go wherever you like. If wings is what you want, wings you will get," he said, tweaking my chin.

He pulled out of the parking spot and merge onto the street. I couldn't stop looking at him as he drove. His beard was shaped to perfection against his light skin. He had lips so pink, they looked like bubble gum and the urge to nibble on them was strong.

"Why are you looking at me like that, girl? You see something you like?" he asked, glancing over quickly.

"I wasn't looking at you. I'm enjoying the scenery as it goes by. What is your nationality?"

He smirked and looked over at me licking his lips. "I'm African American with a touch of other shit. But in my own words, I'm a nigga."

Rolling my eyes at him, I couldn't take his ass serious at all. "Tell me about Carlos. What's your last name?" I asked with my nail in my mouth.

"Damn, shawty. You trying to dig all in my shit today, huh? Are you trying to be my woman or something because I don't let nobody call me by my gov'ment."

"That's the name you were given at birth, right? Oh okay, that's the name I'll use. Now, what's your last name, *Carlos*?" I asked again playfully.

He kept driving without answering my question and turned into the parking lot of the restaurant. Los found a park in front of the door and cut off the engine. Opening the door, he got out and I sat there with my mouth hanging to my chest.

"I know his ass didn't just ignore me like that," I said to myself before I realized he was walking to my side of the car.

Los open the door and waited for me to step out. For some reason, I couldn't unbuckle the seatbelt. He reached over me and pushed the button freeing me. Holding his hand out to assist me getting out, I placed my hand in his. Instead of letting go, he held on tighter and closed the door and set the alarm.

The feeling of his hand in mine was magical, but I tried to think of it as just a friendly handshake. Los led the way to the entrance of the restaurant and held the door for me. I was loving the way he was such a gentleman, but the feeling didn't last long because Dray did all that shit once upon a time, too.

As we chose a booth to sit down at, the waitress came over with glasses of water and menus. I already knew I wanted lots of wings, so I ordered fifteen buffalo wings with fries and a side of barbeque sauce. Los ordered an All-American burger with fries. We both ordered blackberry Izze Sparkling juice.

"To answer your question, my name is Carlos Pedraza. I'm twenty-three years old, no siblings. Born and raised here in Atlanta with my mom and no, I don't know who my old man is. As you know, I work for yo' pops and I'm doing very well in life. I graduated from Morehouse with a Business Administration and Management degree," he said, taking a sip of water.

"Why did you choose drugs rather than going to get a nine to five job?"

"I didn't choose drugs. The game chose me. Like many other young cats out in the streets, I got tired of watching my mama struggle. Stepping up to take some of the pressure off her shoulders was something I was adamant about doing. Lying about how I made my money was what I had to do.

Enrolling into college was the best decision I'd ever made because for one, it got me out of the hood. It's also a nice cover up that kept my mama off my ass every day without her worrying. I'm lowkey trapping and moving silently nowadays whereas back in the day, I was out and about in danger. I'm looking to open up some type of business and thrive off that shit."

"So basically, you're tired of the drug game is what you're saying?"

"I wouldn't say I'm tired of the game, but I know there's bigger and better things out in the world that would make life easier. If that makes sense. What is not in my future is trapping. I won't be thirty years old still doing drops. My goal is to walk into my business calling the shots, legally. Another thing I have to take into consideration is the fact that I want a family. This is not the life I want my kids or wife to be subjected to."

Hanging on to every word that came out his mouth was intriguing because he seemed to know what he wanted out of life. I didn't know why he was trying to know me on a different level, because babies and marriage weren't in my near future. I had one more year of schooling to go and that's when my career will begin. Making a name for myself in the medical field was my focus. I have to secure a bag for myself. I wasn't waiting for anybody to do anything for me.

"You seem like you're sure about what you want out of life. Keep that attitude and you'll be good. The wife and kids will come later. Be patient."

He folded his hands on top of the table and leaned forward. The way he was licking his lips looked magically delicious. I kept fidgeting my ass in the booth and his hazel eyes had me captivated.

"Kaymee, my wife is right in my face. She just don't know it yet," he said, showing his perfectly white teeth.

I glanced around trying to see this wife he was talking about and I didn't see anyone that would be right for him. "Where is she?" I asked confused.

"You, Kaymee. I'm gon' treat you the way you're supposed to be treated. That nigga didn't know what to do with you. In the short time that we've chilled, I knew you were what I needed in my life. I'm not gon' try to rush you into being my woman. That shit gon' happen when the time is right. Just know that I'm ready and willing to put my best foot forward when it comes to you."

I couldn't formulate one comeback from the words that were spoken by him. As much as I wanted to be happy hearing he wanted to be with me, I couldn't. The waitress gave me the opportunity to think about what to say when she came over with our food.

"Who has the wings?" she asked.

I raised my finger in the air and she placed the plate in front of me. "Thank you."

"And this one is for you, handsome. If *you* need anything, don't hesitate to call me over," she said, batting her eyes at Los. Her breast brushed the top of his hand as she leaned down to make the connection.

The fire that was present in his eyes when he glared at her made her smile waiver a little bit. "That was very disrespectful, ma. I'm sitting here with my lady and you outright tried to shoot ya shot. I won't be needing your services. Make sure someone else comes over to check on how we're doing," he said, picking up the knife to cut his burger in half.

"I didn't mean—"

"Save that shit, shawty. That was me being nice. Move around before I embarrass yo' ass in here," he cut her off quickly.

I felt sorry for the girl because I wasn't his lady. Watching her walk away like a wounded animal, I turned back to Los. "Why did you do that? You are single—"

"Not for long. Now eat ya food before it gets cold."

We sat eating quietly and I decided to post the pics I took earlier on my social media page. I was excited to post, so I did it fast not to be rude. Laying the phone on the table I picked up a wing and devoured it. My fingers were covered in buffalo sauce when my phone started chiming rapidly.

Wiping my hands on a napkin, I was eager to see what was being said on my pics. To my surprise, it wasn't my notifications. It was messages from Dray. Opening the inbox message, my breath caught in my throat.

34

Drayton Montgomery: You really showing yo' ass, huh? What the fuck you doing with that nigga?

I was clueless to what he meant and I instantly thought he was watching my every move until I read the next message.

Drayton Montgomery: Is that nigga ready to die behind yo' hoe ass? If I can't have you, nobody will. Stop playing with me and dead that shit. I already told that pussy ass nigga to stay the fuck away from you. He don't listen very well, so I'm gon' have to show him better than telling him.

I went back to my page and looked at the pictures I posted. Sure enough, I had posted the picture of Los and I hugged up in front of the tombs of Martin Luther King, Jr. and Coretta's tombs. We looked like a happy couple if you didn't know we were only friends. Dray must've saw what I was seeing and that's why he was tripping hard.

"What's going on? Is everything okay?" Los asked, taking a sip of his juice.

"Um, yeah," I said in a shaky voice.

"Kaymee, what's wrong?" he asked seriously.

I had promised I wouldn't keep Dray's threats a secret, so I slid my phone to Los and let him see for himself. My appetite was gone even though I was hungrier than a homeless person. Picking up my glass to take a sip, Los was tapping away on my phone and I knew some shit was about to hit the fan.

"I responded to his ass for you. I didn't say anything to bring heat to you, but he is about to get tricked into telling me where his punk ass is hiding out at. Don't be afraid of him. He won't get the chance to put his hands on you again. It's my responsibility to keep you safe now.

When I said you were in the first position to be my wife, I wasn't bullshittin'," he said, sliding my phone back to me. "Let's enjoy the rest of our night together. It's still early, so maybe we can go catch a movie before we go our separate ways. What you think?" he asked.

"I'd like that," I responded, waiting on Dray to respond. I read over the message that Los sent and prayed things didn't backfire on me. Dray was mentally gone and I was scared shitless.

Chapter 4

Poetry

My head was hurting but not as much as before. I was trying my hardest to open my eyes, but I couldn't. The experience was scary because I was trying to stay away from the bright light that was in front of me. It felt like I was being forced in that direction. I was struggling to plant my feet so I could fight the movement.

"Poetry, baby. You've been hanging in this hallway for weeks. This place ain't ready for you. It's time to go back. Your husband and daughter need you and your life is just beginning."

I recognized the voice immediately. It was Big Mama. It was impossible because she passed away when I was twelve years old of a heart attack. Straining to put a face with the voice, I couldn't see anything because of the brightness of the light. After a while, Big Mama stepped out of the light with her arms outstretched.

"Big Mama, where am I?" I asked. "Wait, how did you get here?"

"You came to visit granny, but I don't want you here. Poetry you are stuck between Heaven and Earth. Christine wouldn't be the same if I walked you to my house. I've always told you that my door would always be open whenever you needed to come back. Your mother and father need you back with the living."

"Are you trying to tell me that I'm dead?" Hearing her say I was basically floating aimlessly around, not knowing where to go, was another fear to add to my list.

"No, you're not dead. You're a fighter. I want you to go back in the other direction and make me proud. You will have a long journey ahead of you, but, you will overcome every obstacle and come out on top. I will be there with you every step of the way. Go on now. Get out of here.

Give that beautiful baby a kiss from her Big Mama and love that man you have with everything in you. He is a keeper. Everyone deserves a second chance to right their wrongs and he has earned that ten times fold. I love you, granny's baby. I'll be here when it's time for you to come live with me. It's won't be anytime soon, but I got your back," she said, walking into the light and disappearing.

One minute I was lying in the hospital bed after playing Uno with Monty, the next I was being rolled into the operating room for an emergency cesarean. When I heard my baby cry, everything went black and I was drowning in darkness. The beeping of the machines was loud in my ears and Monty's cries were the last thing I heard.

The fight to see was something I was willing myself to do. Every time I heard voices, I replied but it seemed like I was being ignored. I was screaming bloody murder, but nobody responded to me. They always continued to talk like I wasn't there with them.

I had to be in the vicinity because I could hear them clearly. Hearing me was the problem and I was getting frustrating. Every day I smelled the scent of baby lotion and milk. I knew my baby was lying on my chest, but I couldn't raise my arms to wrap my arms around her. Aria was her name. Monty said it over and over as he talked to me, but he couldn't hear when I responded in return.

"Hey, Wifey. It's just you and me today. I put some moisture on your crusty ass lips today. You almost cut my shit off last night," Monty said, laughing as he ran his fingers down my cheek. "You should be nice and comfy because I got you on a pair of silk hot pink pajamas. That damn hospital gown wasn't bringing out the beauty I needed in my life. It's been two weeks and time for you to open those beautiful eyes of yours.

I miss you Poe. The doctor says your vitals are good, ma. It's up to you, now. I've been praying every day since I almost lost you. God is holding us down and I would forever be in debt with him. Come back to me, baby. I need you," he said sadly.

The hurt in his voice was evident and my heart was hurting listening to the sound of defeat in his words. "I miss you too, Monty," I said, but he continued talking, once again not hearing my words.

"I'm putting things in place so we can be a happy family without me being in the streets. Jonathan found the perfect spot for my soul food restaurant and it's being renovated as I speak. It's gon' be called Poetry's Palace because you are the queen of all of my castles. There will be soul food being sold while we host poetry readings for all the talent that's being unnoticed around Atlanta. Making a life for you and Aria is my main focus and being out in these streets ain't guaranteed.

I'll be around to spoil y'all for years to come. I'm ready to be daddy and husband of the year to get you back on your feet and make sure Aria is good. I get to continue school online and I will still graduate on time. I'm going hard for us, Poetry. It's me and you against the world, baby. I need you to fight this shit so you can shine by my side."

The beeping of a machine startled me. I felt the softness of his lips on the back of my hand. My eyes rolled around in my head like marbles, but it was still hard to open them. It was a task that drained the little bit of strength I thought I had. Sleep took over and I didn't hear anything else for a long while.

"Waaa, waaaa."

"Aria, you want to feel mommy?" Monty asked as I felt my baby on my chest. "There you go. Keep her warm."

She cuddled against me and I felt my shirt being pulled into her little fist. Her scent filled my nostrils and I fought to open my eyes. Tears rolled down my eyes as I saw the curls on the top of her head. I tried to lift my arm, but it was heavy and wouldn't budge. Relaxing for a few minutes, I tried again and wrapped my arm around Aria's back.

Turning my head to the left, Montez was tapping away on his laptop. He looked tired and he had a full beard covering his face. My husband had his grown man look going on and I loved it. The bags under his eyes were huge and I could tell sleep was the last thing he'd made time to do.

"Montez?" Obviously he didn't hear me because he didn't turn in my direction. "Montez," I said again without getting his attention.

I glanced down and saw the call button by my left hand and I pushed the button. "Is there something you need, Mr. Williams?" I heard a voice say.

"Um, no," he said with a look of confusion on his face.

"You must've hit the button by mistake."

Monty looked at the call button and I knew it was my chance to get his attention. He hadn't noticed my arm around the baby, so I had to make him aware. I tried to swallow, but it was impossible. Something was down my throat. That's why I couldn't talk. Moving my finger back and forth, Monty hurriedly put the laptop on the chair beside him without taking his eyes off my hand.

"Mr. Williams, are you still there?"

"Yes, um come in here, please. My wife is moving her hand," he said.

"That's great news! The doctor and I are on our way."

Within seconds, the door to the room was opening and Montez finally looked me in my eyes. His dimples were deep in his cheeks and he noticed my arm around the baby. Intertwining his hand in mine, he continued to look down on me.

"You were trying to get my attention, weren't you?" he asked with tears running down his face. The only thing I could do was nod my head.

"Welcome back, Mrs. Williams," Dr. Brim said happily as she shined a light in each of my eyes. Dr. Brim checked my vital signs and listened to my heart. "Everything sounds good. You had us waiting on pins and needles for weeks. It's great to see those pretty brown eyes.

It's safe to say that this tube can be taken out now. The first thing I will do is suction the tube itself, then I will suction your mouth, Poetry, to clear the secretion that may be in there. I will take down the tubes cuff that helped with your air supply, then I will take the tube out," Dr. Brim explained as she went to the sink to wash her hands.

I didn't understand anything she said, but I wanted the tube out of my throat. Monty reached for the baby and I didn't want to let her go. Watching while he laid her in the baby bed, I smiled seeing her tiny body. Dr. Brim came back over and started suctioning my mouth. It sounded like she was removing snot out of my throat.

"Poetry, now I want you to cough continuously until the tube is removed completely." I nodded my head informing her that I understood. "Give me the first cough and keep going. I'll follow your lead."

I coughed as instructed. It didn't take long for the tube to be removed. My throat felt like it was on fire. The nurse left and came back with a pitcher of ice. Monty didn't hesitate feeding me the chips and it felt good going down.

"I want to administer a little oxygen to you for a couple hours. After that, you should be able to go without it," Dr. Brim said as she placed the oxygen tube in my nose.

The air was cool, going in to my nostrils. "Thank you for everything you've done for me," I said hoarsely.

"You're welcome. I only did what I was trained to do. Your throat will be sore for a few hours and you will be hoarse, as well. Take it easy and you will be good as new very soon."

"Are my parents still here?" I asked, looking at Montez.

"Yes, I'm about to give them a call now," he said, taking his phone from his hip.

"No, let me call. I promise not to talk too much after that, okay?"

"I'll leave you guys to get reacquainted. Poetry, I'll be back to check on you a little later," Dr. Brim said, waving as she left the room.

Montez handed me his phone and I grasped his hand. It seemed like forever had passed since I'd last seen him. Pulling him toward me, he followed my lead and kissed me on the lips. Wrapping his other arm around my neck, he held me tightly.

"I'm glad to have you back, Poe. I love you so much," he said into my shoulder.

"I know you do. You told me how much every day that you sat by my side. I heard every word, Mr. Williams."

"Call your parents so I can hold you in peace." I smiled as I dialed my mama's cell and listened as it rang.

"Monty, is everything okay?" my mama said into the phone. I couldn't utter a vowel and that alarmed her. "Montez, are you there? What's happening?" she called out frantically.

"Calm down, woman. Everything is wonderful now," I said loud as I could.

"Poetry? Baby, is that you?" The joy in her voice was one I could listen to every minute of the day.

"Yes, mommy, it's me. Where are you?" I asked.

"I'm on my way to you, baby. Thank you, Jesus. You heard my cries!" she cried out.

"Chris, baby? What's wrong?" I heard my daddy say in the background.

"She's awake, Stan. We have to get to the hospital."

"Poetry, how you feeling baby?" my daddy asked when he got on the phone.

"It hurts to talk, but I'm alright. I love you, daddy. I'll see you when y'all get here."

"I love you, too. See you soon," he said, hanging up.

Talking to my parents was very emotional for me and I started crying like a baby. In turn, Aria started crying from the side of the bed. Monty raced to her side to calm her. He pinched the front of her pamper and hopped right into daddy mode. Witnessing a new side of him, I was in awe by the way he was handling his daughter.

"Somebody needs a diaper change. Daddy's got you, baby. I have a surprise for you, too. You get to meet your mommy," he said happily, bending down to rub his nose against hers.

I waited for Monty to change Aria and I was fixated on his movements. The way he interacted with her and talked to her throughout the entire ordeal, showed me how much the two of them had bonded. As he moved to place the new diaper under her butt, she pissed on his arm.

"Ari, baby! You get daddy every time. Is that your way of telling me you love me?" he asked, laughing and retrieving another diaper.

42

"That's so cute. I have a lot of making up to do," I said, watching my little family in front of me.

"You have plenty of time, Poe. *We* have plenty of time."

***

Feeding Aria for the first time was amazing. I was excited and she wouldn't take her eyes off me, as if she would miss something. She outlasted me because I fell asleep within the hour. The length of time I slept was unknown to me but when I woke up, the room was packed. Wiping sleep from my eyes, I spotted Kaymee at the same time she noticed I was awake.

"Sista!" she screamed, pushing her way to me. Throwing herself into my arms, we both cried.

"I thought I'd lost you," she wailed into my chest. "Life would not be the same without you, baby! I've missed you so much!"

"I'm okay. We in this thang together. Stop all that crying," I said, trying to pry her arms from around my neck. "Come on, Mee." I tapped her again, but she was holding on for dear life.

"You gave me that bear and I've been listening to your voice every day. I thought I would never hear it again in life."

My best friend was so emotional. The tears filled my eyes and I couldn't stop them from falling. I didn't know how she was feeling, but I knew the love we had was unbreakable. That moment let me know how much we meant to one another. I would spend the rest of my life showing her how much I loved her.

"Mee, you don't have to worry about that. You hear my voice loud and clear right now. It's real, sis. This is not a dream. I'm back. I was resting for a little bit. The next chapter of our lives begins today," I said, patting her on the back.

Kaymee finally released me and kissed me over my entire face. She ran her hand over my face, still in disbelief. Stepping back a little bit, she scrunched her nose up at me and laughed.

"Sis, you need to brush yo' teeth. Your breath is very tart."

"You ain't right, Kaymee," I frowned.

"Get off my wife, Mee. Her breath smells good enough for me under the circumstances," Monty said, taking up for me.

"Thank you, baby. But go get the toothbrush and shit, so I can take care of this mess," I said, chuckling.

Everyone in the room laughed and it was music to my ears. My mama walked to the bed and gave me a hug. She refrained from tackling me like Mee and I was grateful. Feeling her body close to mine was medicine for my soul. When she let me go, my daddy walked over kissing me on the forehead and told me he loved me. I guess he was trying not to smother me.

Noticing all the balloons, envelopes, and gifts that were lined along the dresser, I beamed inside. Jonathan walked to the bed, so I scooted over to give him room to sit down. He looked down on me solemnly, taking a deep breath.

"Poetry, you scared everyone in this room. I've prayed for you to wake up every day. That man over there haven't left your side for more than ten minutes," he said, pointing at the love of my life. "I've watched him go from a young man to a responsible grown man in a matter of weeks. He did all of that because of the love he has for you and I'm proud of him.

Rewarding him for standing up, doing what he was supposed to do would be wrong on my part. But I have a gift for fighting a tough fight of survival. I wanted to present this to you the moment you opened your eyes," Jonathan said, taking an envelope from his pocket. "This is for the Williams family as a whole, from me to y'all," he said, standing up.

Monty, come sit by your wife so the two of you can read it together. I love y'all and want the best for y'all. Don't thank me. I didn't do this for clout. I did it from the bottom of my heart."

After Monty sat in the place Jonathan vacated, he handed the envelope to him and stepped back. My husband handed the envelope to me and I tore it open. Inside there was a check for one hundred thousand dollars. I handed it to Monty and tears stung my eyelids as I shakily opened the other piece of paper.

"Jay, you didn't have to do this. I have more than enough money to hold us over," Monty said.

"I know I didn't. Don't fight me on this. It's all love, brah," Jonathan said.

I continued to read the paper in my hand. I couldn't believe what I'd read. In my hand was a deed to a brand new house that Jonathan put in both, Monty and my name. Monty looked in Jonathan's direction and took the paper out of my hand. Reading the same words, Monty stood up giving him a brotherly hug.

"Thank you wouldn't be enough for what you have done, Jay. I appreciate you, man."

"You have a family now. Take care of them, Monty. That can be your payment to me. I'll be here every step of the way whenever you need any advice. Plus, you will need the room for Mr. and Mrs. Parker while they're here helping y'all out."

I looked over at my parents. "Y'all staying for me? I'm okay. I really am," I said to my mama.

"Poetry, you had major surgery on your head, baby—"

"Wait, what?" I asked as my hand shot to my head. I felt the bandage for the first time and I didn't know what happened. "What happened to my head?" I asked, looking around the room.

"Poe, you had to have emergency surgery after your heart stopped beating after Aria was delivered. The cause of your headaches was found. It was from an aneurysm. Baby, they had to cut your head open to stop the aneurysm from growing," Monty explained.

"My head is still hurting, though. Not as much as before but, it still hurts," I said, trying to understand.

"It's been two weeks. It will take four to six weeks for the incision to heal, the headaches will go away gradually. You gon' be good, ma. The surgery was needed. It was a life or death situation," Monty said, massaging my hand.

"Is the incision big? They had to cut my hair too, I suppose."

"Poetry, we haven't seen the incision. Every time the nurse came in to change your bandages, we always leave the room. Me personally, I wanted to see it for the first time with you," Kaymee piped in.

"I'll take y'all word on this. Would somebody tell them to bring me some damn food? I'm hungry," I said, trying to lighten the mood in the room. The incision in my head was the last thing I wanted to worry about. I was grateful to be alive and sweating the small shit wasn't what I wanted to do. "Hand me Miss Aria, please. Sorry, Los. You are too comfortable with my baby," I said, chuckling.

We all hung out until visiting hours were over. At the end of the day, it was just me, my man, and our baby left in the room. I loved the little family we had created and saw nothing but greatness in the future for us.

Chapter 5

Drayton

It's been three months since I left Atlanta to come back home to Massachusetts. I regret packing up and quitting school, but the things I had done to Kaymee put a target on my back. Jonathan and the Goon Squad probably had a search party looking for my ass. It's a good thing I'd never went into details about my life back home. It would be a matter of time before they tracked me down though.

I found a house to buy and I was waiting on the realtor to get back to me with a closing date. Hopefully, it doesn't take too long. I don't know how long I can go without clashing with my father. The minute I walked into my parents' home the day before Thanksgiving, the atmosphere turned cold. My father and I never really got along and he didn't want me staying under his roof. Of course, my mom intervened and he stopped bitching about me being there.

I was scrolling through Kaymee's social media page when I heard loud yelling. At first, I tuned it out because hearing them argue wasn't anything new. I'd heard it all my life growing up. When my ma cried out in pain, I jumped up and followed the sound of the commotion. My father, Drayton Senior. had my mother against the wall by her throat. I immediately punched him in the temple and he hit the floor.

"Dray, stop!" my mother screamed as I stomped his head re-peatedly.

"Put yo' muthafuckin' hands on her again, nigga!" I grilled him as my mother pulled me off him by the back of my shirt.

"You're wrong, Dray! Stay out of my business!" she yelled at me as she bent down to console his punk ass.

I couldn't believe she was defending his ass after he yoked her up and had the nerve to get mad at me. He was moaning while holding his head with my stupid ass mama by his side. Refusing to watch the bullshit before me, I turned and went back to my room and laid on the bed. Not even thirty minutes later, his ass was yelling again.

"He has to go, Deloris! I won't have him disrespecting me in my house! There's one nigga in charge and that's me!" he screamed at my mama.

"That's your son, Drayton! He was protecting his mother. Both of you were wrong in this situation!"

"No, that's your son! I just gave him my name so he wouldn't be walking around being labeled as a bastard. Had you kept your legs closed, we wouldn't be having this conversation. Tell him to leave. He doesn't have to go back to Atlanta, but he has to get out of here before I kill his ass."

"Lower your voice before he hears you. I didn't force you to stay with me after what I did. You said you forgave me and promised to never bring it up again. It's been almost twenty-three years and evidently, you are still holding a grudge about it."

"Too late," I said, standing in the doorway of their bedroom. "Anybody care to tell me what's going on? I know I didn't hear that nigga say I wasn't his son." One part of my soul was crushed, the other was ready to tear some shit up.

"Dray, baby—"

"Nah, ma. This ain't the time to cry about it. If I heard correctly, I've been lied to my entire life and I need answers. Is this the reason he could never embrace me like a father does his son? Why he never took me to a basketball game or watched one with me for that matter? This muthafucka didn't do shit but send me away to school, I guess so he could whoop yo' ass in peace," I said, crossing my arms over my chest.

"Get the fuck out of my house, young blood," the man I once knew as my father barked.

"Put me out, nigga!" I chuckled. "You will find yourself back on yo' ass. You never taught me to fight, but these hands don't discriminate. I will fuck you up!"

"Both of y'all cut this shit out! Dray, you're my son and Drayton is your father—"

"I heard the words drip from his mouth! He said I wasn't his son, so I'm going off what he validated. Don't try to clean shit up now, the truth is out. I just need you to tell me why I was never told. I've been at the age of understanding for a long time. This shouldn't have been the way for me to find out the truth."

"I didn't think it was necessary for me to tell you because your father raised you as his own. The other man is not in the picture, so it doesn't matter," my mama had the audacity to say.

"It don't matter? Yo' husband never loved me as his own! The only thing he did was beat my ass when I wasn't doing right! He never loved me!"

"I provided your ass with a roof over your head, food in your stomach, and clothes on your back. It was my money that got you into Morehouse to get an education. Without me, you wouldn't be shit!" Drayton Sr. threw at me.

"Nigga, I appreciate all that shit you did for me. As far as me thanking you, I had to send the message through my mama because you did the shit without being there to see my reaction. You was never around for me to tell you how grateful I was. But you know what, fuck you! I'm not gon' stand here while you throw shit in my face that you took responsibility for!

You made the choice to take on the responsibility of being my daddy, so you were supposed to keep the same energy, nigga!" I said before turning to my mama. "You let him ignore the fuck out of me and you knew how it affected me from the beginning. I talked to you about it for years and nothing changed. That was your chance to tell me the real, but you kept it hidden."

"Watch yo' mouth when you're talking to my wife, boy."

"What the fuck you gon' do if I don't?" I asked, walking in his direction.

"Dray, just go," my mama said with tears in her eyes.

"Go? You choosing this muthafucka over me? It's cool," I said, chuckling. "It wouldn't be the first time. I'm witnessing it firsthand today. I'll leave, but don't expect me to come back. You made your choice and I will always love you, from a distance," I said, walking out of their room.

***

I'd been staying at the Marriot hotel since I left my mother's crib. She had been calling every hour on the hour, but she got no play on my line. I would eventually talk to her after I cooled off. My reaction to that nigga choking my moms had me thinking about how I treated Kaymee. If I didn't want it to happen to my mom, why was it okay for me to do it to another female?

The question kept running through my mind so much that I went straight to Kaymee's social media page to send her a message apologizing for my actions. I saw that she had uploaded new pics and I wanted to see her beautiful face. Going through the pictures, I saw that nigga Los in a few of the pics with her and I got heated. Apologizing was the last thing I wanted to do at that point.

I was sending her a message I was pissed and to let her know it, too. She responded but not in the same manner as usual. I couldn't wrap my head around the difference in her response and it was bothering me.

Sassylocs: It's not what you think. We only went out as friends. Whenever you come back, we can see where things go. Don't worry about what's going on over here. Get yourself together so we can be right in the future.

Reading over the message for the third time, I wanted to believe her words, but something was nagging me inside. Kaymee was the woman I loved and seeing her with another nigga, especially Los, had me in my feelings.

I went to google and booked a round trip ticket back to Atlanta for the next day. I was going to have my ride shipped back because I was tired of paying for Ubers. Kaymee would see me too since she wanted to express interest while on the arm of another nigga.

My phone started buzzing in my hand. I saw it was my realtor. "What up?" I asked when I answered.

"Mr. Montgomery, we have a date. The seller has decided on a closing date and we agreed on Monday afternoon. Would that be good for you?" she asked.

"It sure will. I'm going out of town, but I will be back Sunday night."

"Sounds good. I'll see you at the house Monday then. Enjoy the rest of your day, Mr. Montgomery."

"Same to you, Susan," I said ending the call.

I got up so I could take a shower and go out to get some air and something to eat. It was cold in Boston and I was glad I did a little shopping because I didn't need any heavy clothing down south. Entering the bathroom, I turned the water on in the shower and set the temperature to my liking.

Sliding the glass door open, I stepped in and placed my hands on the tiled wall as the water cascaded down my back. Kaymee's face appeared behind my eyelids and I felt my body relax after a few minutes. My stomach growled bringing me back to the task at hand, which was washing my ass so I could go eat.

Twenty minutes later, I was dressed and opening the door to my hotel room. Waiting on the elevator, I thought about my trip back to Atlanta. I didn't want to dwell on it too much because shit may not go accordingly. The doors of the elevator opened and I stepped on and pushed the button for the lobby.

I decided I didn't want to leave the hotel because I wasn't accustomed to the cold since I moved away. Entering the restaurant, I waited for the hostess to escort me to a table. The bitch that approached me was wearing the fuck out of the white dress shirt that she had on. Her titties were double Ds and I pictured my face between the two melons.

"Sir, are you ready to sit?" I heard her say.

Bringing my eyes up to address her, I was disappointed. Her face didn't match the body I was admiring. She looked like a miniature Shaquille O'Neal and my dick died in my pants. All thoughts of sexing her ran off before I could explain what happened.

"Yes, I am. Lead the way," I said, looking everywhere but at her.

Baby Shaq led me to a table with a window view. I missed my city, but I planned to get familiar with it once I come back next week. She left me with a menu and promised to come back with water in a bit. Shid, in my mind, I wanted her to send somebody else over to assist me.

I got the feeling I was being watched and I glanced around. With the Goon Squad out to get at me, I had to still be careful hundreds of miles away. My eyes landed on a pretty little thang sitting at a table diagonal from mine. She glanced up and smiled, holding her head down like she was embarrassed for getting caught staring. The hostess came back with another woman that placed my water on the table in front of me.

"This is Amber. She will be your waitress for the day. Enjoy your meal, sir," she said, walking away.

"Are you ready to order, sir?"

"Yes," I said even though I hadn't given it a thought. "I'll have the prime rib, mashed potatoes and string beans. Would you please bring A1 steak sauce with my meal please?"

"Sure will. Would you like anything to drink?"

"You can bring me a double shot of Remy VSOP if that's okay," I said, smiling.

"I'll bring that right over to you, sir."

I picked up the cup of water and took a long sip. The feeling of being watched came over me and I glanced up, meeting the eyes of the beautiful woman that watched my every move as I was being seated. We held eye contact longer than before and she blushed looking away. She liked what she saw and I wasn't one to miss an opportunity to roll in the hay with a bitch. Rising from my seat, I made my way to her table.

"How you doing, beautiful?" I asked, standing next to her while she gulped water from the glass she held.

Taking a deep breath, she stammered, "I—I—I'm fine and you?"

52

"I'm good. Would you like to join me? I see you can't seem to keep your eyes off me, so I wanted to bring you closer and get to know you," I said with a smirk.

She hesitated and sat thinking too long for my liking. I took her hand in mine and motioned for her to stand. As I guided her out of the chair, she grabbed her water and followed my lead. Pulling the chair out for her, I waited until she was seated before I sat in front of her.

"Thanks for joining me. I'm Drayton and you are?" I asked, staring deeply in her dark brown eyes.

"Koren. My name is Koren."

"Nice to meet you, Koren. That's a beautiful name for such a beautiful woman. You don't have to be shy with me. I was admiring you as much as you were admiring me," I said, trying to make her comfortable. "Why are you eating alone?"

"I'm here on business and decided to take a break from work to grab something to eat."

"They say all work and no play isn't a good thing," I said, licking my lips. "Have you eaten yet?"

"Actually, my dinner is coming now," she said, waving the waitress over to my table.

"Oh my, I thought you'd left. Your order will be coming out in a few minutes, sir," she said as she placed Koren's food in front of her.

"No problem," I said, never taking my eyes off Koren.

She was a chocolate beauty that stood about five feet six, she didn't have the perfect body, but she wore it well. The lounge pants and matching shirt hugged her thighs and ass perfectly. She had a gut, but it wasn't sloppy. It was enough for me to have something to hold on to if I got the chance to bend her ass over.

Koren was sitting with her hands folded in front of her. Every now and again, she would glance down at her plate without picking up her fork. I believed she was trying to wait on my food to arrive before eating.

"Pick that fork up and eat, woman," I said laughing. "Your food will be cold while you trying to be courteous and wait for me. It's cool. Enjoy your meal while it's hot."

"I didn't want to be rude," she said, picking up her fork. "Tell me about yourself, Drayton."

"I'm twenty-three, a graduate of Morehouse College and I work as an engineer with Boeing. Born and raised right here in Boston. I've recently relocated back home."

"Oh, you are an educated youngster, huh?" She laughed, covering her mouth because she had food in it.

"I may be twenty-three, but I'm all man, baby," I said as my food brought out.

The prime rib looked good and I was ready to tear into it. My Remy was brought out as well, but that would have to wait for now. I cut a piece of meat and placed it in my mouth. Once I chewed and swallowed, I gave Miss Koren my attention.

"Back to me being a youngsta. Age ain't nothing but a number. I can have you calling me daddy before I even give you the dick."

Koren choked on the food she was swallowing and I jumped up patting her on her back. She coughed for a few minutes until she composed herself. Koren wiped her mouth and shook her head.

"As delicious as you look and smell, I'm afraid this interaction won't go beyond conversation. I have a family back home. A husband that I love with all my heart. Jeopardizing what I went before God to unite is something I would never do."

"I respect that. Your husband is a lucky man to have a wife that honors and respects him in his absence," I said, continuing to eat.

There was no need to keep pushing up on her, she wasn't going back on her word. You didn't see that type of loyalty no more and I admired her for how she handle herself. I no longer saw her as another bitch I could smash. She was a woman that loved what she worked hard to achieve and that's happiness. If she wasn't happy, she would be heading up to my room with me but that's not the case.

We sat and talked about many things for a while and I enjoyed every minute of it. Koren made me more eager to get to Atlanta to get my woman before that nigga Los got his hands on her. I left the restaurant and went to my room and packed.

Meesha

Chapter 6

Los

After taking Kaymee back to the hospital to pick up her car, I trailed her back to the dorm. When she got out of the car and walked over to the driver's side of my ride, I watched her hips sway from side to side. Kaymee was a beautiful woman that allowed a man to make her look in the mirror different.

She walked with her head down, didn't like to be complimented or should I say, she didn't grasp it with confidence. I was going to do everything I could to bring that confidence that's hiding inside of her out. Sitting back watching her hide in a shell wasn't happening if she was going to be Los' woman.

"Thank you for tonight. I really enjoyed myself. I haven't laughed that much in a while. You have been there through all of my ups and downs with Poetry and everything else. I appreciate you for getting me out even if it was only for a few hours."

"Step back," I said with my hand on the handle. She did what I asked and I opened the door stepping out. My five eleven frame towered over her and I grabbed her around the waist. "You don't ever have to thank me for putting a smile on your face, Kaymee. When I told you I would be there for you, I meant that shit.

I want you to walk with yo' head up, show your beauty for all to see. The things you went through needed to happen. What I want you to understand is it won't continue to happen. Not while you're with me and that's fact. I'm not gon' try to buy, demand, or take your love. You gon' give me that shit. That's how hard I'm about to fight to win you over." I let her know where I was coming from so she wouldn't be confused.

Kaymee wrapped her arms around me and buried her face deeper into my stomach. Holding her close by one arm, I lifted her head and she brought her eyes to mine. Tilting my head to the side, I asked, "You hear what I'm saying?"

"I hear you, Los. Actions speaks louder than words. I had someone that told me he would love me and—"

"Let's get something straight, baby. Don't compare me to that nigga. You got lost in the words of a boy that didn't know what to do with a real woman. He fucked up and I'm picking up what he left behind. I hope you ready for the ride because you won't ever come back from what I have to offer. I know how to put my hands on a female in a way she will love that shit for the rest of her life.

I promise, before you are even mine, that I won't do nothing but love you the right way as long as you will have me. I'm looking for forever. I'm twenty-three and you are eighteen, so what. We have the rest of our lives to get it right. It's on you if we can see what it will feel like between us. I got some business to take care of and I will hit you up later," I said, leaning down kissing her lips.

She didn't kiss me back, but it was cool. I knew she was feeling me like I felt her. After she backed up, I watched her enter the building before I drove off. Making a right on Greensferry Avenue, I cruised thinking about the day I had with Kaymee and I actually smiled. It's been a minute since a female captured my attention.

Like Kaymee, I too had a wall up when it came to relationships. The last relationship I was in, ended fucked up on the female's part. She wanted to have a nigga on the side even though she had all the man she needed in her presence. It was her loss because there was somebody in position to fill that void.

Nearing my destination, I picked up my phone and hit the name I needed. "Yo, I'm about ten minutes away. I'm not trying to be out in these streets too long. Be at the spot and have my money," I said, ending the call.

I had been rolling with Monty for a minute and I'm in a better position now. Dray's fuck up was my gain and I was going to ride this shit 'til the wheels fell off. I was making money before, but my cake was up better than ever and I was loving it. With Monty getting out of the game, Jonathan brought a proposition my way that I couldn't refuse. The opportunity that was presented to me would set me right for life. All I had to do was stay the true nigga I was born to be.

Pulling up to the spot, this nigga was standing out front with a bitch in his face. My money was at his feet in a duffle bag, but his attention was on titties and ass. I guess because these niggas knew Monty was with his wife and not out in the streets, it meant they could slack off. There's no beef, but you have to be ready so you won't have to get ready when shit pops off. I watched his ass for a few minutes before I eased out of my ride quietly.

I crept up on him and pulled my tool from my hip and inched closer to him. Ole girl's eyes got big and fear was etched on her face. Her voice was caught in her throat because she didn't warn his ass at all. I placed the muzzle against the back of his head and he froze mid-sentence.

"Aye, man. Just take that shit. It's thirty thousand in that bag. Just don't kill me, please," he said shakenly. This nigga fucked up because he was a victim of a jack if I would've been anybody else.

"You was a dead muthafucka and my money would've been gone in the wind. This is why we preach to y'all about keeping yo' eyes to the streets."

"Los, I got distracted for a second—"

"As you can see, that's all the fuck it takes, a second. Yo' muthafuckin' body would've been outlined in chalk if I wasn't the one to roll up on you! This was your second strike. There won't be a third. I don't need yo' services no mo'. You done, son. Now you have all the time in the world to do what you want to do," I said, snatching the bag from the ground.

"Wait, Los. I apologized, fam," he pleaded.

"I'm not trying to hear that shit, nigga. You were warned and you thought shit was sweet. Gon' about ya business while you still have the chance."

Poppin' the trunk, I threw the bag in the secret compartment next to the bag of dope I didn't give his stupid ass. I slammed it shut and walked to the driver's door. This lil' nigga was coming toward me as I got in. I started my shit and pulled off on his ass. I didn't want to hear shit else that spewed from his mouth.

I made the other pickups and doubled up at a couple of them because of the bullshit that was pulled at the first spot. Knowing his punk ass, I would be getting a call from Jonathan or Monty but hey, this was business. There was no time for slackers on my team.

Heading to my crib, it was damn near one in the morning and a nigga was tired. I was ready to sleep like a bear in hibernation the way my body was feeling. It took me thirty minutes to get home and I was glad to see my street in view. I squinted my eyes because I knew muthafuckin' well this bitch wasn't at my shit. I pulled beside the car and sat with the engine idling.

My ex, Nicole, jumped out of her ride and stomped over with a frown on her face. The window was down, so I just sat there while she stood without saying anything. "Nikki, why are you here?" I asked irritably.

"Who's the bitch you were hugged up with at the movies, Los?" I laughed without responding and it pissed her off more than she already was. "Oh, it's funny? Who is the bitch?"

"Hell yeah, it's funny because you sitting in my driveway questioning me about something that ain't yo' business. You probably been sitting out here since yo' homegirl told you I left that muthafucka. That means you wasted hours of your time just to be on bullshit. Again, why are you here?"

"It don't matter how long I've been here, Los. Just tell me who she is," she said, pouting.

"Who I spend time with ain't yo' business, Nikki. How many times do I have to tell you that? What we had is over. You're responsible for the single life you obtain right now. Go harass the nigga you cheated on me with," I said, rolling up my window.

She stood firm in front of the door when I tried to open it. "Move, man! I don't have time for this childish shit!"

"I'm not moving until you tell me what I want to hear! Who is the bitch!" she screamed, clapping her hands.

Letting the window up, I pushed the door enough to get out and hit the start button to kill the engine. Hitting the button to activate my alarm, I walked around her ass toward my crib. As I raised my foot to climb the stairs, I was hit from behind repeatedly in the small of my back. Turning around fast, I grabbed Nikki by her wrist and held on tightly.

"Don't put yo' hands on me! You know how I feel about that shit. Get the fuck on before you make me shake the fuck outta you," I said, releasing her hands. At that moment, "Matrimony" by Wale blared from my phone and I saw the horns come out of Nikki's forehead. Hitting the Bluetooth button in my ear, I answered the call.

"Hey, baby. Let me call you back. I'm handling a situation real quick," I explained.

"I know muthafuckin' well you didn't answer the phone calling another bitch baby!" Nikki belted out.

"Los, what's going on?" Kaymee asked.

"Hold on, bae," I said to her as I stared at Nikki. "Nikki, go home. We are done and it's been that way for half a year. Do not come back to my house with this drama. You made your choice and I honored that shit by walking away. I've moved on and I don't need you trying to make my life miserable. Now get in your shit and go home."

"You are my baby's father and we are tied together forever!"

"Nope, not going to work. The only way that would be possible is if the baby was in this world, Nikki. It's not. You got an abortion because you didn't know if the baby was mine or not, so you got rid of it. Go home!" I yelled at her as I turned to walk up the stairs.

I left her ass standing there looking stupid. She tried that silly shit because she knew the woman she was inquiring about was on the phone. When I went into the house and closed the door, I spoke to Kaymee.

"Sorry about that, baby. What's up?" There was silence on the other end. "Kaymee?" I took my phone from my hip and the home screen was on display. I didn't know when she'd hung up because I was too busy setting the record straight with Nikki's ass.

My thumb hovered over Kaymee's name when I heard the sound of glass and my car alarm going off. I threw my phone on the table by the door and swung it open. When I stepped on the porch, there was a huge hole in my front windshield. Nikki was walking along the side of my car with a crowbar in her hand, writing on the side of my 2018 Benz.

My blood pressure was going up with every step she took. It took everything in me not to go ballistic on her nutty ass. She hadn't noticed me standing there watching her, so I eased back into my house and called the law. As much as I didn't like to call them muthafuckas, it was either that, or choke the fuck out of her.

"Nine, one, one. What's your emergency?" the dispatcher asked.

"I need the police at five twenty-four Whitewater Trail. There's someone outside vandalizing my car," I responded as I watched Nikki continue to destroy my Benz.

"A car is in the vicinity and should be there shortly. Stay on the phone with me until you see them outside."

About three minutes later, I saw the lights of the squad car and Nikki running to her car. "They are coming down the street, but the perpetrator is trying to get away," I informed the dispatcher.

Hearing her tap away on the keys, I saw the police car stop in front of my driveway as Nikki was backing out. She had to stomp on her brakes to avoid hitting the vehicle. The cops jumped out with their weapons drawn.

"Get out the car with your hands up!"

"They're here. I'm going outside now. Thanks for your help," I said, disconnecting the call.

Stepping out on the porch, Nikki stood by her car with her hands over her head. She glared in my direction. "Really, Los? You called the police!"

"Don't talk to him!" the female officer yelled as she patted Nikki down. "You are under arrest for vandalism," the officer said as she cuffed Nikki and read the Miranda Rights to her.

"Fuck you, nigga. I never took you as a punk! But it's all good. That's why I did fuck dude and it was his baby, bitch!"

"Put her ass in the car, Murphy!" the male officer yelled at his partner.

Love Shouldn't Hurt 4

Nikki had never acted that way before, but her true colors were showing in rare form. Answering all the questions the officer asked, I didn't press charges on her, but I was going to put a restraining order on her ass. Nikki was kicking the window of the squad car and the officers had to restrain her legs before they drove off.

I went inside and called Kaymee back, but she didn't respond. I called several times, getting the same results. I was pissed because Nikki put doubt in her mind about me and I knew she was going to avoid me at all costs after the bullshit she heard.

Meesha

Chapter 7

Dot

I was let out of the hospital three days after almost dying and transported to Serenity House Rehabilitation Center in Charleston, Illinois. Dirty's ass had to pick a place that was three hours away from the city to force me to stay. He knew I wouldn't be able to leave without money and transportation. I could stop doing this shit on my own, but he wasn't trying to hear any of that. It was either go or get cut off. I agreed to give it a shot.

My phone was taken upon arrival and I was told I wouldn't have contact with anyone from the outside in the first couple of weeks. I was signed up for the four-month program and the drugs were already calling me. While I was in the hospital, the doctor gave me small doses of methadone to help me cope with the withdrawals I was experiencing.

When I was introduced to the counselor that was assigned to me, I was shocked that she was a beautiful African American woman. On the other hand, I was glad it wasn't a stuck up ass white woman that would be quick to turn her nose up at me. The facility looked like one of those cozy vacation resorts on television.

"Ms. Morrison, I am Yvette Ross and I will be your counselor during your stay at Serenity House. How are you feeling today?" she asked with a smile.

"I'm sleepy. Can I rest before we start whatever it is you about to do?"

"Umm, I'm sorry you're tired and I could only imagine the long drive you had to endure, but we have to get you processed in and get you examined."

"What type of examination do I need? I was just released from the hospital for God's sake! Didn't they send my medical file to you?" I asked irritably.

"Actually, Ms. Morrison. I have all of that in my possession. The examination I will be performing is a sleuth of questions that only you can answer. It will give me a better understanding of what level of treatment you will need while you're here. It is very important for you to be truthful about each question. After this, you will go for a physical examination. Are we clear so far?"

"I don't feel like answering questions right now."

"Okay, let me explain something to you, Dorothy. When you stepped through the doors of Serenity House, you let us know that you wanted to be here to get help. I could be the nicest person you have ever met or I can be your worst nightmare. The choice is yours. Which one do you choose?" Yvette asked, staring at me with her hands folded on the desk.

"You don't know what I'm going through! All you know is that I have a substance problem and came here for help. Getting a degree to help people like me don't make you an expert, Miss Ross! So, don't come for me. You have to walk in my shoes to understand where the fuck I've been in life!"

I hated educated, judgmental muthafuckas. She got the right one though. She is lucky I wanted to change my life for the better. Otherwise, I would've gotten up and walked out of there. All I knew was she better change the way she spoke to me before it be some furniture moving in that bitch.

"Are you done?" she asked, sitting up straight. "First of all, I know all about what you've been through. I lived the life you're living from the age of seventeen to twenty-three. I am now twenty-eight years old. Five years sober because someone cared enough to get me out the streets on the southside of Chicago. I didn't get my degree until I got myself together and that was three years ago.

It took a lot of dedication, learning to love myself, and taking the blame for my actions without placing them on others. In other words, I had to grow to get where I am today. You can do the same if you listen and go with what I'm telling you," she said, looking down at my paperwork. "You are a couple years younger than my mother, but age doesn't matter. The time to get your life right is now and I'm willing to help you with that as long as you're willing to help yourself."

Yvette had checked my ass without using one cuss word. Her young ass didn't look like she used a drug a day in her life and I was stunned when she revealed it to me. It showed me to never judge a book by it's cover. You never know the struggle one has been through. I was lost for words, so she continued with the job at hand.

"Shall we get down to business now, Dorothy?" she asked calmly.

"First off, I want to apologize for jumping to conclusions. I would prefer you call me Dot. Dorothy makes me feel old," I said and laughed, trying to break the ice. Yvette didn't laugh in return.

"Tell me a little about your drug history, Dot."

I didn't know where to start, so I began with my marijuana use. "I started smoking weed when I was sixteen years old, the alcohol soon followed. For years, it was just those two substances. About six or seven months ago was when I started using crack. I obtained a laced bag and haven't been able to shake the need to smoke it since."

"That's how many people usually get addicted to the drug, unknowingly," Yvette said sadly, clearing her throat. "What would you like to accomplish while in rehab?"

"Honestly, I don't know. I've never had to get treatment for anything," I said truthfully.

"Okay, we will take things one day at a time. I will ask that question again at some point. When was the last time you used any type of drug?"

"Friday when I overdosed from a bad batch of crack. I was in the hospital for three days, then I was brought here. In the hospital, I was giving methadone, if that counts," I answered without hesitation.

She scribbled on her pad and glanced up at me. "It's been three days since you've used. Have you ever had thoughts of suicide, depression, or post-traumatic stress disorder?" she asked with her pen hovering over the pad.

"I've never thought about killing myself, but I did go into a slight depression when my daughter was given back to me after my mother passed. I also became slightly depressed when I was evicted from my apartment and everyone turned their backs on me. I was stressed over where I would sleep, but I don't think it was too severe."

"Okay, you did good. I will be taking you to see the physician now. Once you're done there, I will show you to your living quarters," Yvette said, standing.

I hadn't been to the doctor for a checkup in years and was afraid of what they would find. Slowly rising from the chair, I grabbed my bag and flung it over my shoulder. Yvette turned to make sure I was behind her and stopped.

"Dot, you can leave your bag on my desk. You will be brought back here after you see the doctor and then we will go through your things together."

Sweat started forming on my upper lip because I had some things in my bag that would surely get me kicked out of the facility. Walking back into the room, I placed the bag where she instructed. I had to come up with a plan and quickly.

"Don't worry. No one will go into your things without you being present. I promise." Hearing her say that eased my mind a little bit and I followed her to another part of the building.

The facility was huge and beautiful. We walked for a while before we came upon a door that had "Medical" printed on a set of double doors. Yvette swiped her key card and they opened. There was a full medical center that looked like a hospital emergency room unit. As we passed each room, there were patients in almost all of them.

"Is this the place for the people that's sick?" I asked Yvette as we continued down the hall.

"Yes and no. Some of the people are here detoxing and some have serious medical issues. We do all we can right here at Serenity House unless there is an absolute emergency to send a patient out to the hospital. Here we are," she said, stopping in front of a desk.

"Hi, Abby. Tell Dr. Sinclair I have a new patient for him."

"Sure thing, Yvette. He was expecting you so he has Ms. Morrison assigned to room twelve," Abby said, glancing at me. "We have a gown already in the room for you. Get undressed completely and wait for the doctor and I to come in. Yvette, I will page you when Ms. Morrison is done," Abby smiled.

Yvette led me to the room and stood in the doorway. "I'll be back after everything is done. Don't be nervous. Everything will be alright, Dot," she said, closing the door.

Slowly taking my shirt off, I placed it on the chair in the corner. I then removed the other items of clothing and did the same before putting the gown on. Out of nowhere, the taste of crack filled my mouth. This had been happening since I came to at the hospital. I started scratching my arms and rocking back and forth.

Knock, knock.

I instantly stopped scratching as the door crept open. An African American doctor walked in with the nurse Abby behind him. My eyes were focused on the file he had in his hand.

"Hello, I am Dr. Sinclair. How are you?"

"I'm alright," I said nervously.

"Relax. I will give you a full exam today. We will be checking for sexual transmitted diseases, pregnancy, HIV, hepatitis, etcetera. The exam shouldn't take too long and you will be out of here and resting in no time. Do you use needles, snort, or smoke heroin?" he asked, reading from my chart.

"It depends on how I feel actually. I've done it all," I replied, scratching my neck.

Dr. Sinclair looked over my arms and legs with a frown on his face. "You look a little bit underweight, but I don't see any signs of needle use. Are you sure you have injected the drugs?"

I didn't want to lie to him, so I lifted my foot and parted my toes so he could see. "I didn't want anyone to know that I was shooting up, so I injected it between my toes," I said, wincing in pain.

He put the file down and removed a pair of gloves out of the box and put them on. As he examined my feet, he sighed long and hard. Moving each toe apart, he glanced over his shoulder at Abby.

"Go get fifty millimeters of penicillin pronto!" Turning back to my feet, he kept moving my toes and the pain shot up my leg. "You have a case of cellulitis, Ms. Morrison. It is caused by inserting the needle in the same spot between your toes continuously. Your case is mild and very treatable. There is redness, shiny patches on the skin, and soreness in in your foot which I noticed the minute you parted your toes.

I will prescribe penicillin for the next fourteen days. You will take that orally. The Mupirocin will be administered between your toes, three times daily for ten days. That should clear up the infection and you shouldn't have any problems thereafter. The only way the medication won't work is if you start using again. That's impossible as long as you are a patient at Serenity House.

Abby came back with the syringe of penicillin, handing it to Dr. Sinclair along with alcohol wipes. I held out my arm so he could inject the antibiotic. Abby shook her head with a smile on her face.

"Nah, you have to turn around for this one. This medication will be inserted into your backside."

"In my ass! Oh, hell nawl!" I yelled.

"It's the only way. Now lie down on your stomach so we can move on to the next step," Dr. Sinclair said. "You won't even feel it, I promise." Doing as I was told, I braced myself for the pain I knew I was about to experience. "Good job," Dr. Sinclair said, tapping me on my calf. Sitting up, Abby was standing next to the bed with everything she needed to draw my blood.

"I will be drawing a lot of blood from you for testing. The results will be back in a day or two. After this, I will need a urine sample, as well."

It didn't take long for Abby to draw damn near all the blood from my body. I was afraid about the results because half the time I was getting high, I didn't remember most of the things that happened. The anxiety was high and all I wanted to do was get high. I needed a hit and I knew there was no way for me to get the drugs I desired.

"Is there something you can give me because I need to get high. I'm feeling nauseated and I'm getting sick."

"The only thing I can give you is a little bit of methadone. We will be able to determine your detox treatments when your test results return. Until then, you are free to go to your room once we obtain the urine sample that's needed," Dr. Sinclair explained.

Abby held out a small cup and I went into the bathroom to give them what they wanted. It didn't take long for me to relieve myself because I had been holding it since earlier. When I left the bathroom, Yvette was sitting in a chair waiting for me.

"I'll take that out to Abby while you get dressed. Meet me by the nurse's station and I'll take you to your room to get settled." I waited for the door to close before taking off the gown.

Five minutes later, I was walking down the hall to Yvette's office. I grabbed my bag and she escorted me to another wing of the building. We entered an elevator and she pushed the button for the third floor. I was so tired that I wanted to just sleep. I realized Dr. Sinclair didn't give me the methadone that he promised and I was pissed. Getting through the night without my medicine was going to be torture.

"Your suite is this way. The way the rooms are set up, every-one has their own space. It's made like an apartment in a way," Yvette explained as we walked down the hall.

She stopped in front of a door that had my name on a name-plate with the number three beside it. Inserting the key into the lock, she pushed the door open. There was a sofa, love seat, and a chair that surrounded a small coffee table. The two end tables had a lamp on each one and there was a small kitchen. On the other side of the living room, there was a door that was closed and I assumed it was the bedroom.

"I get to stay here by myself?" I asked.

"Yes, this is your suite and you are responsible for keeping it clean. This is not a hotel. There's no one here to clean up after you. I will explain everything to you tomorrow because I know you are tired and want to sleep. But first, I must check your bag to make sure there's nothing illegal in it," she said with her hand held out.

I gave her the bag because what I have in there she will never find, I hoped. As she started pulling a bunch of nothing out of my purse, a call came through on her walkie talkie. Yvette stopped rummaging to answer the call.

"Go 'head," she said into the device.

"We have a situation with thirty-seven on the second floor. Come down immediately."

"Ten four," she said, glancing at my purse then at me. "I'm going to trust that you didn't bring shit in here, Dot. If I find out otherwise, you will get locked up for possession of an illegal substance."

"I don't have anything," I said, dumping everything out of the purse so she could see for herself."

"Okay, goodnight and I'll see you in the morning. This is the key to your suite. Don't lose it because it will cost you to replace it. Don't think about going anywhere because the elevators are not in order for patients at this time of the night. So, don't think about running," she said, smirking. They summoned her again on the walkie talkie and she made her way to the door. "Welcome to Serenity House, Dot," she said, leaving out the door.

Waiting a couple minutes to make sure she didn't double back, I went to lock the door and made a dash for my purse. I had four baggies of heroin in a secret compartment and I was like a kid on Christmas.

"Thank you, Jesus! I'm about to sleep good tonight," I said as I dumped it on the table. I went to the kitchen to find something to mesh it up into powder so I could snort it.

Chapter 8

Montez

Poetry has made great progress in the past couple days. She freaked out when she insisted on seeing the scar on her head. With the staples that were used to hold her scalp together and her hair being gone, she started crying louder than Aria. It took Kaymee and her mother to convince her that it was only hair and it would grow back. Dr. Brim told us the incision was healing nicely and they would be removing the staples in a week or two.

Aria was staring at Poetry as she held her in her arms. Seeing my little family always brought a smile to my face. I was twirling Poetry's wedding ring around in my pocket because it was time to put it back where it belonged, that's on her finger.

"Babe, I have something for you," I said, standing from the chair I was sitting in.

"You better stop buying me stuff, Monty. I'm not moving all this stuff when I leave this hospital," she said, laughing.

"I'm gon' take care of all that. Don't worry yourself about it. As your man, that's my job. All you have to do is hold our baby and stay beautiful," I said, taking her left hand into mine. Kissing the back of her hand, I slid the ring on her finger.

Poetry looked down and the tears slid down her face. "Aw-www, Monty. It's beautiful! Wait, are you proposing to me?" I cocked my head to the side and stared at her. "What's wrong bae?" she asked.

"Poe, we were married the day after Christmas. You don't remember?" I asked, reaching behind me to pull the chair closer to the bed. Sitting down, I rubbed the back of her hand while she fought hard to remember the day that we'd professed our love to one another.

"I'm sorry, I don't remember getting married," she cried. "That was supposed to be a moment to never forget and I have no recollection of it. I feel horrible."

"What are you sorry for, Poe? You didn't know the things that happened to you would occur. I have pictures and video of our special day. You have plenty in your phone and on social media, too," I said, reaching for my phone on the nightstand. "We can reminisce together. I'm all for taking you back to the day you agreed to be my wife."

I started going through the photos in my phone and Poetry looked on with a gleam in her eyes that I hadn't seen in weeks. It felt good to see her smile and gush over the photos. Playing the video from our wedding day, she placed her hand over her mouth.

"Turn it up so I can hear better," she said, shifting Aria in the crook of her arm. We were saying our vows and I couldn't do anything but smile.

"Poetry Renee, I knew from the first day I laid eyes on you that you would be my wife someday. I messed up and almost lost you forever. Fighting with all my might for forgiveness and giving up on the love I have for you wasn't an option. I can't imagine choosing anyone else other than you to marry. Your smile and laugh are only part of the reason I fell in love with you.

But your loyalty, dedication, and love for me, let me know you were the one. Our baby was the icing on the cake. I promise to support, honor, and love you unconditionally, until I take my last breath. I'm looking forward to spending this undying love journey with you. I love you, baby."

With every word I professed to her in front of the preacher, a tear fell from her face. I watched her watch our union for the first time. The nervousness was just as strong as it was the day of. I meant every word I recited to the love of my life. I knew that after that touching moment, she almost left this world leaving me alone.

"Oh Monty, that was so sweet!" she said, wiping the tears with her free hand. Pausing the video, I gave her my undivided attention. "I don't remember what you did to mess up, but I'm glad it's over. It doesn't matter because if a man is pouring his heart out to the woman he loves like that, there's nothing getting in the way of this love." Poetry leaned over and planted a wet kiss on my lips and my lil' man jumped in my pants.

"There's more. Let's watch." Pressing the play button, her voice filled the room.

"Montez, we had our ups and downs throughout the years and I'm glad I didn't let another day go by without you. Life is too short not to follow your heart. The love you have shown me has actually taught me, there's only one love for me and that's yours. I'm ready to spend the rest of my life loving you, baby. Nothing will ever keep us apart. Ain't no breaking up once I say I do. I'm ready to be your ride or die chick," she said and chuckled. *"I love you so much."*

When we got to the part where I got to kiss my bride, "Monty! How the hell were you groping me in front of them folks like that? I feel violated!" she yelled.

"Waaaa waaaaa." Aria was startled by her mama's big mouth.

"Now look what you've done."

Poetry rocked Aria, trying to calm her down, but it was not working. She laid her between her legs and checked her diaper. "She's wet. Hand me a diaper and the wipes." Handing her what she needed, I watched with admiration because I prayed for hours on in to have the chance to see her be a mother to our daughter.

After she dried Aria, Poetry grabbed the bottle off the nightstand. The baby didn't hesitate latching on to the nipple. We watched her for what seemed like an eternity and she drank two ounces of milk in record time. When Poetry took the bottle out of Aria's mouth to burp her, she screamed like she was pinched.

"Okay, greedy," she said, putting the nipple back in her mouth. "I can't wait until I'm done taking these meds. Breastfeeding is what I want to do with Aria."

"You missing suction on them titties, baby? I got you. I've always wondered what titty milk tasted like."

"Shut up, fool. You got jokes. You won't be suckin' on nothing anytime soon, get ready to jerk that bad boy," she laughed.

"I need you to be fully healed so I can drill you the way you like. You gon' get the business. Be ready because you gon' be the mother of two babies in diapers," I said, smirking.

"Shit, you a lie! We ain't trying to do that," Poetry's mama said, entering the room. "Y'all already made me a grandma before my damn time. It's only been two weeks and there's still a month to go. Hey, baby," she squealed, kissing Poe on the cheek and Aria on her forehead.

"Hey, ma. Where are you going her so early?" Poe asked.

"Your husband has some things to take care of, so I agreed to come sit with you and the baby."

"Even you knew he was my husband and I didn't. Why don't I remember anything from my past?"

"Dr. Brim did tell us that you may experience some memory loss and it will come back gradually as you continue to heal. We won't worry about that right now. The important thing is that you are here with us in the flesh. Anything you want to know, we will gladly fill you in on," Chris explained.

I draped a blanket over my shoulder and took Aria from Poetry's arm to burp her. She sounded like a grown man that drank a couple beers. I kissed her all over her face because it would be my first time leaving the hospital for a long period. Leaving my girls wasn't what I wanted to do, but I needed to handle business.

"Monty, stop kissing on her before she starts breaking out," Chris said.

"Mama, no disrespect, but I'm gon' give my baby lots of kisses and can't nobody stop me," I said, kissing Aria once more before putting her in the baby bed. Walking over to the bed, I leaned over and planted a kiss on Poetry's lips. "I'll be back. Call me if you need anything, beautiful. I love you. Peace out, overprotective granny," I said, rustling Chris' hair.

"Keep it up and get whooped, Monty. Get out!"

"This is my house, woman. I pay to lay up in here as long as wifey is here. I'll leave, but I'll be back," I winked at her and left out the room after grabbing my phone.

***

I was meeting Jonathan at the house that he'd purchased for Poetry and I. When I pulled up to the address that was on the deed, I was in awe. The two-story brick house was beautiful with a well-manicured lawn and three-car garage. Jonathan stepped onto the porch and I got out of my ride.

"I thought you were gon' sit out here forever, nigga. Get yo' ass in this house," he said as I walked up the steps.

"What's up, Jay?" I said, slapping hands with him.

"Shit. I just wanted to get yo' ass outta that hospital for a lil' bit. How's Poetry doing?" he asked, leading the way into the house.

"She's a lot better. I put her wedding ring back on her finger this morning and she didn't even know we were married. It hurt for a minute, but things will start coming back to her soon, I hope."

"Yeah, she had major surgery to her head. That's one of the side effects. It's usually not long term, so we just have to keep the prayers going up for her. Come on so I can show you around yo' new crib. Take ya shoes off at the door. This is the only spot that don't have carpeting other than the bathrooms."

"Damn, fam. This is nice. How many rooms in this joint?"

"There's four bedrooms, a living room, dining room, kitchen, two baths, full basement, and a laundry room. The backyard is huge and will give the baby plenty room to play. I got first dibs on a barbeque once y'all are settled in."

"You got it," I said as I glanced around.

I walked through my new crib in awe. Coming from the North side of Chicago, I've never had the privilege to live in a house, let alone own one. Every room I stepped in was furnished. The kitchen had stainless steel appliances, marble counters, and a dishwasher. The cabinets were oak wood and filled with food and dishes.

"I appreciate everything, but I can't let you foot the bill for all of this, Jay," I said as we entered the only bedroom downstairs. It had been transformed into a duel office for me and Poetry.

"Ain't shit you can do about it, young blood. I don't want anything in return. I don't want you to look at this as an act of charity. You earned this. You have been a true nigga and you love Poetry. I don't want you to have to worry about nothing but your family. Everybody needs a little help sometimes."

"Thanks. I'll leave it alone, but this is not the end of this conversation. Why the hell did you buy food? We will be at the hospital for a while. It will go bad."

"Nah, it won't. Chris and Stan will be coming later today. Come on, let's go check out upstairs. I have a surprise for you."

"You've surprised me enough, Jay," I said, going up the stairs behind him.

We went to a room right off the staircase to the right and Jonathan opened the door. There was a king-sized bed with black bedding on it with lots of pillows. Poetry loved pillows. She needed at least three to herself. Me myself, only needed one. There was a sixty-inch TV mounted on the wall and a vanity for my wife.

There was a walk-in closet big enough to be another bedroom. It was set up so my clothes would be on one side and Poetry's on the other. I was really pleased with the set up and I couldn't wait to move in.

"I had this put in for you," Jonathan said, walking to the back of the closet. He pushed the wall slightly and it opened. "You will need a safe to hold your money. I know you only put so much in the bank, which is smart. You can set the code to whatever you want it to be. I left it on the factory setting which is one, two, three, four. Enter that first, then set the new code."

Doing as he instructed, I set the new code and the safe opened. It was small but deep. I would be able to fit plenty inside. "Good looking," I said, closing the safe's door and pushing the wall back in place.

"Check out this bathroom, Monty," Jonathan yelled, forcing me to follow his voice.

As I stepped into the bathroom, I started thinking about all the nasty shit me and Poetry could do in there. There were his and hers sinks, the shower sat alone on one wall, and the tub on the other. It was a Jacuzzi tub with about ten jets.

"I had this shower custom designed because it was something I wanted, but Katrina didn't. She kept talking about how much her hair would get messed up," he said, shaking his head. "It is a chrome finished sixteen-inch shower system with a hand shower, as well. There are six body sprays as well as a rainforest shower-head. The water changes color with the temperature."

"That's dope! I've never seen anything like that."

Ding, dong,

"You expecting somebody?" I asked Jonathan when I heard the doorbell. I didn't want anyone to know where I laid my head at night with my family.

"Yeah, that's Los. He called and said he needed to talk to us, so I invited him over."

"A'ight, I'll go let him in," I said, leaving out the bathroom.

I bounced down the steps, looked through the glass paned door, and saw Los standing on the other side with his back turned and his phone to his ear. Opening the door quietly, I heard the end of his conversation.

"Come on, Kaymee. Call me back. I've been leaving voicemails for days. Let me explain what's going on before you jump to conclusions. I'm trying not to show up at ya spot, ma. I want to clear my name. Hit my line soon."

"What the fuck you do?" I said, catching him off guard.

Los turned around looking like a pitiful teenage boy. "That bitch Nikki did it. I didn't do shit," he said, walking past me. "Oh, this is tight, son!" he said, stepping into the house.

"Get back on the subject at hand, Los. What happened with Nikki?"

"She showed up outside my crib the day I took Kaymee out. One of her hoe friends told her they saw me at the movies. Nikki called herself questioning me about who I was with and I ex-plained that it didn't matter. Kaymee called and I told her I was dealing with a situation and I'd call her back. Nikki started talking about I was stuck with her because I was her baby's father.

Monty, the bitch got an abortion and I didn't even know if the baby was mine because she was fuckin' wit' another nigga. She admitted that it wasn't that night when her ass got arrested for fuckin' up my ride. That's the reason I stopped messing with her ass. I caught her at the club fuckin' the nigga in the men's bathroom. Now Kaymee won't answer any of my calls," he explained.

"Give her a minute. That nigga Dray did her dirty, so she is being cautious. I know the history between you and Nikki and the bitch is crazy. Handle that shit because sis has been through enough."

"I know. That's why I'm trying to get in touch with her. I don't want her to think that every nigga is like that pussy, Dray. Monty, I want to show her what it's like to be treated right. You know, what love really feels like. I'm a patient man and I will get your sister and do right by her," Los said.

"Honestly, she's worth the wait. We're upstairs looking around. Jonathan really decked this muthfucka out for us. I'll show you the rest of the house afterwards. Shoes off at the door, if you don't mind," I said before leading the way upstairs.

"It's about time y'all decided to come up here," Jonathan said, coming out of the master bedroom. There are two more rooms to see, then we can go out back and chop it up." Passing the door that had a sign on it, we went to the room that was at the end of the hall. It had a king-sized bed, a TV on the wall, and dressers to match the bed. "This could definitely be a guest room. I only put the necessities in this one. Now, for my surprise."

Glancing into the second bathroom, it was a little smaller than the one in the master bedroom, but it was still nice. There was a regular shower and tub in that one, but it was bigger than the average size. Jonathan stood outside of the room that had the sign on it, but the sign was now in his hands.

"I had this room designed my way. When Kaymee was born, I didn't get the opportunity to give her all that I wanted her to have. So, baby Aria got it all when I decided to buy this house for y'all," he said, holding up the sign. It read, "Princess Aria" in calligraphy letters.

When Jonathan opened the door, he ushered me in first. I strolled in slowly with a big smile on my face. There was a grey crib that had a throne like scheme. There was a crown above it that had a sheer covering that draped around it.

"The bed will convert as she grows. When the time comes, she will have a twin-sized bed. There's a rocking chair in the corner for when you guys want to soothe her in the middle of the night. I made sure that you guys had a video monitor so you can keep a visual sight of Aria from anywhere in the house.

All the gifts y'all received, were brought them in here and put where I wanted them to go. All of the clothes are hanging on little hangers in the closet. She has diapers for every stage of her life. There's a changing table and one of those diaper things that prevent the room from smelling like dirty diapers. There's a bottle warmer and a breast pump over there on the royal table. I didn't know if Poetry was breastfeeding or not, but just in case."

"This is too much. I will be thanking you for the rest of my life, fam. I'm a man. How am I not gonna repay you for this? I fell less than a man accepting all of what you did without hittin' you with something," I said, turning to Jonathan.

"Bro, you do a lot for many people. The last thing you need to worry about is getting a whole house together. Poetry needs you to concentrate on helping her get better and taking care of Aria. You are an honorable dude that's hustling, going to school, being a husband, and a father. I salute you, my nigga," Los said, patting me on the back.

"I'm tryin' to tell his ass. Don't worry about shit," Jonathan chimed in. "I've showed you everything except the laundry room. You can find that shit on your own. It's time to go outside and blow somethin'."

"I second that," I said, staring at the wall memoir on the wall. It was a drawing of Aria sleeping in a pink and purple onesie with the words, 'Princess Aria' above it. "That is beautiful! Who the hell drew that? And I love the way they captured her," I exclaimed.

"I did, my nigga. A nigga can do more than sell dope," Los said, beaming with pride over his work.

"Damn, I didn't know you had talent like that! Good looking, my nigga. That's why yo' ass was pressed to see everything. You were in on this shit," I said, punching him in the arm before I pulled him in a brotherly hug. I couldn't stop smiling as we left Aria's room.

"What do you need to talk to us about, Los?" Jonathan asked when we got outside.

Chapter 9

Kaymee

School started back the end of January and I've been studying and kicking ass. I was on the Dean's list and ahead of my class. My advisor Ms. Parker called me in her office, telling me what I already knew. She told me when the time was right, I would have recommendations from the Dean, her, and many of my professors. I was ecstatic because I had people that were proud of me and they weren't family.

Speaking of family, I hadn't heard from Dot in a while. That could be a good or bad thing with her ass. You'd never know. Poetry was doing better as the days went by and I couldn't wait for her to get out of the hospital. She had a little case of memory loss, but I was filling her in on what she didn't remember.

She was in touch with her advisor and they were working with her through her situation. Poetry received the assignments that she missed as well as exams to complete online. At first, she struggled with it, but she was catching on. Aria won't let her work in peace. She was going to be spoiled.

I was on my way to West End mall before going to the hospital. Poetry told me that Aria was discharged two days ago, but Monty didn't want to leave without her. The house my father bought for them was beautiful. Chris cooked and I needed some of that pasta in my life.

Aria's room was fit for her. She was going to be the diva of that household, Monty better get his gun ready. When mama Chris told me Los painted the picture on the wall, I couldn't believe it. He didn't seem like the type that would be interested in art. He never brought it up during conversations.

As I parked my car, Los' name appeared on my phone as it vibrated in the cup holder. I had been ignoring his calls for almost two weeks. He had to take care of his drama before he came at me again. I'd been through enough in my past relationship and I wasn't going through that shit again. Fighting a bitch over a nigga was something I wouldn't subject myself to.

Throwing the phone in my purse without answering it, I got out and set the alarm on my car. I truly didn't know what the hell I was at the mall for. Being cramped in the dorm without Poetry and only studying was driving me crazy. I just wanted to get out.

Victoria Secret was the first store I saw when I entered and I headed straight for it. Buying panties and bras never got old to me because I always needed them. Vickie had a sale going on and I loved a good discount. There was a pretty green bra and panty set that called me from the doorway. I had to have it.

I grabbed a basket that somebody's trifling ass left in the aisle and threw my garments inside. I felt my phone vibrating and knew it was Los, so I didn't even look at it. When it buzzed again, I had to see what was up. There was a message from Dray. I hadn't heard from him in a while. Opening the message, I read what he had to say.

Dray Montgomery: You looking good in those tight ass pants. I see you dropped that nigga since he ain't wit' you.

Dray Montgomery: You shouldn't ignore the nigga that loves you, Kaymee.

His ass was like a magician, popping up at any given time without me knowing where he was. I glanced around frantically and my heart was racing a mile a minute. This was a man that didn't love me. He was psychotic and possessive. I was outright scared of him.

I couldn't spot him, but I knew he was around. The enthusiasm that I had when I stepped in the mall was gone. Leaving suddenly wasn't an option because then he would know that I was afraid. Plus, I didn't want him to catch me outside alone. I was safer in this mall in case he wanted to act stupid.

Moving to another section of the store, I saw a variety of pink leggings with the shirts to match. Rummaging through the rack, I chose one in green and black, adding them to my basket. One of the pants fell off the hanger and onto the floor. Bending over to pick it up, I felt a presence behind me and I went still as a board.

"Hey, baby. You didn't respond to my message."

I rose up slowly and my heart was in my throat. Dray was so close to me that I could feel his thigh on my ass. He placed his hand around my waist and eased me upright. Pressing my back against his chest, he whispered in my ear.

"I've missed you. It's good to finally have you in my arms again."

I shrugged out of his grasp and took a couple steps back. "Hi, Dray," was all I could muster up to say.

"Why are you so timid? I'm sorry for putting my hands on you. I love you, Kaymee. I would like for us to start over, come together as one again," Dray had the nerve to say.

"Apology accepted, but I want you to know that we will never be together again. You had your chance and didn't do right by it. Threatening me, frightening me and, basically, stalking me were true signs to get away from you. When you tried to run me off the road, I covered for you, Dray. But when you put your hands on me, that was the last straw."

"What the fuck do you want me to do? Get on my hands and knees and beg you? I said I was sorry," he replied with gritted teeth.

I didn't want him to get angry in the store. Smoothing things over was all I could think to do. I had no choice but to tell him what he wanted to hear. Dray had shown me in the past that he would do something drastic anywhere.

"Calm down, okay. I was telling you about the things that you did to me because you seemed to have forgotten. Let's go to the food court and get something to eat. Maybe if we sat and talked about this like adults, we will be able to get a better understanding," I said, dropping the basket on the floor.

"What about your stuff? You not gon' buy the shit now?"

"Nah, talking to you is more important than shopping right now," I said, walking toward the door.

Dray followed me as I led the way to the food court. I was trying to figure out a way to alert somebody that he was back in Atlanta, but nothing came to mind. He was on me like flies to shit, barely watching what was happening in front of him as we walked. When we arrived at the food court, I wasn't hungry but I made the suggestion to go there. I had to eat something.

"Do you want Chipotle?" he asked.

"Yeah, I'll take a steak burrito bowl with extra steak and chicken, brown rice, lettuce, salsa, sour cream, and no beans. I will also have a medium pink lemonade, no ice," I said, removing a twenty-dollar bill from my wallet.

"Kaymee, I'm not letting you pay for anything. I got this. Find a table and I'll order our food."

I was thanking God when he offered to go to the counter to get our food. Hurrying to find a seat, I chose a booth that would hide my hands so he couldn't see what I was doing behind the partition. Dray was in my sight, but he couldn't see me, so I knew I had to be quick with what I was doing.

My daddy was the person I called. His phone rang several times and I thought the voicemail was going to pick up, but he answered right on time. "Hey, baby girl," he sang into the phone.

"Daddy, I need you to listen to me. I went to the mall just to get out of the house. To make a long story short, Dray is here. He snuck up behind me. I'm at West End mall. I'm about to try to see if he will tell me where he's been staying. I'm scared, so come and sit in the cut or something. We're in the food court. I gotta go because he's coming back to the table."

I hung up my phone just in time and dropped it in my purse as soon as he walked by the table. "Hey, I'm right here," I said cheerfully.

"You had a nigga thinking you ran off or some shit. I wanted to see what table you were at while I waited for the bitch that's at the front of the line ordering everything on the menu. I'll be back, beautiful," Dray said, kissing me on the cheek before walking back to the counter.

Wiping off the spot he kissed, my phone vibrated and Los' number appeared on the screen. I was still mad at him, so I didn't answer. A couple seconds later, a text followed.

Los: You don't have to answer. I just wanted you to know that I was here. Get any information outta that nigga because I got a bone to pick with his ass. It was good to see you disgusted with him putting his lips on you.

Scanning the food court, I didn't see Los anywhere. He knew Dray had kissed me, so I knew he was there somewhere. My eyes landed on my father as Dray was heading back to the table with a tray in each hand. I threw my phone back in my purse so he wouldn't be suspicious of anything and bolt.

"Here you go," he said, placing the tray in front of me. "What have you been up to?" he asked, after sitting down.

"School, basically."

"Did you stop seeing that nigga Los?" he asked, taking a bite of his burrito.

"There's nothing going on between the two of us. I told you we were just friends." That wasn't a lie because I wasn't fucking with Los.

"Those pictures told me something different. Y'all looked cozy as hell and very comfortable with each other."

"Everything that has nothing to do with us as a couple will look a certain way to you, Dray. I'm sorry to keep saying this, but we won't mesh as a couple. We had some good and bad times and I want us to be cordial as friends. I need to know if you can handle that."

A grimace appeared on his face but quickly disappeared. His nose flared wide and he started breathing heavily. I knew he was mad and was trying to hide it. Dray's deathly stare shook me because he was capable of hurting me when he was angry.

"Do I look like I want to be your *friend*?" he asked, gesturing with his fingers. "Come on, Kaymee. Don't patronize me, man. I came back to Atlanta just for you."

"You came back for me? Dray, where have you been? I need to know in order to give you the answers you are seeking. The last time we talked, you told me you were out of town on business. When did it go from business to you coming back just for me?" I asked as he looked around the food court. I was afraid he would see Los or my daddy, but he never looked behind him.

"What are you looking for?" I asked softly.

"I don't know. Something don't feel right," he said still scoping out the area.

"What have you done, Dray? You are running from something? What is it?"

"You think I'm stupid!" he screamed, jumping up.

Both Los and my daddy started heading in our direction. I shook my head no to stop them from coming any closer. They got the hint and went back to their spot out of sight. Continuing to shake my head, I finally found my voice to respond.

"No, I don't think you're stupid. Sit down, Dray. Why would you think that?"

"Kaymee, I know that your daddy and Monty are looking for me for what I did to you," he said lowering his voice as he sat down. He pushed his food away and folded his hands in front of him. "You are still scared of me and you may have called them while I was getting the food."

"Dray, I didn't call anyone. I may be scared of you because of what you did to me, but I don't think you meant to hurt me. Everybody is entitled to a second chance. To ease your mind, my father and Monty aren't worried about what you did to me. I told them that I didn't want them to do anything to you. Both of them promised to leave it alone. You have nothing to worry about.

Come back to Atlanta, Dray. You are almost finished with school. You've worked too hard just to throw your education away. I'll help you with your drug problem and whatever else you're dealing with. Until you get yourself together, we can't move forward.

I'm willing to give us another chance." I had to make what I was saying believable. It was the only way to get any information from him.

"I can't come back to Atlanta. There's other shit going on that you don't know about. I want you to leave with me, Kaymee."

"I can't leave, Dray. You know how important school is to me. I won't give up on my education for anything in this world, not even you. Coming to visit every other weekend or something, I can do that. Before I agree though, where did you move to and why?"

"The why is not important. Just know that I was a little homesick. If you were paying attention when I talked, you would know where I live now. I won't tell you where exactly because like I said, there's other shit going on and I don't want to put you in harm's way. I'll be leaving tomorrow at noon, but I had to see you before I left."

My daddy stood up and held his arms wide. He looked like he was getting impatient. I knew there was be nothing I could do to stop him from approaching Dray. Nodding my head, my daddy took that as go and started making his way over to us.

"I understand. We have nothing but time to figure out what to do," I said as Los and my daddy stood next to our table.

"What's up, Drayton? Long time no see, playa," Jonathan said with a smirk. "Where ya been hiding and where's my money?"

"You ain't gotta come at me like that, brah. That's the reason I came back. I got yo' shit at my hotel," Dray said, glaring at me.

"What is he talking about, Dray? You owe my daddy money?" I asked.

"Stay out of this, Kaymee. This is business that I'll settle with this nigga. Now, why didn't you hit my line and tell me you had my shit? Don't let another lie come out yo' mouth either, nigga!" Jonathan snapped.

"You set me up, bitch? I knew I shouldn't have trusted yo' muthafuckin' ass!"

Before Dray could get another word out of his mouth, Los punched him it. Dray fell over in the booth and Los grabbed him by the front of his shirt, dragging him out. Dray tried swinging but missed and that only pissed Los off. He punched Dray in the ribcage, making him double over,

"Call her out her name again, muthafucka!"

The people that were eating scattered away from the commotion and out of the food court. Los was beating the hell out of Dray when security came from every direction. The presence of security didn't stop Los from beating the hell out of Dray.

"We don't allow this type of behavior in our establishment sir," one of the security guards said, grabbing Los.

"Nigga, if you don't get yo' hands off him, you will wish you had stayed wherever the fuck you was before bringing yo' ass over here!" Jonathan yelled, pushing the guard.

"The police are on their way and you will get arrested for disturbing the peace," another guard said.

"Fuck you and the muthafuckin' police! Get the fuck outta my business!" Los shot back.

Dray took that moment to high tail it out of the food court. He was running like a skilled track star, too. Jonathan and Los took off after him. The guards weren't far behind, and I was keeping up the rear. All of them were running too fast, but I had them in my sights.

Dray pushed a lady out of his way and she fell hitting her head on the window of the Champs store. I wanted to help the woman, but I had to make sure my daddy was good. If he got his hands on Dray, his time breathing on earth would be over. Dray ran out of the exit door and cut left and Jonathan was right behind him. By the time I made it outside, Atlanta police were jumping out of their cars.

I saw Los cut the corner and I hurried to my car to pick both him and my daddy up. When I reached my car, I saw Los running and there weren't any police behind him. Backing out, I drove beside him and honked my horn. I popped the locks so he could get in and pulled off.

"Where is my daddy?" I asked.

"He ran down Lee Street Southwest. The law is on his ass and that nigga Dray got away. If I catch his ass, he's dead. That ass whoopin' I gave him wasn't good enough for me. How the fuck did you end up with him anyway?" he asked as I drove, trying to keep an eye out for my daddy.

"He came up behind me while I was in Victoria Secret. I don't know how he found out where I was. He came out of nowhere."

Los phone rang and he answered on the first ring. "Yeah, Jay. Where you at?" he asked quickly. "A'ight, I'm in the car with Kaymee. We're on our way. Stay put," he said, hanging up. "Go to the Popeyes on Oak Street. Jonathan dipped off in there hiding from the law." As I left the mall's parking lot to pick up my daddy, Los took another shot at questioning me about Dray. "Where is Dray laying his head, Kaymee?"

"I don't know where he is here, but he told me that he was homesick," I started saying as I pulled up to the restaurant. Jonathan came out and jumped in the car and I sped off. "I think he went back to Massachusetts."

"Who went back to Massachusetts?" Jonathan asked.

"I was telling Los what I learned about Dray. He didn't tell me where he was staying here, but he told me that he got homesick and I should know where he lives now. All I know is that he was born and raised in Boston. Monty may know more details than I do," I said, keeping my eyes on the road.

"I'll find out. Take me to the crib. I'll come back later to get my car. Shit too hot for me to double back now. Dray will be a distant memory very soon. Did his punk ass tell you how long he will be here?"

"His flight leaves at noon. That's all he would say. He wanted me to leave with him, but I refused."

"I'm about to make a call because he won't continue to walk around with my muthafuckin' money," Jonathan said as he made a call and put it on speaker. "Aye, G? That nigga Dray is in Atlanta, but he got away from me and Los. I need one of the lil' niggas from the Chi to get on the next thing smoking so they can take a flight to Boston tomorrow."

"Is that right? He really thinks he's gonna get away with fucking over my money, huh? I got just the person to send down there. Don't worry, he will be dealt with and I will keep you posted. You know what to do if you see his ass again, Unc.

Tell Kaymee to stay the fuck away from him. I gotta go. Ryleigh is about to whine because I'm on the phone. You know how that goes," he said, laughing.

"Yeah, give my niece a kiss for me with her spoiled ass and tell Nova I said hello."

"Will do, fam. Be easy and keep ya eyes open."

"Daddy, I didn't know Dray—"

"I believe you, baby girl. Stay at the house tonight until I know for sure that nigga got on that plane. I will kill his whole family if something happens to you."

"Or I can stay guard at her dorm," Los said slickly.

"Nah, I'm good on that," I said, rolling my eyes. "I'll stay at my daddy's house. Thanks, but no thanks. You tried it though. You have a lot of shit to clean up beforehand, don't you think?" I said sarcastically to Los.

"If you would've took the time to hear me out, you know, let me explain the situation, you wouldn't be categorizing me with that nothing ass nigga that did you wrong," he snapped back.

"Save that shit for another time. Let her ass drive. I'm not trying to hear all that back and forth shit right now. If y'all gon' try to build something together, both of y'all need to talk that shit out and get over it or go y'all separate ways," Jonathan said, ceasing the bickering quickly.

I was fuming like a kimono dragon because Los was wrong and he knew it. Niggas always had an excuse as to why they fucked up. I wasn't trying to hear the bullshit he was spitting. He could kiss my ass because I was done with the situation altogether.

Chapter 10

Drayton

That bitch Kaymee set my ass up and she was gon' pay for it. I was watching her while I was in line and her head was down. Knowing that she was afraid of what I did to her, I should've known she would contact them niggas like I was trying to kill her or something. That was the reason I went back to the table to see what her ass was doing. But she was quick as hell because I didn't see any indication of her being on her phone.

When I heard Jonathan's voice, my heart stopped mid beat because I feared the worse. Taking his product and fleeing the state after assaulting his daughter was a death sentence. The lie of having his money rolled off my tongue without thought and if looks could kill, Kaymee would be dead. She was sitting there looking just as surprised as me at seeing her daddy.

"You set me up, bitch? I knew I shouldn't have trusted yo' muthafuckin' ass!"

The blow to my jaw came out of nowhere unexpectedly. I thought Jonathan was the one that rocked my ass, but it was Los' bitch ass. He hit me so hard that I fell over into the booth. I was yoked up and beat the fuck down. Catching me off guard gave him the upper hand and there wasn't much I could do to redeem myself.

"Call her outta her name again, nigga!" was all I heard as he kicked me in my ribcage.

I was stuck in a fetal position until I heard somebody trying to break up the commotion. I used the distraction to formulate a plan to get away before they killed me. Jonathan never went anywhere without a piece and I knew he was ready to pop my ass for everything I'd done.

"We don't allow this type of behavior in our establishment, sir," one of the guards yelled, grabbing Los off me.

My eye was throbbing and I could taste the metallic flavor of blood in my mouth. While the guards were trying to diffuse the situation, I hauled ass. Dashing for the nearest exit, I ran like my life depended on it. Muthafuckas were in my way and I was pushing pass their ass without stopping.

"Move!" I yelled out to a woman that was walking slow as fuck. She didn't get out of my way fast enough and I pushed her ass hard to get past. I trained my good eye on the exit in front of me as I fought hard to get to it.

Bursting through the door, the air hit my face as I cut through the parking lot. My ride was on the other side of the mall and I needed to get to it in order to save my life. The sound of some-one's feet pounding the pavement behind me was deafening in my ears. Glancing behind me was out of the question because that would slow down my pace.

"You are dead when I catch yo' ass, nigga!" I heard Jonathan scream from behind me.

When I saw the lights of the squad cars, I thanked God. Nothing drastic would happen because Jonathan was still on papers and he wasn't ready to go back to jail. He veered off in the other direction and the law pursued him. I slid under a car until the coast was clear before coming out jogging to find my car.

Finally reaching my rental, I slid into the driver's seat and peeled out of the parking lot. I headed straight for the hotel because it was time for me to lay low until I got on the plane the next day. I had been back in Atlanta for four days and had been scoping out Kaymee's dorm. It didn't dawn on me to track her through her phone until that day.

She had deleted me the day I led Monty to the mall her and Poetry was at back in Chicago, but I remembered her login information. I was surprised she didn't change that shit but was happy when it worked after entering it into my phone. When the dot started moving, I headed out the door.

I kept leaving messages on her social media as I drove, but she hadn't responded. Shit, she didn't even look at them. It only pissed me off more, but she would get what was coming to her. Kaymee was not going to get away with what almost happened to me. I parked the car and got out and rushed inside the hotel.

I wanted to pop a pill badly, but I didn't bring any with me because I was traveling by plane. But I needed to get my mind right. Settling on a drink instead, I sat on the bed and sipped slowly as I thought back on the events that took place. My phone chimed and I picked it up. Jonathan was calling my phone, but I didn't answer it. As I placed it back on the bed, it rang again.

"What are you calling me for, nigga?' I barked into the phone.

"I didn't hear all that hoorah when we was face to face! Your chest swole like a muthafucka now that yo' ass got away. Yo' day coming. Keep hiding, but you won't be able to hide much longer. You got fifty thousand outta me, but you won't live to spend that shit," Jonathan threatened into the phone.

"Look, Jay. I told you I had yo' money, nigga! Ya boy got in his feelings and prevented me from getting that package to you. My life is on the line here and I can't trust you to even meet up to handle that business. I didn't run with yo' loot, nigga! I got that!" I continued to lie about giving him his money. He wasn't getting shit.

"Keep it, Dray. That money won't make me or break me. I want ya life, muthafucka and I'm gon' get it. Stop contacting my daughter and watch ya back! Remember, the Goons are every-where. There's no way you will live to enjoy that bread," he said, hanging up.

Jonathan's words rang in my head constantly after he hung up. He wanted me to stop contacting Kaymee, but it wasn't going to happen. I went straight to her social media and she had made a post that read, *"When you leave a situation, but the situation doesn't want to let you go."* She was out of her mind calling me a muthafuckin' situation. I'm a nigga that loves a bitch that's dirty. I went straight to her inbox.

Drayton Montgomery: You playing games with the wrong muthafucka, Kaymee! Why would you call them niggas even though I wasn't trying to hurt you? All I was trying to do was talk to yo' ass and this how you do me! I've already apologized for the shit that I'd done and you said you understood, but you had already set me up to be killed!

I waited for her to respond and when she read the message and didn't reply, I wanted to find her ass and choke her out. I opened the "Find my Friend" app on my phone, but nothing came up. She couldn't have figured out I was following her through the app that fast. Logging out, I put her information in again, but it said the login information was incorrect.

Downing the glass of Hennessy I had in my hand, I got up and grabbed the bottle and drank from it. My phone rang and I glanced down and saw Melody's name on the screen. I didn't want to answer because she had no clue I was back in Atlanta. She had my son and I didn't even attempt to see them when I landed.

"What's up?" I asked, answering the phone.

"What's up? Nah, how about you tell me why people are constantly coming to my house looking for you? What the fuck are you into, Dray?" she screamed in my ear.

"I don't know what the fuck you talking about! Shouldn't nobody be coming to yo' crib looking for me. I don't even live there."

"I know that! This is the second time these niggas been here. I was told you are back in Atlanta. Stay yo' ass far away from here! I don't want whatever you are into around my baby. You weren't hear for his birth, so you are not on his birth certificate. I'm all the daddy he needs, Dray. Get yo' life in order before you even try to be a part of my son's life. All this drama is exactly what I don't need."

"Listen to me, Melody. I haven't don't anything to anyone, okay? I don't know who has come to your house, but they are lying. Tell them the truth, you haven't seen me. That's all you have to do."

"You must think I'm stupid, don't you? I know you put your hands on that girl, Dray. That's why you upped and left, leaving everything behind, including your son. I also know that you stole some shit that didn't belong to you. Don't bring that shit over here because I will call the police on all you muthafuckas.

I'll be changing my number. Get out of Atlanta because they are talking about killing your stupid ass. I don't understand you at all. You had everything going for yourself and you threw it all away," she said as I heard my baby crying in the background. "I have to go. My baby needs me," she said, hanging up before I could say anything else.

Melody sent me a couple pictures when my son was born, but I hadn't seen him in the flesh. He was the spitting image of me and she named him Xavier Carter. She didn't even give him my last name. I couldn't be mad at her because I did leave both of them behind. I didn't want a baby to begin with, so it didn't bother me.

There was so much I had to digest in a short amount of time and I wanted to shut everything out. The only way to do that was to go through the fifth of alcohol I held in my hand. I drank until nothing was left in the bottle and passed out.

***

I was awakened by the sound of my phone ringing. Rolling over, I grabbed it off the nightstand. It was the transport company that was picking up my car from the apartment I used to live in. "Hello," I said into the receiver.

"Mr. Montgomery, I wanted to inform you that I had your car loaded on the truck. I will be heading out later this afternoon and I will be in Boston tomorrow morning."

"Okay, that's cool. I will be there whenever you arrive. Thank you and drive safely with my baby. Don't damage my shit," I warned him.

"You don't have to worry about that, sir. I'm very good at doing my job. I haven't had a complaint yet," he said, laughing. "But I will see you tomorrow. Enjoy your flight."

Rolling out of the bed, I headed to the bathroom to take a shower. My flight left at noon and it was already after nine. I always wanted to be at the airport waiting to board versus rushing to catch the flight. The hot water hit my body and soothed the aches I didn't realize I had until that moment. Thoughts of Los stomping me the day before had me angry at myself for running like a bitch.

I washed my body thoroughly and got out snatching a towel off the rack. Walking out of the bathroom, I grabbed my bag and pulled out a black sweat suit with my black and white Nikes. I dressed quickly to leave because my mind was on slapping Kaymee around before I left, but I knew that wouldn't be a wise choice to make.

Surveying the room to make sure I hadn't forgotten anything after tying my shoes, I clutched the handle of my bag and left the hotel room. After checking out, I went outside and hopped in my rental. The weather was nice. I wish it would be the same in Boston, but it wouldn't be. Removing my phone from my hip, I went to Kaymee's social media and saw she was online. I called her through her messenger and was surprised she answered.

"Nigga, weren't you told not to contact Kaymee? You don't follow directions well I see."

"When it comes to my woman, there's no direction to follow, muthafucka! Put her on the phone," I said, backing out of the parking spot.

"Nah, homie. See that's where you're wrong. You had her and didn't know what to do with her. Now I have to show her what it's like to be with a real nigga. Don't call her no mo'," he said calmly.

"Who are you talking to on my phone, Los?" I heard Kaymee ask before the line went dead.

I tried calling back, but she had blocked me from contacting her on messenger. Now there was no way I could call her if I wanted to because I also was blocked from calling her phone. The minute I got back to Boston, I was buying a prepaid phone to call her ass. I thought to myself as I drove through the heavy traffic.

I finally arrived at the airport thirty minutes later. Heading straight for the rental facility, I followed the signs to the designated return area. The line was short so I wouldn't be waiting too long. When I got to the window, the attendant showed me where to park the car and instructed me to wait for someone to inspect the vehicle. I prepaid when I arrived so I took my receipt and went inside to go through security.

Once I was finished getting searched like a criminal, I went to Dunkin Donuts to get a croissant, hash browns, and orange juice to eat while I waited to board the plane. I decided to sit in a seat that was next to an outlet. Taking a bite of the croissant, it was pretty good. I took a sip of the orange juice and continued eating.

This beautiful light-skinned honey stood in the middle of the gate entrance scanning the area for an empty seat. She stood about five feet four and petite with a slim waist and a plump ass. The way she was standing sideways put her figure on display. She wore her hair curly and it flowed down her back and it was hers.

She had on little to no makeup, but I could tell she was naturally beautiful. I couldn't take my eyes off her, so when she turned her head in my direction, our eyes connected briefly. The beautiful woman looked down at her phone, grasped the handle of her luggage and walked in my direction. My dick jumped in my sweatpants because she was bad.

"Is this seat taken?" she asked, standing in front of me as she placed her phone in her purse.

"No, no it's not," I stammered. "Have a seat," I said, motioning to the seat next to me.

"Thank you," she said, sitting down and positioning her luggage in front of her as she sat down.

I couldn't take my eyes off her ass, but when she turned her head, I shifted my eyes away just in time. Taking a bite of my sandwich, I wished in my head I was tasting her instead of the bacon and eggs.

"I'm MaKenzie. Thanks again for allowing me in your space," she said, holding out her hand for me to shake.

Accepting her hand, I shook it lightly. "Drayton. My name is Drayton. Nice to meet you, MaKenzie. This is a public airport, so it's far from *my* space," I said, smiling. "Do you live in Boston?"

"That's true. I'll take that. To answer your question, no, I'm not from Boston. I'm heading there on business. I've never been there before, so it will be an adventure."

I had to shoot my shot. She was too fine not to try to get to know. Clearing my throat, I took a sip of my orange juice. "I was born and raised in Boston. Maybe we can get together and I'd show you around, if you have time, of course," I said.

"That sounds like a good idea. I will be in Boston for a few weeks. It would be great knowing I wouldn't have to maneuver around a foreign city alone. Here's my card. I look forward to seeing your city and with such a handsome man." She smiled as I took the card from her.

Sexing her was the first thing that came to mind and I couldn't wait. She looked like she had a gold mine between her legs, too. That camel toe was on full display and my mouth was watering. I had plans to take my time with MaKenzie. *She was going to be my forever,* I thought to myself. We boarded the plane about forty-five minutes later and talked the entire time.

Chapter 11

Dot

Being in the treatment center was for the birds. I was trying my best to continue the journey of staying clean. The drugs I had smuggled into the center were long gone and I wanted to get high every time I thought about it. I faked ailments every chance I got just to get some type of drug to chase a high. Nothing I took got me to the place I was seeking.

I was lucky I didn't get tested for drugs while I was using. I didn't go anywhere, so it wasn't necessary for them to test me. It had been over thirty days since I was forced to come to Serenity House. Dirty called to check on me daily and I appreciated him for doing so. I hadn't tried talking to Kaymee because I was still upset with her for not helping me keep my apartment.

Yvette scheduled counseling sessions with me twice a week and I hated them. She asked me questions about my past that I didn't feel comfortable answering, so we weren't getting very far with those. During the group sessions, I also refused to participate. Everyone who spoke about their addictions sounded pitiful as hell and I wasn't trying to spill my dirt the way they were. I didn't know them like that.

It was Wednesday and, of course, the day of my counseling session with Yvette. I wasn't in the mood for this shit. I wished she would just cancel them and just let me suffer with sobriety. As I laid in the bed snuggled under my blanket, I wanted to get up, but my mind said fuck it. Closing my eyes to go back to sleep, there was a loud knock on my door.

Ignoring the person on the other side, I rolled over and put my head under the blanket. The sound of keys in the door pissed me off because I have told them muthafuckas about coming in my shit unannounced. I kicked the blanket back as Yvette appeared in the doorway of my bedroom.

"Get up, Dot. You have five minutes to get up and get to my office," she said, aggravatingly.

"I'm not a child—"

"I'm not trying to hear any of that!" Yvette yelled, cutting me off. "I've let you refuse talking long enough! It stops today! Now get up!"

"This is bullshit," I mumbled.

"What was that?" she asked.

"I need more than five minutes. I have to take a shower and brush my damn teeth!" I snapped.

"Brush your teeth and slip on some shoes. I don't care what you have on when you come down. I'm here to talk to you and make sure you get through this program the correct way. How you look while doing it is not important. You now have three minutes," she said, turning around and walking out.

I took care of my hygiene and slipped on a pair of flip flops. Tying a scarf around my head, I snatched my keys from the dresser and walked out of the room. Yvette was standing by the door with her arms folded over her chest. When she saw me, she opened the door and walked out. I didn't need an escort. I knew where the fuck her office was.

Locking the door, I walked to the elevator that Yvette held open for me and got on. I stayed in the far corner with a scowl on my face. When the doors opened, I rushed off and headed straight to her office and took a seat. She entered and closed the door behind her, taking a deep breath.

"Dot, I want you to know that I will not tolerate you sitting there silently. These sessions are for you to talk about what led you to your drug use. If you don't open up, I won't know how to help you, help yourself."

"My past don't have nothing to do with my drug use! How many times do I have to tell you that? My daughter's father laced my weed over six months ago! I didn't choose to start using drugs! The shit was forced upon me!"

"Why do you think that?" she asked.

"I don't think shit, I know!"

"I want you to lower your voice, Dot. I've respected you since the moment you stepped through those front doors. Give me the same respect. We will be in this room until you let out everything you have been holding in. I don't care how long it takes. I have all day," Yvette said, sitting back in her chair.

"Jonathan did it!" I screamed. "He's trying to destroy me!" I screamed. Yvette continued to sit back without saying anything. She sat that way for about five minutes before she spoke again.

"Are you done screaming? I told you I had all day. Is this the way you want to handle this, Dot?" she asked calmly.

I was frustrated and just wanted to leave. Yvette was working my nerves and I wanted to beat her ass. Talking about the shit I'd been through was something I wasn't ready to do and she was forcing me to relive everything.

"Let's start at the beginning. What was your relationship like with Jonathan?" she asked.

Thinking about where to start, I took a long sigh. "Jonathan was my first love. We started dating when I was fifteen. I found out I was pregnant at seventeen and I was ecstatic about carrying his baby. When I told Jonathan the news, he wanted me to get an abortion.

I was crushed because he told me he loved me, but wanted me to terminate the life we created together. He thought we were too young to have a baby and was worried about what his mammy would think.

Jonathan moved to live with his grandmother and I ended up having the baby alone. I hid the pregnancy from my mother because I was adamant about having our baby, hoping he would have a change of heart," I explained with tears falling from my face.

"How did your mother take the news that you were with child?"

"She was pissed because she had five other kids to care for. We lived in a three-bedroom apartment in the projects. There was barely enough room for the people that lived there. She helped me get an apartment in the very housing projects that we lived and I went to the welfare office and applied for food stamps. I was forced to become an adult before my time and Jonathan was still a no show."

"I'm sorry that happened to you, Dot. How old is your daughter and what's your relationship like with her?" Yvette asked. I started breathing heavily at the mention of Kaymee. My nose flared and the tears stopped immediately.

"That bitch is eighteen. She will be nineteen in July."

"Tell me why you are so angry with her, Dot," Yvette said with a confused expression.

"She destroyed my life! If I hadn't pushed her outta my pussy, Jonathan wouldn't have left me! It's because of her I lost the only man I loved!" I cried.

"Dot, no child asks to be born. You do understand that was a decision you made, right?"

"I didn't have a choice! He was supposed to help me raise her! We were supposed to live happily ever after together, but he didn't show up! I had to drop out of school to take care of her muthafuckin' ass! My life went from sugar to shit because of a baby I should've never had!" I cried.

Yvette held her head down for a few moments and stared me in the eyes. "Again, that was the decision you made on your own, Dot. You can't continue to blame your daughter for things you chose to do with your life. There are many single mothers who have graduated from high school and college and have successful careers. She didn't hold you back. You have to take full accountability for your actions. Be real to yourself, Dot. You gave up on your own life."

"No! I couldn't do shit with a baby! My mama only babysat when she wanted to. Not when I needed her to do so."

"Okay, let me ask you this. Where you trying to go back to school? Get a job?"

"Hell nawl! I was getting enough money from the government to take care of my monthly bills. I needed my mother to watch the little girl because I needed a break. She reminded me of Jonathan everyday because she looked just like him. I couldn't stomach looking at her. That's the reason I took her to my mother's house one day and left. If her deadbeat ass daddy could do it, why couldn't I?"

"So, you thought passing your daughter on to your mother to raise was the best thing for her?" Yvette asked.

"Yes, it was. If I hadn't given her to my mother, I would've hurt her. My mother was the best person to care for her, not me."

"Your mother raised her from a baby until today?"

"No, I got the girl back when she was six after my mother passed away," I said, hunching my shoulders.

"Sorry to hear about the passing of your mother," she said sadly. "Dot, why do you refer to your daughter as bitch or the girl? What is your daughter's name?"

"Her name is Kaymee, but she will forever be bitch to me."

"You mean to tell me that you still hold your daughter responsible for the way your life turned out?"

"Yes, she is at fault!"

"When you got Kaymee back, was it an easy adjustment having her back in your home?"

"Easy for who, me? I didn't change anything about my life. As long as she had a place to lay her head, food in the kitchen, and a school to go to, she was fine. My mother had raised her to take care of herself. She didn't need me!"

"She was six years old, Dot!"

Yvette was shocked at what I said, but she wanted the truth, so I gave it to her. There was no reason for me to start lying about what I had done. "And she's still breathing, so she was fine. How do you think I felt finding out that Jonathan was going to my mother's house to see his daughter, but couldn't come see me? He even gave her money every month to take care of her. That was money he owed me, not my mother!"

"Your daughter was living with your mom, correct?" Yvette asked.

"Yes, but I'm her mother."

"Jonathan did what was right for the child. He took care of his responsibilities and made sure Kaymee was taken care of. You should be happy that your mother wasn't struggling to care for your child."

"What would've been right was giving the money to the mother of his child. It doesn't matter though, because I eventually started getting the same payments after my mother's death," I said, smirking.

"I'm glad you and Jonathan learned to work together to raise Kaymee. Bickering between two parents is not healthy for the child."

"Jonathan didn't show his face again until Kaymee's eighteenth birthday. He didn't help raise shit! She fell right in his lap and clung to him like he was there all of her life and said fuck me! Both of them are on my shit list. I'm going through everything because of the two of them. I'm done talking about this shit. We have been going at this too long and I'm tired."

"I want to ask you something, Dot. Will you be willing to have a session with your daughter present? I think it will help you let some of this resent me go. What do you think?" Yvette asked.

"It's not time for me to talk to her face to face. She has turned her back on me too many times to count and I don't want to see her. I've done some fucked up shit to her, but she is supposed to love me regardless."

"That's not how life works, Dot. You have so much built up anger inside of you and from the sound of it all, you directed it at the wrong person. Kaymee was innocent in this entire scenario. She endured the pain that you put her through without having a say in the matter. I believe a counseling session with the two of you is long overdue and I want to give you the opportunity to talk it out with her," Yvette said.

"That will be impossible because she moved to Atlanta with Jonathan. She also attends Spelman College and thinks she's too good for Chicago. She won't answer my call anyway."

"Congratulations to her. Maybe I can give her a call and talk to her on your behalf," Yvette said hopefully.

"I'll give you her number, but I don't want the meeting to take place just yet. I'm not ready," I said.

"Okay, Dot. We covered a lot today and I'm glad you finally opened up about a lot of things. There's still much more we have to discuss so I will see you Friday to do it again."

"Yeah, okay," I said, getting up leaving her office.

Meesha

Chapter 12

Poetry

I finally got the okay to go home and I was so ready to leave the hospital. Being in one room for the past five weeks has been hard for me. Monty made my stay very bearable by being there with me every step of the way. The staples were removed from my head a week ago and now I couldn't wait for my hair to grow back. The first thing I wanted to do was go to the salon to get a bomb ass short-styled lace front.

When I saw my head for the first time, I cried. My self-confidence went out the window. I thought I was the ugliest woman alive, but Monty cut that shit short. He didn't let one day go by without telling me how beautiful I was. Being alive was a blessing and I was given another chance to make the best of it. I was ready to push through every obstacle to get back to the person I was before the surgery.

Knock, knock.

Dr. Brim walked into the room with a huge smile on her face. "Hey, beautiful. Are you ready to blow this joint?"

"Yes, I am. I've been a prisoner under your care long enough, don't you think?" I said, chuckling.

"I wouldn't use the word prisoner, but it was a pleasure taking care of you. Do not worry about anything once you get home. Like I explained to you and Monty, the headaches will take time to completely go away. I'm sending you home with enough pain medication to help you as needed. Poetry, don't take a pill every time your head throb.

Try to bear the pain most of the time. Only take them if you really need to because the pills are easy to get addicted to. That's the reason we brought them to you the entire time you were here. I will explain this to Monty, as well."

"What about my memory? It hasn't come back and I don't know how life was before all of this," I asked sadly.

"It will take time for you to start remembering things. You had major surgery to your brain, Poetry. We will be doing CT scans every visit to make sure everything is still on the track. You are a strong woman. For now, make new memories to add to the ones that will eventually come back to you. Whatever comes back good or bad, remember, the past is the past. Okay?"

"I'll keep that in mind. I wanted to ask something of you," I said, sitting up on the bed. "Monty, Kaymee, and myself would like for you to be Aria's second Godmother. Kaymee won't give up her spot," I said, laughing. "Without you and your staff's help, me and Aria wouldn't be here today.

Words can't express how much I owe you for going over and beyond to save my life. If you hadn't reacted the way you did, I could've died. It was because of your actions that the umbilical cord was released from around Aria's neck. Not to mention, you never left my side. You checked on me every day since the day I was admitted in January," I cried.

"You don't have to thank me. I did my job and along the way, grew attached to a young lady that I adore. To answer your question, yes, I will be honored to be Aria's Godmother," she said, hugging me tightly.

"Hey, get off my wife," Monty said, coming into the room.

Dr. Brim released me and looked over her shoulder and stepped back. My husband stood with his legs slightly parted wearing grey sweatpants that showed his dick print vividly. I drooled down my chin and he walked over laughing, using his hand to catch it.

"Hey, Monty. I'll be back with your discharge papers and the instructions I want you to follow at home," she said, leaving out of the room.

"Why are yo' ass slobbin' all over yourself?" he said with a smirk.

"You must be outta ya mind walking around with ya dick sitting up for every bitch to see. I'm well enough to kick your ass, Montez."

"I know what I'm going home to, no need to worry about the small shit. You looking real good today, Mrs. Williams," he said, trying to butter me up.

"Don't Mrs. Williams me! Say it again," I said, wrapping my arms around his waist.

"Mrs. Wiliams," he whispered in my ear as he picked me up by my ass and kissed me deeply. My lady parts started tingling as our tongues intertwined. A moan escaped my throat and Montez pecked my lips one more time before placing me on the floor. I was upset because he ended our bonding time, but we could continue when we got home.

"Your six weeks ain't quite up yet. That kiss made my shit rock hard and now we can't leave until it goes down. I don't need you snapping on every female that looks down when I'm walking pass them."

"You should've worn something other than those damn sweatpants! Here, wrap this around your waist," I said, throwing the sheet off the bed.

"You gotta be shitting me right," Montez said, laughing as he tossed it back on the bed. "I'm not walking around looking like I'm wearing a skirt. I'm too gangsta for that, Poe." He laughed as he hiked his pants and sat in the chair.

"Play with it if you want to. I'll slap you upside your head," I said as two rapid knocks on the door filled the room.

"Don't do it, Poetry. I don't feel like stitching anyone up this morning. I'm trying to get home to my babies," Dr. Brim said, walking in with my papers. "I wrote you a prescription for birth control, as well. That jail sentence is almost up, so I want you to be careful since my God baby is only a little over a month. Take care of her, Monty. I'll see you I guess back here for your first outpatient appointment in two weeks," she said, giving me a hug.

"Monty, I want you to hold on to these pills. They are for Poetry's severe headaches and she gets them only if her headaches are unbearable. I don't want her to get addicted to them, so they have to be taken responsibly."

"Okay, I will remember that. Thank you for everything. You were placed in our lives for a reason and I appreciate you and your staff," Monty said, giving her a quick hug.

"Get out of here and enjoy your new home and that beautiful baby. I brought a wheelchair for you so you can go out of here in style," Dr. Brim said and laughed.

As much as I wanted to walk out of the hospital, I was still kind of fatigued and accepted the chair without argument. Monty and my parents hauled all the gifts that Aria and I received to the house a couple days prior. He placed the small bag that contained a few items I needed on my lap, wheeling me out of the room. Nurses and doctors hugged me, giving kind words of encouragement as we moved through the halls.

"Bae, you are a hospital celebrity," Monty said, patting me on the shoulder.

"I was here long enough, shit. I've met everybody on the payroll in this place. I'm glad the worse is over and I'm going home," I said as we got on the elevator.

"You damn right about that. We made it through the tough times. Now I have to wait on the day I can slide into something wet and feel that headlock grip on my joint."

I couldn't believe he said that and he was serious, too. Pondering over his statement, I didn't realize we were at my truck until Monty took the bag and lifted me out the chair. Once I was comfortable and strapped in the seatbelt, he closed the door and got in on the other side. When he pulled out of the parking lot, my thoughts flowed out of my mouth.

"Montez, why is sex the first thing on your mind? There are other things you could've mentioned like cuddling watching TV, cooking together in our new home, or finally being able to enjoy Aria outside of the hospital. Better yet, how about giving your wife a massage or something? The kitty will forever be yours. it's not going anywhere," I said, rolling my eyes.

"Sex is always on my mind, Poe. A nigga got blue balls and I'm on the verge of falling in love with the palm of my hand from all the attention it's been giving my mans. I didn't need to hear the

112

last part of what you said though. That pussy got my name written all over it. Ain't no nigga gon' ever get to sample that shit.

I fucked up and took our relationship for granted, almost losing you one time too many times. It will never happen again. It's me and you forever," he said, grabbing my hand, kissing my fingers as he drove.

"What do you mean you almost lost me?" Tell me about it."

Monty stopped at a red light before turning to me. "I don't want to talk about it now. We can snuggle like you want and discuss it later. Right now, I just want to enjoy being in your presence as we drive to G's new crib before we go home."

"When did G move here?" I asked confused.

"He bought a crib not too far from Jonathan's place a few weeks ago. I have to handle some business with him, but it won't take long. I will have you home in no time," he said as the light turned green.

Sitting back watching the scenery fly by as we sped on the highway, I thanked God for giving me another chance at life. I thought about the day I almost died daily and it frightened me. Being able to see and hear things gave me a new prospective on life. Many take the little things for granted and I was one of those people. After what I went through, I was going to cherish every minute of my life.

I fell asleep and woke up when I felt the truck slow down. Glancing out the window, I notice we were in a neighborhood with many beautiful houses. As we cruised down the road, I noticed there was a lot of construction going on. There was a sign that announced the new development of houses that were being built.

"I've always dreamed of getting a house built from the ground up. G was lucky to get a home nobody had ever lived in. I can't wait to see it, babe. Maybe we can invest in one someday."

"We will see what we can do," he said, sneaking a peek at me.

Monty pulled into a driveway of a two-story brick home. It had huge bay windows and a glass-paned door. The house looked like one out of the movies. My husband pushed the button to turn the truck off and got out. I pulled the visor down and made sure my scarf was in place. I wasn't confident enough for anyone to see the scar on the side of my head.

Opening the door for me, Monty held his hand out for me to grasp. I placed my hand in his and stepped down from the truck. There were many cars in the driveway and knew some of the other guys were there, as well. It would give me a chance to check out the house G had purchased while they conducted business. Monty had his phone in his hand texting as we walked slowly up the walkway.

"Somebody is barbequing and it smells good," I said, sniffing the air.

"Yeah, that shit do smell good. Come on before you have me walking door to door to find the culprit of that meat," Monty said, laughing.

"I'm all for finding cuzin Pete and nem."

"You know you're stupid, right?" Monty said, laughing hard as we climb the stairs. The door opened when we reached the top and G started laughing just because we were.

"What the hell are we laughing about?" he asked.

"We were about to go searching the neighborhood for whoever is grilling around this muthafucka. That shit got a nigga's stomach growlin'," Monty said.

"Look no further. Ya'll at the right spot, my nigga. Come on in and don't forget to take off y'all shoes. I'm not getting cussed out by the Mrs. because you muthafuckas got dirt on her white carpet. Hey, Poe. It's good to see you. Lookin' good, ma," G said, pushing Monty out of the way to hug me.

"You don't have to lie to me, G. I look a hot ass mess with this scarf on my head."

"I wouldn't do that to you, cuz. You are just as beautiful now than before the surgery. Don't start getting self-conscious because of a scar. It will heal and you will be good as new in no time. As a matter of fact, when you're ready, your first hairdo is on me! You can make it a spa day and I got you covered. A'ight?"

I nodded my head as I stepped out of his embrace and slipped off my shoes. My feet sank into the carpet and I fell in love.

Monty came inside behind me and gave G a brotherly hug after removing his shoes.

"Stop hitting on my wife before I go find Nova and trick on yo' yella ass," Monty said, slapping him on the back.

"Man, gon' head wit that shit. Nova already know that my loyalty with her is solid. Poetry ain't trying to let no nigga disrespect what ya'll got going on. She's ready to throw that big ass rock in a muthafucka's face telling his ass to back the fuck up," G said, laughing. "We in the yard. Come on before that nigga Scony burn my damn meat."

The inside of G's house was gorgeous. I couldn't help admiring everything like a love-struck groupie. The décor was so homey, greatly placed and well thought out. I would love to sit in the living room in front of the fireplace with a good book or playing with my princess.

"Hey, Poetry!" Nova screamed happily, entering the house from the patio as G and Monty went out. "How are you feeling?" she asked hugging me.

"I'm maintaining. Glad to be out of that hospital," I said, chuckling. "Thank you for checking on me and for the gifts. This house is everything! I can't wait to see the rest of it."

"Girl, we have plenty of time to walk through this place. Let's get outside and enjoy this food my husband cooked while these fools talk business."

Nova led the way outside and from my view, it was huge. There was a basketball court and a spot to barbeque. The smoke was coming out of the grill followed by the smell that had my mouth watering for a beef rib. I stepped out of the sliding door and "Surprise" filled my eardrums.

To the left of the yard there were many people smiling. I was confused as to what the surprise was all about. The entire Goon squad and their wives were present, along with Kaymee, Los, and my parents. My uncle Charles was even there with his wife, Shirley.

"Hey, my baby! I'm glad to see you up and about. Sorry I couldn't make it while you were in the hospital. I was out of town on business and ya daddy said you were good," my uncle Charles explained.

"It's okay, Uncle Chuck. I know you were praying and thinking about me the whole time."

"His motherfucking ass wasn't out of town on business! Lie again, Charles, and I'll slap the fuck outta of you in front of these people," Shirley yelled, spilling the tea. "Yo' ass was at that bitch Belinda house! If you gon' tell the story, tell it right, you lying sack of shit!"

My hand flew to my mouth and I looked at my daddy. I knew the day would come for Shirley to find out about my uncle's other family. She'd been waiting on the right time to let his ass know that his secret wasn't a secret no more.

"Shirley, this ain't the time for this. We are here to celebrate Poetry coming home from the hospital. Hold that shit in for a couple more hours," my daddy said to Shirley.

"Stanley, yo' ass knew about this shit from day one! Don't try to shut me up now. We've been married almost thirty years and this bitch got a twelve and ten year old by another woman!" My uncle's eyes got big as saucers and he couldn't say nothing. "You thought I was never gonna find out, huh? Well I did!"

"We can talk about this later, Shirley," Charles said.

"Don't worry about it, motherfucker. I already talked to your young bitch and she told me all I needed to hear. When we get back to Chicago, I want you gone!" Shirley screamed as my mama led her into the house.

I blinked a couple times and noticed the sign that hung from two trees. "Welcome Home" is what the sign read. Finding Monty in the crowd, tears filled my eyes. "Awwwww, ya'll didn't have to throw me a party. Y'all have done enough for me and Aria already," I said as a lone tear fell down my face. Monty walked up and embraced me in a hug.

"This isn't just a party, baby. Everything that you admired when you walked into this house is ours. G didn't purchase a home here in Atlanta. This is our house."

"What? This can't be the house Jonathan gave us as a gift. It's too much!" I said, looking around at all of the smiling faces. The incident with uncle Charles was a distant memory.

"Yes, it is and it's never too much for you, Poetry," Jonathan said.

Nova stood back smiling the hardest because she knew about this and had me thinking this was her house. "I'm gon' kill you, Nova! Why didn't you tell me this was me?"

"You didn't ask. All you said was you loved it and can't wait to see the rest of the house. I told you we had plenty of time for that. You assumed and that wasn't my fault."

"Don't come for me, sis because I was warned not to tell you," Kaymee chimed in before I could chew her out.

"Where does your loyalty lie, Mee? Can't nobody tell you what to do but me! You should've told me about this! Got me wishing and praying this house was mine and it really is!" I said, smacking her on the arm playfully.

"Poe, don't do me. You already know I'm holding you down through everything. This was something I had to keep from you because it was important to bro. You are gonna love this place and I can't wait to spend lots of time here," she chuckled.

I walked around hugging everyone and thanking them for always showing up for Monty and I. There was a lot of food on the table and my stomach growled. There was going to be many days that I sat outside enjoying the weather. Jonathan came up to me and I couldn't stop myself from giving him another hug.

"Thank you so much, Jonathan."

"Stop thanking me, Poetry. I don't do anything I don't want to do. I meant what I said. You are a part of my family and I take care of mine. Kaymee is going to want a house now, but I'm not worried about that. She'll get a little something," he said as Kaymee came up behind him.

"A little something? You better go all out when it comes to me, daddy!" she pouted.

"Girl bye, with yo' spoiled ass," I said, looking amongst my guests. "MaKayla, how are you? Where's MaKenzie?" I asked.

MaKayla looked at Kaymee and smirked. "She's out of town conducting business. Hopefully, the mission is accomplished soon. How are you feeling, boo?"

"I'm okay for now. All of this excitement and my head is hurting a little bit."

"Your head hurting?"

Monty was by my side before the words left my lips with Aria in his arms. He didn't miss a beat when it came to making sure I was okay. I wanted to tell him so badly that he didn't have to do that, but I knew he wouldn't listen.

"Just a little, babe. I'm okay," I said, taking the baby. "Hey, beautiful. How's mama's baby?"

"Poe, sit down. I'll fix you a plate so you can eat," Monty said.

Los walked over and Kaymee turned to walk away, but he grabbed her elbow. The way she looked down at his hand let me know that something was going on between the two of them. Kaymee hadn't been talking about him much, but I didn't think anything of it. But she would be giving me all the tea soon.

"Can I talk to you for a minute?" Los asked

"There's nothing to talk about, Carlos," Kaymee said with an attitude.

"Mee, whatever it is, hear the man out. Communication is the key with any situation. Don't make it harder than it already is. Get whatever you're harboring off your chest for yourself. Stop holding shit in and speak your mind. You can't keep running away from everything."

"Poe, let her deal with her own issues the way she feels fit," Monty said, leading me away from them.

I sat in the chair while my husband fixed me a plate as my mama and Shirley came out of the house. Uncle Charles was in for a rude awakening when he got home because Shirley was pissed. I knew shit was gonna hit the fan and was glad they were in my home to hash that shit out.

Chapter 13

Kaymee

Poetry was right. It was time for me to stand up for myself. I was tired of being taken for granted. My relationship with Dray was the first I'd ever had and it left a bad taste in my mouth. I liked Carlos, but I didn't need any more drama in my life. There was enough bullshit I had to deal with already knowing Dray was still on the loose.

When I saw him walking toward me, I wanted to walk away, but it would've been rude to leave Poetry while she was talking. We walked to the other side of the yard in silence. Los looked at me and sighed heavily.

"Kaymee, you have been avoiding me for a minute without giving me a chance to explain what happened. Would you listen to me, man?"

"It really doesn't matter at this point. Whatever you have going on, take care of that shit before you come for me again. We can be friends but anything serious is out the question until you exclude the extra from your life. I've been through the back and forth bullshit with females and that shit is dead. If you want—"

"Are you gon' let me talk or not?" he asked, cutting me off. "I don't know how much you heard that night, but shit between me and Nikki been dead. When I found out she was cheating, I ended things with her and she came back talking about she was pregnant. I was ready to be a father and was willing to wait until she had the baby to get a DNA test done. Nikki got an abortion without talking to me about it.

When she terminated the pregnancy, the ties were cut between us. The night you heard her at my crib, I didn't invite her. One of her friends saw us at the movies and called her on that messy shit. Nikki was parked outside my shit when I pulled up. She got mad when you hit me up and I called you baby," he explained.

I hung up when I heard the Nikki bitch questioning him like a jealous female. It didn't dawn on me until now that if it was his woman, he wouldn't have answered the phone the way he did. I still didn't want to jump into anything because she was going to be a problem and I wasn't going for it.

"Obviously, she still wants you, Los. She's not trying to let you go and I'm not dealing with that again."

"She don't have shit to hold on to because I let go. Worry about us, Kaymee. I'll handle Nikki. I can't control the feelings she has for me, but I can guarantee that I don't have feelings for her. It's been over for six months. There's no communication between the two of us. When she calls, I let it go to voicemail and then she starts texting and leaving fucked up messages."

"Okay, well it's time to cut her completely off then. Why are you still entertaining her by giving her an outlet to text and call you? Block her ass! Don't give her a fuckin' choice! Fix that shit, then come talk to me. Until then, I'm good on you. I've been through too much with Dray—"

"I'm not that nigga, Kaymee! We are not comparable. Whatever his stupid ass did to you will never happen with me. I stand on that shit. When I'm with someone, that's what it is, me and her. That playing the field shit is for these dumb niggas out here. There's too much shit going on out in these streets for me to jump pussy.

But I'll give you your space, Kaymee. That nigga fucked you up being a goofy and every man ain't like him, especially not me. I don't want to see you with nothing but a smile on your face. You will never shed a tear behind me unless it's in pure ecstasy. We ain't at that level yet. You know how to reach me when you get yo' mind right," he said, turning away as his phone rang.

Los took his phone off his hip and glanced at it shaking his head. "You talked her ass up, man," he said, stopping it from ringing.

"Why didn't you answer it?" I asked.

"I already told you, I don't entertain her crazy ass." Before he could clip his phone back in place, it rang again. I smirked at him and folded my arms, tilting my head to the side because I knew it was Nikki calling again. Los answered the phone and put it on speaker. "What, Nikki?"

"Where are you, Los?" she said with attitude.

"That's not your business. What can I do for you?"

"I want to know where you at and who you wit'!"

"Let me tell you for the last time, we are not together. I'm with someone now and all of this calling and questioning is putting a strain on my relationship. So, to stop all confusion, you won't be able to contact me after this conversation. I will do all that needs to be done out of respect for my woman."

Hearing Los set her straight and call me his woman had me beaming inside. I was still going to make him work hard to prove he's not on dumb shit. I'm not up for the job of being loyal to any man, then I'm out in the streets looking like a fool for the second time.

"You are not about to be parading another bitch around when you know how I feel about you, Los! Stop fronting for this broad because I know that's the only reason you're talking this way. You've told me how much you love me and you can't take that shit back now."

"Nikki, I had love for you when we were together and all of that went out the window when you made the decision to be with another man. There wasn't anything lacking in our relationship. You had money at your fingertips, me at your beck and call, and a place to come for a piece of mind when your mama was giving you shit. I didn't hound you when you wanted to go out with your friends and you were free to do you.

The words I love you were spoken when you deserved to hear them. Give it up. You haven't heard me utter those words to you in a very long time. So, who's fronting?" he asked. "Don't get quiet now, Nikki."

She sounded pitiful and I was done listening. "I'm going over to talk to Poe. Finish your conversation," I said, whispering in his ear.

"You don't have to go anywhere. I'm about to end this right now," Los said.

"Los! Los!" Nikki screamed into the phone. "Don't' turn your back on what we have! I love you."

Chuckling loud enough for her to hear, Los looked into my eyes and held my hand tightly. "Nikki, we don't have shit. I got what I want right in front of me. It was fun while it lasted, but it wasn't meant to be. Enjoy the rest of your day. I'm out."

Los ended the call and lowered his head, kissing me deeply. I backed up and wiped the lipstick from his lips and smiled before walking away. Poetry was smashing a rib tip with one hand, struggling to hold Aria. I reached for the baby and she let her go without question. I sat in the chair across from her and she stared at me while she chewed her food.

"What was that all about?" she asked, taking a sip from her water bottle.

"Los has a crazy ass ex that don't want to let him go. I told him he needed to get that hashed out before we could move forward."

"Shid, that kiss told me something different," she said, laughing. "You got a man and don't' even know it."

"I've been through enough with Dray. I want to be with him but I'm scared. My heart is not a toy that can be played with and put back on the shelf. These muthafuckas don't want to do right by a woman. They want that for right now situationship and I want love, Poe."

"Believe me, I know. Love don't come instantly, sis. It's something that comes with time and dedication. Some spend a lot of time doing everything right, living life being faithful, loyal, and true to someone that chooses the next one over them. It happens sometimes, but it doesn't mean give up. It's called a work in progress.

You have to continue to live, have fun, and take care of your business. Secure the bag for yourself so when the right man comes along, you will be ready to build together. If he's not on the same page, you'll still be good. It's that simple."

I listened to what she said and it made sense to me. The funny thing about it was the fact my eyes didn't leave Los' from the time

I sat down. He was still standing in the same spot hitting a blunt and looked sexy. My daddy walked in his direction and they started talking.

Every once in a while, I saw my daddy motion his hand in my direction, but I knew they weren't talking about me. At least I hoped they weren't because he was good for threatening anybody nicely. I was glad to have him as my protector because my life has been everything since he's came back into my life.

"What are you over there thinking about?" Poetry asked, looking over her shoulder. "Oh, damn. Jonathan over there probably giving Los the 'that's my pussy" talk," she said, laughing and choking on the water that went down the wrong way.

"That's what I was afraid of. It is what it is though," I said as my phone rang in my purse.

I looked at the number and there was a Chicago number displayed on the screen. Hesitating to answer, I caught it before it went to voicemail. "Hello," I said softly.

"May I speak with Kaymee, please?" the caller asked.

"This is she. Who's calling?"

"My name is Yvette Ross. I'm a counselor at Serenity House rehab center and I'm calling on behave of your mother, Dorothy. How are you?"

"I'm fine, thanks for asking. She finally checked herself in for help I see."

"She actually didn't have a choice in the matter. I'm about to break all types of rules by explaining things to you over the phone, but I have to fill you in. Dot was entered into the program once she was released from the hospital. She overdosed on heroin, Kaymee. The nature of my call is to ask you to come to the rehab center for a family meeting.

Your mother has a lot of issues that she needs to talk about in order for her to get through this program successfully. If she keeps harboring the feelings that she has pinned inside of her, she will leave here and pick up right where she left off before she came here. We don't want that to happen, do we?"

"Truthfully speaking, I want her to get her life together, but she doesn't care about me. Never have. The last person she wants to see is me."

I really didn't know why this woman was calling me about Dot. Nobody could help her if she wasn't trying to help herself. I gave up when she proved I didn't mean shit to her. There was nothing I could do right in her eyes and staying away from her was the best thing to do. I didn't want any parts of her dilemma.

"That's not true. She's willing to talk things out if you agreed to attend the meeting," Yvette explained.

"Did she tell you I no longer lived in Chicago? I reside in Atlanta now."

"Yes, she informed me of that. We usually do meetings during the week, but I'm willing to make an exception and schedule one for a weekend that you're available."

"Can I call you back? I have to check my schedule and consult with my father first," I said, trying to get off the phone with her.

"Speaking of your father, do you think he will be willing to come, as well?" she asked.

"You're pushing it, Mrs. Ross. The only way that will happen is if you have the police on the premises. The two of them in the same room is a disaster waiting to happen," I said seriously.

"From the things she had to say, I know there's tension between the two of them, but I think it's time for them to put the past to rest. The relationship your parents had is a major part of Dot's emotional state."

"I'll ask him, but I don't think he will come. I'll call you back sometime today," I said.

"Okay, this is my personal number. You can call me back here when you're ready. Thanks for hearing me out and I can't wait to meet you, Kaymee," she said, hanging up.

I sat with the phone still to my ear after Yvette was long gone. Poetry stopped eating and stared waiting for me to say something. No words came to me, my mind was blank.

"Mee, is everything okay?" she asked, wiping her hands on a napkin.

"I don't know," I said, focusing on my daddy. "That was a counselor at a rehab center asking me to come for a meeting with Dot."

"She finally checked herself in?"

"Nope, she almost overdosed and was forced to go. Yvette, her counselor thinks it will be a good idea for me to come talk out our problems. She wants my daddy to come, too. I don't know about that. Nothing good can possibly come from going there, Poe. You know how Dot is."

"This meeting is probably what she needs, Kaymee. Plus, you can get to the root of why she treated you the way she did your entire life. I think you should go to be honest. It will help you heal and get some type of insight so you can get over that part of your life. Most of your trust issues stem from how Dot treated you."

I looked down at Aria and she was knocked out. She was so beautiful and I loved her. Just looking at her made all my thoughts of Dot go away, but it was short lived when my daddy walked up on me. Los walked past the table and joined the guys at the table where they were playing cards.

"Baby girl, let's walk and talk," he said, lifting Aria out of my arms, taking her to the playpen that was open for her.

"Poe, I'll be right back. We will walk through this beautiful house when I finish talking to my daddy," I said, standing from my seat.

Thinking we would walk around the yard, Jonathan had another idea. He led me out of the yard and we started walking down the street. The neighborhood was quiet and all and the yards were well kept. There were kids riding their bikes up and down the street and playing like kids should. It was going to be a great place for Aria to grow up.

"I had a conversation with Los," he said, breaking the silence. I try to stay out of your affairs, but I had to go see if everything was good with him. When a man hit a blunt as hard as he was, shit is not all right. He told me everything, Kaymee.

To me, it seems like he really wants to build something with you. I won't tell you what to do with this situation because you have to make your own choices. Every nigga is not like Dray. The things his punk ass did to you were fucked up on every level and karma will catch up with him.

Love is a powerful thing that can't be taken lightly. The only advice I can give you is to take things slow and let shit happen as it may. If it was meant to be, it will be. Los has a situation that is out of his control. People tend to hold on when they fucked up a good thing." He explained.

"I hear what you're saying and I don't mean to compare him to Dray but I can't help it when I see the same shit happening again."

"That's where you're wrong. Dray was playing games and thought he would get away with it. Los is nipping shit in the bud and the female ain't trying to hear that it's over between them. There's a big difference. Los told his ex he was in a relationship and respect his woman, grown man shit in my eyes. Dray tried to hide everything he had going on in his life. I don't see that happening in this situation."

"I'll see where it goes. I like him, but I have to be cautious. You should understand that. I just got out of what I thought was a relationship with Dray and I'm not sure if I want to do it again so soon."

"Okay, I'll leave it alone. I think you'll figure it out and do what's best for you. It's good to see Poetry out of the hospital, huh?" he asked, changing the subject.

"Yeah, her whole ordeal scared the hell out of me. I don't know what would've happened had we lost her. She is my everything and been there for me through so much."

"We don't have to worry about that because she is on the road to recovery. God is good and is always on time. Have you heard from your mama?"

"It's funny that you asked about her. I got a call back at the house from a counselor at a rehab center. She wants you and I to come for a meeting," I said, looking up at him to see his reaction.

"I'm glad she checked herself in for help. Kaymee I have always been truthful with you. I was the one that started your mama on drugs."

"Why would you do something like that? She has been a shitty parent but she's still my mother!" I stopped walking and waited for him to explain his actions.

"When she shot us and I had to fight for my life, she had to pay for that shit. Not to mention how I felt finding out how she was treating you in that apartment. Not taking care of you, and spending my money on everything but my daughter. That shit was unacceptable. It was wrong for me to do what I did, but I don't regret it. I didn't keep her going back to the shit, that was all on her."

I couldn't believe he stooped that low to get back Dot. It was wrong and I didn't know how I felt about it. He could've just left it alone and let her drown in her own sorrows. She didn't need help to fall on her face. That would've happened when he stopped her money flow.

"I'm upset to hear that you had a hand in something like that, daddy. You were supposed to be the responsible parent and you stooped to her level," I said sadly.

"I'm sorry, baby girl. I'm a street nigga and she violated in the worse way when she shot us. Dot is lucky I didn't follow my first mind and killed her muthafuckin' ass. So, I set her up to kill herself. I wanted you to hear it from me before you heard it in the meeting because we are going. When is it?" he asked.

"I don't know. I told the counselor I would call her back."

"Okay, dial her up and set everything up and let me know. We will be on the next thing smoking to get the ball rolling. Your mother needs help and it started way before the drugs. She needs to face reality. I'm ready to clear the air because I believe deep down inside, she blames me," he said as we turned back around to go back to the house.

Meesha

Chapter 14

Monty

We were sitting playing a game of spades and things were getting personal at the table. G and Scony were partners and Los was mine. The game was competitive as fuck and I loved a good challenge.

"Stop stalling and play, lil' nigga!" Scony screamed across the table. "Take this ass whoopin' like a G!"

I was studying my hand to see how I was about to pop this Boston on their ass. I had a hand full of spades from the ace down to the two, the only one I didn't have was the six and nine. I also had the ace and King of hearts. There was no way we would lose this hand. Both of these old heads were about to be pissed when I ran this shit by myself.

Leading off with the ace of hearts, G played the deuce, Scony played a three, and Los played a jack. Scooping up the book, I looked at my hand again and smiled. I stood up and let the cards rip, smacking the ace of spades on the table and it was on from there.

"I don't hear you muthafuckas talking now!" I yelled every time I smacked another card on the table.

"Fuck you, lucky bastard!" Scony said, playing his cards lazily. "You cheated, nigga!"

"How the fuck I cheat and yo' busta ass shook the cards? Thanks for giving me the tools to spank y'all ass," I said, placing my king of heart on the table ending the game,

"Damn, nigga! You ran that shit on yo' own because I didn't have shit!" Los said, standing up to give me dap.

"Give me my fuckin' money! Game ova!" I said, laughing at Scony since he had the biggest mouth.

"A couple bands ain't shit to me, youngin! But I want a re-match. You ain't about to get away with that shit. Double or nothing, muthafucka!"

"That's some sucka shit right there, Scony! We ain't running shit back. You lost and I'm done," I said, laughing at his ass. "I will be a dummy to sit down playing the same game I just won at. Now, if you want to throw these dice, we can do that. I'm quite sure there's more where this came from," I said, taking the five stacks from his hand."

"You don't' want to see me on no dice, nigga!" Scony said, standing up.

"But I do! Where's ya money, brah? I got mine right here," I said, counting out Los' cut.

"Monty," I heard Poe calling my name.

"I'll be right back. Wifey needs me," I said, going over to Poetry.

"I need to lie down. My head is killing me," she said, holding her head.

Mama Chris came over and bent down in front of her. "You okay, baby?" she asked.

"My head hurts."

"Monty, I got her. Go back to the guys," she said.

"Nah, I'll carry her upstairs. Go to the car and get the white bag off the backseat. Her pain pills are in there and bring them upstairs with a bottled water.

Putting the money in my pocket, I placed one of my arms under her legs and the other around her back and lifted her out of the chair. Kaymee opened the patio door for me and followed us inside. Carefully climbing the stairs, I kissed her on her head to let her know everything would be alright.

I stood to the side as Kaymee opened the door to the master bedroom. Poetry's eyes were closed and I knew she was in pain. Laying her on the bed, I went into the bathroom and wet a towel to put on her forehead. Mama Chris entered the room with the medicine and shook a pill out, putting the bottle on the nightstand. Immediately picking it up, I put them in my pocket remembering what Dr. Brim said to me before we left the hospital.

"I'll get her undressed, Monty. Go back outside with your company. She will be fine," her mama said to me.

130

I was reluctant about leaving, but I knew she was in good hands. Slowly leaving out of the room, Aria was fussing and I followed her cries. MaKayla was struggling to change her pamper and she didn't like it. I stood in the doorway laughing because I could tell she didn't know what the hell she was doing.

"Need any assistance?" I asked, still laughing.

"This shit is not funny, Monty. Come help me!"

I strolled over to the changing table and peeked down at my baby. Aria opened her pretty doe eyes and when she saw me, she instantly stopped fussing and smiled. It took me no time to get her cleaned up and dried. MaKayla picked her up and stared at her.

"You little faker," she said, swinging Aria around.

"Did she eat yet?" I asked MaKayla.

"Yes, I just fed her before we came up here to get her changed up."

"I think you should stop shaking her up then," I warned her.

MaKayla didn't listen. As she held Aria above her head still shaking her, baby girl gave her a little present that fell all over her face. The shit looked like it happened in slow motion and I grabbed my baby before MaKayla could react.

"Aria, that was gross!" she shrieked, wiping her face with a baby wipe.

"I told you to stop shaking her," I said, laughing. "You got her good, Pooda," I said, giving her a kiss.

MaKayla left out to go wash her face in the bathroom down the hall and I sat in the rocker to spend time with Aria. She was dry and had been fed, so I knew she would be sleep before long. Never in a million years did I think I would be married and have a kid at this point of my life, but it happened.

So much had transpired and I was ready to see what else was in store for me. The past few months forced me to grow up and become the man I've always wanted to be. I was determined to be a better father than my sperm donor was to me. My daughter won't ever have to worry about me walking out of her life. Poetry didn't have anything to worry about either because we were in this marriage together.

A few minutes later, MaKayla came back into the room and shook her head because Aria was knocked out in my arms. I was deep in thought and didn't even realize she had fell asleep. I stood and placed her in her crib and covered her with her blanket. Turning on the baby monitor, I motioned for MaKayla to leave out of the room.

Before we went back out to the yard, I stopped in my bedroom to check on Poe. Mama Chris was sitting in the chair by the bed watching TV and Poetry was sleeping. "Hey, Aria is sleeping in her crib. I turned the baby monitor on. Would you listen out for her?"

"Get out of here. You know damn well you don't have to ask me that. I got both of my girls, Monty. Keep an eye on Shirley though. She's ready to bust Charles upside the head," she said and laughed. "I told his stupid ass to tell her about that shit years ago, but he wanted to be a playa. Don't be like Charles, Monty. It's not worth it."

"Nah, I've learned my lesson and I'm married now. I won't put my wife through that. We did that as boyfriend and girlfriend. It's a new ballgame now. I'll try my best to keep everything peaceful."

Going down the stairs I thought about the pictures I had in my phone of Poetry. She was pregnant and I'd captured many great shots. I will have them printed and enlarged to hang along the staircase. Every inch of this home will show the love we shared throughout our union.

I heard voices coming from the bedroom on the first level of the house. I almost ignored it until the voices started getting louder. Heading in the direction of the room, I could clearly hear the bickering of Shirley and Charles that was getting louder the closer I got to the bedroom. They were not about to tear my shit up before I could spend one night in it.

"How long did you think I was going to be your fool, Charles? Thirty years of marriage and you have another family out there?"

"Shirley, lower your voice when talking to me. I won't deny having two children outside the marriage because they are mine.

To answer your question, I don't think you are a fool. I cheated and kept it to myself," Charles said.

"I love how you said that nonchalantly. You should've been a man and told me just like that years ago, I shouldn't have learned about your children from anyone else! She knew where the fuck I laid my head, but I knew nothing about her! If she wanted to kill me, she could've. I wouldn't have known because of your sneaky ass.

I looked dumb as hell when she rang my doorbell and told me she was the mother of your kids. The only damn child I'm aware of is Charles Junior and he's a grown as man at twenty-five. I didn't know shit about Charles the third and Charlotte until a couple weeks ago!"

"We haven't been happy in a very long time, Shirley. It's not a secret. When was the last time we had sex? We don't even sleep in the same damn bed! Did you think I was in there fucking myself? If so, you *are* a got damn fool. My dick still works!"

I had heard enough. I walked into the room without knocking and both of them closed their mouths. This was something they were going to have to take somewhere else. My wife and daughter were upstairs sleeping while they were down here acting like they were at their own house.

"Aye, y'all gon' have to take that outside or something. Poe ain't feeling good and my baby is sleeping. This not the place for all the yelling and cursing."

"I'm sorry for disrespecting ya home, Monty. I didn't know we were loud," Charles said, glaring at Shirley.

"You can stop looking at me like that. This conversation is far from over, bastard," she said, walking out of the room.

"Uncle Charles, what you gon' do about this, old head? And how the hell did you hide two kids in the same city you live in?" Shid, I needed to know how he pulled that off. That was a playa move I'd never even heard of before.

Stan showed up leaning against the doorframe. "Brah, you know my name's all in this shit, right? Shirley is ready to go back to Chicago. She booked a flight and it leaves in three hours. How did she find out about the kids?"

Sighing deeply, Charles ran his hand down his face. "Supposedly, Belinda came to the house and told her. It was bound to happen, Stan. You of all people know we haven't been happy for a very long time."

"No, you haven't been happy for a long time. I've told you to talk to her and follow your heart, but you are too cheap to give Shirley what she deserves. You'd rather sneak around behind her back, dish out your cash to her, and hide your kids. That shit is too damn stressful. Now Chris is going to be looking at me sideways like I got a damn family tuck away somewhere."

"I would cut yo' damn balls off if I suspect some shit like that. Charles, you're wrong. I arranged for you to fly back with Grant and his family. Shirley didn't want to take that flight because it leaves tomorrow. My daughter doesn't need this bullshit while she's trying to recover from surgery. I hope y'all fix this before I come back home because ain't nobody staying in my house," Mama Chris said, walking out the room.

That was my cue to go. This old school shit was too much for me. I went out the patio door and the guys were cleaning up while the ladies were taking food inside. Jonathan was emptying the grill and I walked over to him.

"Man, I don't ever want my marriage to end up like that," I said, running my hand over my face.

"Communication is key. The only way it gets to that point is when there's no talking going on. Someone should've been the bigger question and brought the problem to the table. It's fucked up that she had to learn about his infidelity like that after damn near thirty years though," Jonathan said, moving the charcoal around.

"I'm done talking about that subject. Anything new on that nigga, Dray?"

Scony came over with a spiff and flamed it up. "That nigga is in good hands with Kenzie," he said, smirking. "Pussy will have a nigga forgetting he fucked with the wrong muthafuckas. His days are on a timer."

"Damn, you cool with yo' sister going out taking on an assignment like that?" I asked.

"You don't know the twins very well. They're not new to this, they're true to this. Kenzie can handle a muthafucka almost better than any of us can," G said, joining us. MaKayla walked out as G said her sister's name and jumped right into the conversation.

"Speaking of Kenzie, I just spoke with her on the phone and she said he is smitten with her. He has been calling her to go out on the town every day since they arrived. Dray had forgotten the code of not telling his business to strangers. He's bragging about the lick he came up on and dragging Kaymee's name through the mud. Kenzie almost killed him tonight, but she composed herself."

"Knowing my crazy ass sister, she's holding off to see what that dick do with her nasty ass," Scony said, choking on the gas he inhaled.

"Keep me posted. I hate that I won't be the one to put a bullet between that nigga's eyes. Tell MaKenzie to make his ass suffer," I said, turning as I heard the patio door open.

"What are y'all out here talking about?" Kaymee asked, walking with an extra swing in her hips.

Los met her halfway and hugged her and she was hesitant to return the gesture. He was whispering in her ear and her cheeks were turning redder with every word spoken. That was my nigga. He took her mind off what we were talking about and gave her something else to think about.

"I'll keep you informed on that situation. We're about to get out of here because the jet will be ready in the morning. Charles is rolling out with us and Jade and Nova took Shirley to the hotel, then to the airport. Take care of Poetry and princess Aria with her cute self. Congratulations again on yo' crib and joining the daddy club, nigga," G said, giving me a brotherly hug.

"Similac finally filled his grown man shoes. I'm proud of you," Scony said, holding his hand out for me to shake.

MaKayla was hugged up with Conte and they looked happy together. From the stories I've heard, the whole squad had been through a lot of shit in the past couple years. There was nothing in store for us but greatness going forward.

"We can discuss the business for the restaurant next week. Things are going good with the remodeling and everything. I can't wait for you to see the changes," Jonathan said proudly. "Baby girl, go tell ya step mama to bring her ass on. We're about to roll."

Los' wasn't trying to let Kaymee go. She reeled her head back and laughed. He shook his head no and she placed her lips on his and pushed him back.

"Kaymee, are you staying here or you're rolling with me?" Jonathan asked before she went into the house.

"Negative, she's coming with me," Los said, smirking. "Hurry and come back, bae so we can go."

Kaymee glanced over her shoulder, smiled and stepped through the door. Los licked his lips while rubbing his hands together as he sat at the table with his legs parted.

"Hurt my baby and I'm gon' hurt yo' ass, nigga. Remember what the fuck I said to you earlier. Kill that shit with that bitch because I will shoot that hoe and make her disappear," Jonathan said seriously.

"I'm only trying to love her, Jonathan. I got Nikki's ass and she won't be a problem because we ain't been together and never will be again. Kaymee is who I want. She will be mine. I'll do right by her and I will be your son-in-law in no time," Los said, draping his arm on the back of the chair he was sitting in.

"I'm with Jonathan, fam. Mee has been through too much to be fucked with. I'm not her brother for nothing. You know how I roll, Los. Don't play with her emotions," I told him.

Katrina and Kaymee exited the house. Los got up and Kaymee walked right past him to Jonathan. "Daddy, I'm gonna leave with Carlos. I'll call you tomorrow and let you know what the counselor said about the visit,"

"Call me tonight if you need to," he said, hugging her neck.

"See ya later, bro. Tell Poe I'll see her tomorrow since she's sleeping. Safe travels you two," she turned to G and Scony. "I'll pay y'all a visit when I come back to the Chi," she said, giving us hugs before she headed for the gate.

"Aye, Kaymee!" Scony yelled. "You better sit on one side of the couch and he on the other. Won't be no fuckin' tonight!" he said, raising his shirt showing his gun.

"Scony, please. I'm grown. I won't do nothing you wouldn't do," she said, smiling.

"That's what I'm afraid of. Los, keep yo' hands to yo'self, nigga!" he screamed as they disappeared through the gate. "Jonathan, yo' daughter is about to give up the ass, man. You ain't gon' stop her?" Scony asked.

"Nope, I'm not about to tell her what she can and can't do. Like she said, she's grown. I'll be there when she needs me. That's all I can do. Come on baby so we can get home. I'm tired as hell."

Jonathan said his goodbyes and G and Scony followed behind him because Nova called saying she was out front. I locked the gate and made sure everything was straight. I walked into the house and locked the door, making my way upstairs to cuddle with my wife.

Meesha

Chapter 15

Los

I wanted Kaymee to come home with me because I didn't really get a chance to spend time with her at Monty's crib. All that shit Scony was talking about wasn't what I had in mind. Shit, she could sleep in the guest room if she wanted to. The only thing on my mind was being in her presence and conversation.

"What are we about to do, Los?" Kaymee asked as I cruised down the street.

"I figured we could sit back, watch a movie at my crib. Or we can go out for drinks and chill. It's up to you, beautiful."

"Seeming I'm not old enough to drink publicly, maybe we can catch a movie at the theater," she replied.

"Come on now, you're with me. Do you know how to shoot pool?"

"No, I've never tried to play."

"Today is your lucky day. We're about to have some fun," I said, heading for a little bar not too far away.

We rode in silence for a few blocks before I reached up and turned on the radio. Tank's "Dirty" blared through the speakers. I'd never heard the song, but Kaymee was singing her little heart out. The lyrics to the song was explicit as hell, but hearing the words fall from her lips made my joint brick up.

You like when I do you dirty
Yeah, yeah
Like when I do you dirty, oh
I'll put your face in the pillow
I'll be smackin' on that ass
I grab your neck, choke you real slow
You ain't even gotta ask
You like when I do you dirty
I ain't gon' tell nobody
Oh, tell nobody
Oh, tell nobody

She switched the lyrics up and it seemed as if she was low key sending me a message. I leaned back in my seat and acted like I wasn't locking the subliminal in the back of my mind for a later time. I really wanted to say fuck going out and head straight to my crib, but I didn't want to give off the wrong impression. Instead, I pulled into a space outside the pool hall, cutting the engine off.

Getting out of the car, Kaymee was already out by the time I could open the door for her. That told me Dray didn't treat her right in several departments. It was time for me to change that and show her how it's done. The jeans she wore hugged her thighs for dear life when she sashayed in front of me. I moved in behind her and wrapped my arms around her waist and pressed my joint against her backside. The lyrics to "Dirty" played in my head, making my lil' nigga rise.

"Los, get yo' perverted body parts off me," she said, trying to wiggle away.

"If you really mean what you said, I'll oblige. I don't think you do," I replied, kissing her neck.

"Don't start anything we won't finish. We're here to play pool," she said, reaching out to open the door.

"I got that," I said, smacking her hand down playfully. "I'm the man. It's my job to open doors, pull out chairs, and carry you over puddles from this point on."

"That's cute, thank you," she said, chuckling.

"What's up, Los? Who's your lady friend?" An older guy asked as we entered the hall.

"Back up, playboy. This is my future wife. How ya been, Al?"

"I won't complain as long as the money still rollin' in. You got a beauty on yo' hands this time around. What happened to you and Nikki?" Al asked.

"Nikki is long gone. Don't talk her up. This is my girl now. Her name is Kaymee. On another note, is there a table available for me? I'm about to give a quick lesson."

"Nice to meet you, cutie. There's a table in the back you can grab. It's money in the building too if you want to empty some pockets," Al said, grinning.

"Nah, I'm cool on that, old timer. I got my lady with me and I don't need her to see me fuck somebody up about my money."

"I'll watch her for you." Al thought his ass was slick. Kaymee wasn't like some of the bitches I brought to Al's place. He didn't have a chance with her.

"Don't start that shit, man. Kaymee ain't one of them throw aways. She's a keeper. You won't get my sloppy seconds this time around. She don't need yo' money. She has her own and mine, nigga. I don't think Jonathan would approve of you hitting on his daughter," I shot back at him.

"This is Jay's daughter?" Al asked surprised. "Gone over there and rack them balls. Not you, baby girl. Don't touch no balls. As a matter of fact, don't touch the sticks either. I don't want no problems with yo' daddy. Drinks are on the house. Y'all enjoy yourselves," he said, going behind the counter.

Kaymee laughed so hard, she had to rush to the bathroom. I walked over to the available table and racked up the balls. Reaching for a stick, I felt my phone vibrate on my hip. I looked at the screen and it was the same number that called earlier. Wondering who it was, I decided to answer the call.

"Yeah," I said smoothly.

"Why did you block me? I have to call you from somebody else's phone in order for you to answer. Los, stop playing with me because I'm not the one!"

"Nikki—"

"Don't Nikki me. Hear me out! What I did was wrong and I can't apologize enough for my actions. Dude didn't mean shit to me. I regret it ever happened. I love you. Don't do this to me, Los."

Nikki must've thought I was a stupid nigga. I couldn't believe she was on my phone begging and pleading like that was going to move me. She was wasting her time begging and pleading because I could care less. Nikki wasn't sorry for cheating, she was sorry she got caught.

"You done? All that shit that fell from yo' lips is hilarious. It's been six months and I stand on my decision to not fuck with you ever again. I won't be hittin' you up and I'd appreciate if you stop blowing my shit up. A muthafucka don't miss a good thing until it's gone and you that muthafucka.

Go find that nigga that had you throwin' that ass back like you were single. I guess you trying to come back to me because your lifestyle changed drastically. His ass ain't good for shit but dishing out dick, huh? That's what you get. Now live with the consequences, bitch!"

"I'm sorry, Los—"

I hung up on her ass because I wasn't in the mood to listen to her crying in my ear. Putting my phone back on hip, I grabbed the cue stick and chalked it up. I aimed the stick and broke the balls, sending several solids into the holes. My phone started vibrating continuously breaking my concentration.

"What, Nikki?" I growled into the phone after ignoring several of her calls. Kaymee walked out of the bathroom at that precise moment, stopping in her tracks.

"Would you listen to me for a few minutes? Can we try one more time to make this work? I promise not to take our relationship for granted again."

"Actually, I'm tired of listening to you, Nikki. I need you to comprehend the words I'm about to say for the last time. We're done!" Then I hung up.

Motioning for Kaymee to come over, I racked the balls up again and used the table to lean on. I tried to calm myself down because the whole conversation with Nikki irritated me. I wasn't about to let her get under my skin. All I wanted to do was have a good time with Kaymee.

"Everything okay?" she asked, rubbing my back.

"Yeah, that was Nikki. There's nothing to worry about. She don't want to accept the fact that we are over. Even though it's been six months, I guess knowing I'm pursuing something with you is getting to her. She will be alright though. Let's get this pool lesson under way."

I explained the rules of the game to her and showed her how to hold the stick. The first couple of tries, she fucked the table up by

142

scratching it with the tip of the stick. I was going to have to pay for it, but I didn't mind. She was enjoying herself.

"This is not the game for me, Los. I will never learn how to do this. I quit," she said, placing the stick on the table.

"Nah, you ain't about to give up like that. I don't have quitters on my team, pick up that stick and try again." She glanced at me sideways and did what I told her to do. When she bent over the table, I eased behind her and connected my hands with hers. "Loosen up on the stick, babe. It should be able to glide between your fingers with ease. You have too much tension on the stick," I explained to her.

"No, the tension is pressed against my ass," she said, laughing. "Back up a little bit, you are distracting me from focusing on the balls."

I laughed because I wanted her to focus on my balls, but I didn't want to stress that thought to her. "Come on, let's get a drink." I held her hand and led her to the bar. We sat on two available stools and Al was waiting for us to give our orders. "What are you drinking, Kaymee?"

"I will have a Sex on The Beach. Heavy on the vodka please," she mumbled.

Once again, I took that as another subliminal message that she was throwing at me, but I was going to let things flow at her pace. Kaymee didn't come out and say she wanted to fuck, but there was no doubt in my mind that she wanted to. Al mixed her drink and gave me a bottle of MGD.

"What do you know about that drink that you ordered?" I asked after taking a sip from the bottle of beer.

"I had one at my birthday party last year and I liked it. I wasn't about to *not* drink while you were."

"You not even supposed to be drinking, legally," I said and grinned at her.

"What you gon' do, turn me in?" she asked smartly.

"Nah, you're too beautiful to be locked up. Your secret is safe with me."

She smiled and swirled her straw around in her drink before taking a sip. The drink had to be strong because her face scrunched up and she coughed a little. Taking another sip, she coughed uncontrollably. I patted her on the back and waved Al over.

"Let me get a cup of water, old man. You trying to kill my girl making that drink strong as hell," I said when he walked over.

"Shit, I gave her what she asked for," he said, handing her a bottled water. "Here's some more juice so you can even it out in this glass."

"Old man Al don't water down drinks, so when you ask for more alcohol, remember there's already plenty in the glass to start."

"Thank you," Kaymee said, twisting the top off the water bottle quickly.

"Al, have the cook whip up twenty wings, catfish, and fries for us. Oh, you may want to put a sign on the table we had because my baby scratched the fuck out of it. I'll hit you with some cash before I leave."

"It's all good. You're good for it. I'll put that order in for you now," he said, picking up the phone.

We sat listening to the music that was playing around the hall and I couldn't stop looking at how beautiful Kaymee was. Her locs were full and complemented her face well. Being out with her was like a breath of fresh air. We laughed, joked, and we didn't argue.

"You want to talk about what happened earlier?" she asked, taking a sip from her glass.

"I won't lie to you, Nikki called talking about she's sorry for what she did to me. I've blocked her from hitting me up but, she's calling from other numbers. The only reason she's doing the most is because she knows I'm with you," I explained.

"We're not together, so there shouldn't be a problem. I don't understand how these females get all in their feelings about a man that don't want shit to do with them. All I know is, she better keep that bullshit between y'all because I'm not for it," she said, sipping her drink deeply.

144

"You don't have nothing to worry about. Leave Nikki to me because she is far from stupid."

The cook from the kitchen walked over, placing our food in front of us. Kaymee snatched a wing and bit into it closing her eyes. I watched her lick her lips and I wanted a taste, too. The catfish was what I went for, and it was cooked how I liked it, crispy.

"You killin' them wings, ma," I said and laughed, watching her reach for another.

"They are so good and the fries are seasoned just right! Here, try one," she said, holding a fry out for me to taste.

I knew how the fries were, but I allowed her to feed me anyway. It's been a while since I've had feelings like this for anyone, I was going to enjoy every minute. We were enjoying our meal when the doors to the hall opened and the sound of a female made my ears perk up like a K-9.

"Yeah, I'm about to have a couple drinks. Fuck these niggas. I'm not sweating no muthafuckin' body to pay attention to me," Nikki said as I watched her through the mirror.

She waltzed to an empty table on the other side of the room and sat with her back towards the bar. I was glad she didn't notice me, but I wanted to keep it that way. "Umm, Kaymee? How about we take this food to go? A problem just walked in,"

"Please tell me that was not Nikki," she said with a raised eyebrow.

"I'm afraid it is. Hey, Al. Let me get a couple to go boxes. I have to leave because I don't want no trouble in your place of business," I said lowly.

"What's going on, young blood?" he asked, scanning the hall. "Ohh, I see what you talkin' about. I think it's a little too late to leave peacefully. Her friend just spotted you," Al said, coming from behind the counter. "Don't start no shit, Slim. This is not the place for you to let your feelings out."

Glancing in the mirror, Nikki was storming towards me like a raging bull. "I'm not trying to hear none of that, Al. This is a public place. I have a right to use freedom of speech and I have plenty to get off my chest today."

"I will toss yo' ass out of here on your ass! Don't play with me, girl," Al said, stepping in front of her.

Ignoring everything that was said to her, Nikki sidestepped Al and headed straight for Kaymee. I stood from the stool with my arms outstretched, preventing her from moving any closer to my girl. "Yo' ass ain't about to pull that bullshit! What the fuck you mad at her for?" I asked her stupid ass.

"Los, you don't have to protect me," Kaymee said calmly, taking off her earrings. "She can come over her and get this Chi-town ass whoppin' if that's what she's looking for. See, your problem is not with me because I've never laid down with you. That's what's wrong with simple-minded hoes. It's always the female who gets approached. Check ya nigga!"

"Bitch you must not know how we get down in the A, but I can show you," she said, swinging around me.

I swung my arm upward, blocking the blow she threw at Kaymee and pushed her back. Neither me nor Al saw Kaymee come from behind us and jaw check Nikki. She wasn't ready for it either because she went down on one knee holding her head. The female that was with her charged Kaymee and before we knew it, they were going heads up.

Ole girl was about four inches taller than Kaymee, but that didn't give her an advantage. Kaymee somehow wrapped her hands around the girl's weave and was tagging her ass. Arms were flaring about but my girl had them hands. Every punch she threw hit its target.

"Let her go, Kaymee!" I yelled. It took everything in me not to let her continue to beat this bitch ass, but I had to break that shit up. When Al and I were able to get them apart, Nikki came out of nowhere hitting Kaymee while I had her wrapped in my arms. That sneaky shit was fucked up and I didn't have a choice but to let Kaymee go."

"How the fuck that feel, bitch?" Nikki screamed with her fist up in a boxer's stance.

Kaymee responded with action instead of words. When I released her, she faked a right hook and Nikki fell for it. Kaymee rocked her ass with a left-hand uppercut. Nikki had the boxing experience, but Kaymee looked like she was a street fighter to heart. Blood dripped down Nikki's chin because her two front teeth were embedded in her bottom lip. That's how hard Kaymee hit her.

"Aaaaargh!" Nikki screamed out in pain.

Kaymee went for Nikki again and I grabbed her shirt pulling her back. "That's enough, bae. She's hurt."

"This is the shit I was talking about, Los. I'm not about to be fighting every time we're out. That's not the way I operate. I've seen and heard you tell her y'all was done but at the same time, I'm not doing this high school shit. It's your job to get the word out to this hoe in a way she will understand that ya'll are done!

She will not destroy what we are working towards and I won't be fighting to prove you're my man. Step the fuck up and tame yo' gorilla, Los. If she steps to me again, the outcome will be far worse than the little blood you see now. I'm tired of muthafuckas taking this pretty face as a sign of weakness. Give me your keys. I'm going to the car while you pull that bitch teeth out of her lip," she said, holding out her hand.

I gave her my keys and she stormed out of the hall. There was a crowd of people standing around watching the commotion. "There's nothing to see over here! Go back to playing pool, drinking or whatever, but get out of this section!" Al yelled at the patrons of his establishment.

"Damn, Al. I was just trying to make sure baby girl is okay. She did just get fucked up quickly," a big nigga said, making everybody around laugh. "Pretty girl pulled a Mike Tyson tonight. My money was on her from jump after the forewarning she gave."

"Big Mike!" Al snarled. He was pissed because Nikki brought drama to his place of business and I didn't blame him for being upset. "Los, I got this. Go with ya girl," he said snatching a towel his barmaid brought to him.

"My bad about this, Al," I said, reaching in my pocket.

"Yo' money ain't good here, Los. Don't worry about it. All I want you to do is make it right with that cutie. If you're not serious about pursuing her, leave it alone. She's different and too beautiful to be whoopin' ass every day.

I felt what she said to you, young blood. Pay attention to what she's talking about. I can tell she's been through a lot and you have to show her something new to win her over. It won't be easy, but you can do it."

"Fuck that bitch! You see what she did to my girl?" Nikki's friend screamed, walking over to where me and Al was talking.

"I don't know you, but this ain't got shit to do with you. That's why you got jaw jacked for putting your nose in mutha-fuckas shit! If anything, you should've been telling Nikki to stay off the dumb shit. I don't want her ass. Be the little birdie and tell her to let it go. There will be nothing between us!" I said calmly to her.

"All you niggas the same. Get a bitch hooked on ya'll and then want something new! That shit fucks with a woman's mental, but y'all don't care."

"See, you don't even know the situation but want to ride with ya girl! Tell her to run the truth by you first before you step to me. Get yo' pussy ridin' ass out my face! Al, I'm leaving before I hurt this hoe's feelings," I said, walking toward the door.

"Los!" Nikki called out to me and I ignored her and kept going until I was out of the door.

Chapter 16

Kaymee

That bitch showing up talking crazy shot my blood pressure through the roof. I hated a "check the female" type of hoe. How about you address the problem at hand? Her problem was with Los, not me, but she learned that shit the hard way when she swung on me.

I went to the car to wait on Los to come out. My phone rang and it was the number from the counselor that reached out to me earlier. I forgot to call her back, so I answered without hesitation.

"Hello," I said, pausing.

"Hi, Kaymee. This is Yvette again, I'm sorry for calling so late. Have you decided if you will be able to come for the family session?"

"Yes, I actually forgot to call you back. My dad and I will be coming whenever you give me a date. We agreed that everything needed to be put on the table if it will help Dot with her problem."

"That's great to hear. One thing I want to say is this, Dot doesn't have a problem per say. Drug usage is a disease," Yvette tried to explain.

"I understand the terms you were taught in order to become a counselor. In my opinion, you can't walk down the street and contract addiction. That was a choice she made on her own."

"Well, your mother said she was forced on the drugs by your father—"

"I don't know anything about that. It can be discussed during the meeting. Dot's issues go beyond her drug usage. It's been ongoing for years. What would be a good date for you?" I asked nicely.

"How about next week Saturday, say about three o'clock?"

"That will be fine. I'll inform my dad of the appointment. You may want to have security on hand because she is expecting me, not my dad. I think that's where all of her anger stems from, their past relationship. She may not take it well. You should inform her that he's coming," I suggested.

"If he's a trigger, she may not want to attend the meeting. I think her not knowing is the best way to go with this." I didn't agree with keeping Dot in the dark, but who was I to argue a point to someone that obviously knew everything about the person she was trying to help.

"Text me the location and any rules we may need to follow. We will definitely see you next week. Thanks for calling," I said.

As I hung up the phone, Los came walking out of the pool hall with a look of frustration on his face. I wanted to be mad at him, but the incident was not his fault at all and I refused to blame him. Honestly, he did everything necessary to get his point across to Nikki. One couldn't control another person's actions.

When he reached for the door, a woman ran out of the building with a bag. Los paused and waited for her to reach him. Taking the bag, he reached in his pocket and peeled a couple bills from the knot he held in his hand. She turned away going toward the building and he opened the car door and slid inside. Los pushed the button to start the car and placed the bag in the back seat.

"I'm sorry, Kaymee. I didn't know Nikki would show up here tonight," he said, before pulling off. "Shit shouldn't have gone in the direction it did and I can't be mad if you don't want to fuck with me. Nikki's not gonna stop until I'm no longer with you. I didn't have these problems from her until now. I'll take you home so you can decide what you want to do."

On the inside I wanted to go home and get far away from him and the drama he had in his life. Then I had to think about the reason I really took him up on his offer to leave Poetry's and Monty's house together. The way he had been watching me ignited a fire that I'd had trouble distinguishing alone. I needed a man's touch to get my kitty right and I thought Los would be the perfect candidate to get the job done.

"I'm not going home. We agreed to hang out and that's what we will do. Head on to your crib and we can Netflix and chill for the rest of the night. All that other shit is behind us. What was in that bag?" I asked, changing the subject.

"It's a fresh food order that Al sent out for us since we didn't get to finish eating."

"Good shit because I'm starving. Do you have anything to drink at your house?"

"Yeah, I think I have some soda and water in the fridge," he said glancing in my direction.

"I'm trying to drink! My Sex on The Beach is still sitting on the counter back there," I said, pointing my thumb behind me.

"Ohhhhh, you want a drink drink, huh? The only thing I have his Remy at my crib. We can sip on that."

"I don't drink dark nothing! I would be sick as a dog, I need some light in my life."

"Okay, I'll stop at the liquor store. We have time to get there before it closes," he said, pressing his foot on the gas. We pulled up to the store and he got out and poked his head back in the door. "What do you want to drink?" he asked.

"Get a bottle of Coconut 1800 and some pineapple juice."

"What are you trying to get into, Kaymee? That's a sinners drink."

"Would you stop asking questions and get in there before the damn store close!" I said, shooing him out the door.

Los closed the door and walked into the store. In my mind, I was trying to contemplate how I was going to initiate this night I had conjured up in my head. Fucking was in the forefront of my mind because my pussy hadn't been tampered with in a while. It was time for me to moan in ecstasy.

He came out of the store carrying a bag and he looked sexy as hell. He didn't even have on anything spectacular. The jeans he wore were black, the black and white polo was hugging his chest just right. He also wore a silver chain around his neck with a diamond earring in his ear. The thing that made my girl tingle was his goatee that outlined his lips.

I wanted to see what it'd look like if my juices coated it. My eyes were focused on him and I couldn't tear them away. When the door opened, I was still lusting and got caught.

"Why are you staring at me like that?" he asked, getting in the car. He reached between the seat and put the liquor bag in the back on the floor.

"Maybe I was admiring the way you look, damn!"

"Well voice that shit, Kaymee. Don't stare at me like a creep, yo'," he snickered, shifting the gear in drive.

"Now I'm a creep?"

"I didn't call you a creep. I said stop looking at me like one. Don't twist my words around to fit your thoughts. If I like something about you, I'm gon' let you know about it, plain and simple," he said without taking his eyes off the road.

"Yeah, yeah, yeah. Turn on the radio, please."

"What's wrong with your hands, Kaymee?"

"It's not cool to touch a black man's radio. I don't want any problems," I said, hunching my shoulders.

"What type of shit is that? Turn the radio on, woman," he said, laughing. "I got a lot of work to do if we will be together. What's mine, is yours. There are no stipulations at all. You don't need permission to do anything around me. All I want from you is four things, respect, honesty, loyalty, and love. It takes time to receive all of the things I ask for and we will move accordingly to get there," he said, reaching for my hand.

What he said sounded good, but I wasn't trying to think about commitment at that time. The only thing on my mind was sex and he was going to give it to me. Los acted as if he wasn't interested in having sex, but he wasn't going to turn me down.

He took the initiative and turned on the radio and I bobbed my head to the sounds of Beyonce's song "Hold Up." The beat was crazy on that track and I loved it. I received a notification on my phone, which was still in my hand. Opening the messenger, I received a photo message from Dray and I wanted to see what type of crazy he was on. When the photo downloaded, I clicked on it and there was a picture of him and a woman.

152

The female looked familiar, but I didn't know anyone in Boston. They seemed happy with one another and I was happy for him because that meant he wouldn't be bothering me. Zooming in on the picture, I started laughing uncontrollably.

"What's wrong with you?" Los asked.

"Dray sent me a picture showing that he has met someone. The one he's with is Scony's sister, MaKenzie. He has no clue that he has stepped into a trap he's never gonna get out of. Karma is a bitch and he's a great candidate to receive it."

"Yeah, that nigga is going to get what's coming to him in due time. Just say something nice and keep it moving. Don't feed into it. Try not to say too much to him. He's trying to get a reaction out of you," Los said nonchalantly.

"You already knew about this, didn't you?" I asked as I replied to Dray's message.

"That's not important," he said, pulling into his driveway. "Just know that he will be taken care of.

Los shut off the car and got out after grabbing the bags from the back seat. He came over to the passenger side, opening the door for me. Hand in hand, we walked up the stairs and he fumbled with the keys before they fell out of his hands. Bending down to retrieve them, I stumbled and grabbed his leg to prevent myself from falling. His third leg was the one that saved me and lawd, it was huge.

"I'm sorry about that," I said, feeling my face heat up with every dirty thought that swam through my mind. I stood up and looked down at the keys. "Which key belongs to your house?" I asked, trying to avoid eye contact.

"It's the key with the silver and black ring on the top. When you go in, put two, five, fifty-six into the alarm keypad." Doing what he instructed, I was able to get into his home without any incidents.

"Whose birthday is February fifth ?" I asked out of curiosity.

"It's my mom's birthday, lil' nosey."

"I'm not nosey. If I want to know something, I'm asking. My days of keeping things inside are over. I'm going to inquire about any and everything so get ready friend."

He walked to the kitchen while I stood by the door admiring the artwork he had on the wall. I loved beautiful African American art with my people with melanin. He had a picture of a black man that was naked from the waist up, wearing a crown representing he was a King. His queen was leaned against his chest looking up at him, while he protected her with his arms around her breast. The picture showed the love he had for her.

There were hand painted images of Martin Luther King Jr., Malcolm X, Barack Obama, Maya Angelou, Tupac, Eazy E and countless others throughout the room. The art was impressive and I loved it. I had to ask where he purchased them from because I wanted some in my home, whenever I bought one. Los came back into the living room with the bottle of tequila in his hand looking like a drink himself.

"Are you gonna stand there for the rest of the night or are you drinking with me?" he asked, holding up the bottle.

"I have to eat first, Los. Throwing up on you is something I don't want to happen. By the way, where did you get these paintings from? They are beautiful," I said, glancing around at them once more.

"I drew them myself. I see you like them."

"Wow, that's impressive. You are very talented. You could make lots of money off your work, why haven't you looked into it?" I asked seriously.

"I don't have time to paint all day. I'm trying to stack this bread to open an art studio. I've been looking into some things so I'll be ready when the time comes. I want to show you something I'm working on," he said, placing the bottle on the island.

Following him to a room down the hall, he opened the door and I walked into a full art studio. He had easels, paintbrushes, paints of all colors and a cover on the floor. There were paintings lining the wall, but he led me to a covered easel and summoned me over.

"I've been working on this one for a couple weeks. I wanted to surprise you with it but since you're here, I may as well show it to you now. There will be plenty of time for me to capture other moments to bring to life."

He stepped to the side of the easel, slowly revealing what was underneath. My breath caught in my throat when he let the cover fall to the floor. The painting was of me from the day we went to the Martin Luther King Jr. National Historical Park. Los caught every feature I possessed and it popped off the canvas like 3D. I was very impressed with his work.

"Oh my gosh, this is beautiful! It looks finished to me. What else needs to be done?"

"There's lots that I have to do before it would be ready. Be patient and I will deliver it when it's done. Come on so we can enjoy the rest of the night, you're wasting the time I have to spend with you."

"Los, it's Friday night. I don't have class in the morning. I'm too grown for a curfew, so we can watch movies all night if you want," I said, leaving out of the room. "Where is your bathroom so I can wash my hands? That chicken is smelling too good."

"It's straight ahead to your left. What movie do you want to watch?" he asked.

"Scarface, I want to get my Al Pacino on. The world is mine," I said, laughing in my imitation Tony Montana voice.

"You're silly. Hurry up, I'll warm your food for you. Meet me in the living room then we can head to the theater."

"The theater?" I said to myself. His house didn't look big enough to have a theater in it. It was two levels and I haven't seen the entire place yet. Los definitely had a nice bachelor's pad going on and it was very cozy. I washed my hands and made my way back to the kitchen.

"Your phone was ringing," he told me as the microwave buzzed.

I didn't realize I had left my purse in the living room until that moment. As I reached inside my purse, my phone started ringing again. When I looked down at the screen, it was Dot calling.

Everything in me wanted to decline the call because I didn't want to be bothered with her bullshit.

"Yes, Dot?" I said when I answered.

"You still disrespecting me by calling me by my name? I'm your mother!"

I knew from that point that the conversation wasn't going to be a good one. Taking a deep breath, I held the phone to my side before bringing it back to my ear. "*Dot*, I'm not about to go through this with you tonight. You have never wanted me to call you mama, mommy, mother, or any of that shit. My mother passed away when I was six and I haven't been loved the same until my *daddy* came back into my life. Now, what are you calling me for?"

I hated talking to Dot like that, but I was tired of her and everybody else's shit. There wasn't going to be a push Kaymee down session ever again. It was time for me to live my own life and if that meant standing up for myself, so be it.

"That was my mama, not yours! She only had you because that's what I wanted her to do. Anyway, enough about that shit. I'm calling because you don't need to come here next week. I don't want to participate in no damn family meeting.

I've been dealing with this shit alone for months and my family ain't did shit to help me. It would be a waste of time and money for you to come here. Shit, send me the money and call it a day," she had the nerve to say.

"I will never give you a dime of my money. You haven't done anything for me, but you are always calling me to help you when you're in trouble. You can't keep blaming me for your downfalls in life. I will see you next week because I want you to get the help you need. Even though you never cared for me, I care for you because it wouldn't be right if I didn't. I'm hanging up and I will see you Saturday."

"Don't you dare hang up, bitch!" she screamed in my ear.

"Things don't actually change with time, I see. The shit you used to say before doesn't work today, Dot. Go lay down somewhere and whatever you want to get off your chest, we will hash that shit out on Saturday. Until then, goodnight." I said, disconnecting the call before she could say anything else.

My heart was hurting because I didn't want to turn my back on her. My mother wasn't giving me much choice and I was still willing to show up at the rehab center to hear her out. If she got her shit together, I wouldn't mind using my own money to get her a place to stay and doing things for her. But if Dot continued to talk sideways to me, she was going to be ass out.

"Is everything okay, Kaymee?" Los asked, coming up behind me.

"It will be," I replied, wiping a tear from my eyes. "I'm tired of muthafuckas trying to run over me! I've been hurt too many times, starting with my mama. I'm trying to be the bigger person and be there for her and she continues to talk to me like I'm not shit. Then tries to come back to me only when she needs money.

Dray convinced me that we were a match made in heaven and when we got here, his true colors started to show. He started putting his hands on me, controlling me, and making my life a living hell by threatening me. It was no different than the things my mother did to me for years," I cried.

"You don't have to worry about any of that again, I promise. Kaymee things happen for a reason and you can't allow it to hinder you for the rest of your life. I'm sorry you had to go through all the shit you did with that nigga and your mother, but I see a strong, determined, intelligent, and beautiful woman in you. Nothing will stop you from getting where you want to be in life," Los said, gathering me in his arms.

At that moment, I made a declaration to myself, never shed another tear for anybody that didn't give a damn about me. Faulting myself for things I couldn't prevent, had no control over, or could do nothing about were over. I was ready to move on to the next chapter of my life and happiness was what I was seeking.

I calmed down and finally ate before settling down to enjoy a night with Los. Poetry had called asking why I left her. Explaining that I would be over the following day, I sat back and sipped my third drink as we watched Venom. The movie was crazy, but I was tipsy as hell and that made it funny.

"What's so funny, Kaymee?" Los asked.

"He's talking to that thing like it's human! Did you see how he was fucking up that meat?" I said, laughing. My head fell onto his shoulder because it was heavy as hell. The tequila was taking over my body.

"Give me that glass. You've had enough," he said, reaching for my hand.

Switching hands, I leaned over and downed the rest of the alcohol that was in the glass. That shit burned, but I finished it and wiped my mouth. I passed him the glass and he stared at it before turning to me.

"Why would you do that? I'm gon' be up holding your damn hair back as you're throwing up for the rest of the night. You about to be fucked up!"

"I'm straight, Los. Trust me. What you can do is bend me over this couch and kiss me on my neck," I said, whispering in his ear.

"Kaymee, you don't mean that shit. Pay attention to the movie because ain't shit happening."

The tequila gave me liquid courage that had me feeling like a sexy super hero. Running my hand up and down his leg, I eased my hand to the zipper of his pants to see what his reaction would be. Glancing up at his face, he looked down at me and I licked my lips.

"Stop, ma. You're drunk. Come on now, watch the movie," Los said, moving my hand.

"What if I don't want to stop, Carlos? We're both grown and I want to feel your dick on my tonsils," I replied, placing my hand back on his dick. He grew rapidly with each rub I ran across the front of his pants. Los was working with a big one.

"Kaymee, I won't be having sex with you. The alcohol got you acting up. Go to the bathroom and splash your face, then come back and relax."

I stood and walked down the hall to the bathroom. Doing what Los suggested, I splashed my face and used a towel out of the

158

linen closet to dry off. Instantly, my body got hot and I started snatching my clothes off. When I was completely undressed, I hopped in the shower and turned the cold water on.

My kitty was tingling and my hand went to directly to my clit and rubbed vigorously. Lifting my leg and planting my foot on the edge of the tub, I stuck two fingers inside my tunnel. A low moan escaped my lips, making me go harder on myself. The heat I experienced down below was like an inferno, so masturbating wasn't working this time around.

Stepping out of the shower, I grabbed a big bath towel out of the closet and wrapped it around myself. As I opened the door and headed back to the living room where Los was, I was determined to explode on his dick. His back was to me and he was into the movie that was on the TV, so he didn't hear me come back. Standing behind him, I ran my hands over his shoulders and down his chest.

"Kaymee, why are you wet?" he asked, trying to turn around.

"I was wet before you sent me to the bathroom, Los. I thought I told you that already," I said, slipping my tongue in his ear. "I need you to put out this fire between my legs. Would you do that for me?" I asked, releasing the towel so it could fall to my feet.

My breasts were resting on his back and my nipples protruded outward. Los ran his hand up and down my arm, but he had yet to respond to my question. Giving him the option to say no was something I didn't want to do. I moved around and stood in front of him stark naked. His eyes roamed my body and stopped on my clean shaved mound.

As I wrapped my arms around his neck, I placed one foot on the side of his leg on the couch and hoisted myself upward. Standing with my treasure in his face, I ran my fingers along my lower lips getting them nice and wet. Bringing one of my fingers to his lips, he opened his mouth and encircled it with his tongue.

Motioning me forward while his hands palmed my ass, all bets were off. I was about to get what I wanted. Los kissed the top of my kitty repeatedly then snaked his tongue between my slit. My legs trembled with anticipation as he slid down a bit before lowering my love box onto his tongue.

"Mmmm, shit," I moaned, grinding my hips in a circular motion. My legs were shaking and standing was becoming a hard task to master. Los was caressing me with his tongue so good that I grabbed his head for leverage. Flicking his tongue quickly over my bud, my stomach tightened and my river overflowed. "Oh shit!" I yelled trying to unattached my kitty from his lips.

"Where the fuck you going? This is what you wanted right, Kaymee?" he said, smirking.

"Yeah, I wanted to see what that mouth do but, it's doing too much," I said, swinging my leg over his head, falling onto the couch on my stomach. Los followed me and pulled me up by stomach, tooting my ass in the air. His tongue slid between my cheeks and I crawled forward. Los wasn't letting up because he pulled my love box back into his mouth and held my thighs in his hands.

"Aaaah, fuck," I moaned, rocking my hips back and forth. Reaching behind me to grasp his head, he held my hand and pinned it behind my back. A sista was stuck, but I wasn't complaining. The massage I received on my lower region was just what the doctor ordered.

Los removed his right hand from my thigh and I heard his belt buckle rattle. Glancing over my shoulder as his pants fell below his waist, my eyeballs almost popped out my damn head! His manhood was long, thick, and had veins that looked like they were on steroids, right along with his meat.

His ass was high yella and his dick was a caramel color. It looked like one of those caramel candies that had the white center and I wanted a taste. Planting my feet on the floor, I turned around with a little spittle on my lip.

"What are you doing, Kaymee? I wasn't finished feasting on that pussy."

"Oh, that can wait. There's something right there that I want to get acquainted with," I said, pointing between his legs.

Smirking, he leaned back on the arm of the couch as his lil' man jerked slightly. Without using my hands, I French kissed the tip. His thigh muscles flexed and he braced his head against the arm of the couch. I wasn't very skilled in this department, but I was going to give it my all. Using both hands, I grabbed his pole and inserted it into my mouth as far as I could.

Closing my eyes, I envisioned the porn videos I'd watched on many occasions and tried to suck the skin off his shit. The way he moaned told me I was on the right path and it excited me. Taking in a few more inches, I started humming while I swallowed in between sucks.

"Damn, ma. Get that shit," he groaned, lowly as he cupped the back of my head. I was trapped and there was nowhere for me to go but down, so that's what I did. Gagging a little bit, I relaxed my throat and felt his member glide slowly to the back of it. "Shit, damn," he growled lowly as his grip tightened on my locs.

Los started feeding my mouth and I was taking it like a pro. The alcohol helped a bitch out in this situation because I was super head at that moment. My mouth was wet as hell and his dick went in and out of my mouth with ease. The more I sucked, the more he grew on my tongue. My kitty was thumping and I couldn't let her react alone.

Releasing one of my hands, I played in my silky fold and felt an orgasm coming immediately. Los' hand traveled down my back and I felt his fingers tracing my ass crack. He started playing with the forbidden hole and I tensed up for a second because I wasn't ready for that action.

"Relax," he said as he put the tip of his finger inside. An electric like current shot through my stomach and I assaulted my clit faster. The penetration of his finger sent me into a frenzy and I found myself meeting his finger thrust for thrust. It felt good and I was loving it.

"Oh shit!" I screamed, letting his joint slip from my lips. He released my head and guided it back to my lips, but my concentration was on what he was doing to my asshole. "Go deeper," I said, cupping his balls. "Yes," I said, bouncing my ass on his finger. "I'm about to cum!"

"Stop talking about it and let that shit go, ma."

The urge to pee was what I felt, but I remembered that during sex, that meant something else. Trying to hold back, I knew I was about to fuck up the upholstery on his couch. It was going to be on him because he was the cause.

"Aaaaaah," I screamed as I released a bucket of cum everywhere. Feeling the wetness on my thighs and legs, and my clit jerking in the pam of my hand, I fell forward and my head landed in his lap.

"Shit and you're a squirter! I'm gon' need you to do that shit on this dick, baby. The faces you make when you're about to cum is the sexiest shit to me," he said, tapping me on the ass.

My energy level was spent and I couldn't move. Los held my chin with his hand, while he eased from under my head. He put his hands under both of my arms and picked me up, cradling me like a baby. I wrapped my arms around his neck as he palmed my ass and walked across the room. I opened my eyes as he climbed the stairs and I knew the night was far from over.

Chapter 17

Poetry

Waking up to the sound of Aria crying, I sat up and snatched the baby monitor from the nightstand. She was lying on the changing table and Monty was standing over her unsnapping her sleeper. He had a pamper, wipes, and another sleeper next to her, everything was within arms reach.

My heart swelled every time I saw him interact with the baby and tears always threatened to fall. The thought of him having to raise our daughter alone did something to me. I thank God every day for giving me a second chance at life to be there for Monty and Aria.

"You're finally awake," my mama said from the doorway with a smile on her face. "How are you feeling?" she asked as she walked in taking a seat beside me.

"I'm feeling good, actually. Sorry for leaving the party early. I couldn't bare the pain. Mama, how long is this going to go on?"

"It depends on your body, baby. Give it time. You will be good as new. I'm about to cook breakfast. What do you want to eat?"

"Ma! You know I'm not picky about any food that you cook. It doesn't matter," I said, turning my attention back to the monitor.

Monty was sitting in the rocker with Aria cradled in his arms. His mouth was moving, but I couldn't quite hear what he was saying. Turning up the volume, I caught on to the conversation he was having with the baby.

"You are so beautiful, Princess. Daddy loves you with all of his heart, always remember that. A man is not complete until he sees the baby he's made and you have completed me, Aria," he said, raising her up to kiss her cheek.

The words that Monty spoke were from the heart, but Aria wasn't trying to hear any of it. She started fussing as she swung her little fists in the air. Letting out a loud wail, Monty bounced her up and down a little bit to no avail.

"Okay, with your little feisty self. You get that shit from yo' mama. I only wanted a father daughter moment and you want to eat. My bad for being inconsiderate of your needs. You lucky you're daddy's baby and can get whatever you like or I'll leave your ass in here to cry a river by yourself."

"Montez! Bring my baby to me so I can feed her!" I yelled loud enough for him to hear me.

Looking at the monitor, I saw him look down at Aria, shaking his head. "See, you got me in trouble. Come on so I can get you to that titty milk you cravin'. Are you sharing today? The way you be sucking on that shit, I want some too," he said, standing up from the rocker leaving the nursery.

"He is a whole mess," my mama said, getting up to leave. "I'll bring your breakfast to you when it's ready."

"No, I'll come down. I'm not staying in this room. I have to go check out this beautiful home I didn't get the chance to see last night. Plus, Kaymee will be coming over sometime today, as well."

"Oh, you're going to love it. We can walk through together because I want to see your reaction. Especially the nursery," she said, leaving out the room as Monty and Aria appeared.

"Good morning, mama," Monty said, giving her a kiss on the cheek.

"Hey, Monty. You better stop cursing at my grandbaby before she grows up doing the same to you. It's cute now, but it won't be later," she told him.

"To be honest, your grandchild will be the first toddler with dentures if she every part her lips to cuss at me. That's me keeping it real with you. Do as I say, not as I do. That will be the first thing taught in my house. Ass whooping's will be dished out around these parts.

That's what's wrong with kids of today, parents are too busy trying to be the child's friend. Mine will have guidance *and* her daddy to regulate what the fuck goes on in her life. No disrespect to you, but I understand where you're coming from. We will be raising Aria the old school way and I dare the law come for me."

164

Monty was serious and I was with him a hundred percent on what he said. My mama smiled and nodded her head because that old school ass kickin' kept me in line for the most part. But I was a kid once and I knew what to look for. If I had to pull out the book of hard knocks that I went through growing up to raise mine, that's what I'd have to do.

"Okay, breakfast will be ready soon," she said, leaving.

"There's mama," Monty sang, bringing Aria over to me.

"Hey, pretty girl! Was daddy being mean to that baby?" I asked, kissing her on her nose after taking her from Monty's arms. She cut her eyes at him and if looks could kill, Aria would've been the first infant serial killer in history.

"Feed her evil ass. She gon' be one spoiled ass little girl."

"Monty, that's on you. Every time I look up, you have her in your arms holding her."

"That's what I'm supposed to do. She's my first born, Poe. But she ain't about to be acting funny when she gets hungry and want to switch sides," he said, climbing into the bed beside us.

Positioning Aria in the crook of my arm, I removed my breast and she latched on immediately. Breastfeeding was something I still had to get used to because it hurts when she suckles. I would rather pump and freeze the milk instead. Mama insists that allowing Aria to drink from my breasts is bonding time for us, but that shit is painful.

"How are you feeling this morning, baby?" Monty asked, watching me nurse the baby.

"I'm feeling a lot better than yesterday. Hopefully, these headaches let up sooner than later. I don't want to have to pop pills just to cope with the pain. I'm good right now though."

"For the next couple days, I want you to just chill, Poe. Your body needs to heal without stress. You will bounce back from this soon."

Watching Aria suckle on my breasts with her eyes closed, I smiled. Being a mother was never in my plans, but I'm glad I didn't go through with the abortion because I love my baby with everything in me. I've thought about the photoshoots I wanted to have, dressing her up in different outfits and just raising her to be the best she could be.

"Your advisor called to check on you yesterday, but you were sleeping. She emailed you all your assignments for your classes, but I told her that you needed to rest. She understood and said she was just trying to make sure you had what you needed so you wouldn't fall behind."

"Okay, thank you for taking that call. The last thing I want to do is fail my classes," I said, removing my nipple from Aria's mouth. She was full and knocked out. Placing her on my shoulder, I burped her, then handed her to Monty. "Put her in the bassinet and cover her up for me, please."

After making sure the baby was comfortable in the bassinet that we had by the side of the bed, Monty crawled back over to me as I covered my breast. He put his hand on top of mine to stop me. With a smirk on his face, I knew he was up to no good.

"Don't put that away just yet. Aria said she was going to share her milk with me this morning. It's my turn."

"Get your silly ass out of here, Monty. This is not adult milk," I said, laughing. "We can use this time to talk about some of the things we have endured that I don't remember. Let's start with what happened between us that broke us up." Monty was quiet for a spell and I had a feeling whatever happened wasn't good.

"Poetry, what I'm about to tell you may hurt. I'm sorry for putting you through all of that shit and I want you to know that I love you with all of my heart. We were apart for months before you gave me another chance, I hope that doesn't change after I reveal this to you," he said, bracing himself against the headboard.

"Montez, tell me what happened. It's in the past and I just want to remember," I said sincerely.

"I cheated on you with someone for two years while I was with you. She didn't mean anything to me, but we did have sex. You found out about it and I lied to keep the secret going. Breaking off things with Mena made things worse and the two of you got into a fight after she bragged about being with me."

"What happened in the past is just that, the past. There is only one Mrs. Williams and it's me. Is there anything else that I need to know about?" I asked.

"Mena has reached out to me via social media and has called me from various numbers, but I haven't talked to her. There's nothing that will every allow me to break up my family. I love you and only you, Poetry."

"Babe, you have shown me that love is more than a word. Monty, you were by my side for countless hours while I laid in that bed fighting to stay on this side of life. I heard every prayer you recited to me, my baby's cries, and how you tended to her needs. They were the main things that pushed me through. Knowing that you were doing all of that and staying on top of your schoolwork, makes me so proud.

We will continue to move forward together as a family. As long as we stay true to one another, never keep secrets, and communicate, we will be alright. It takes more than love to stay solid in a marriage."

"I promise to love, honor, and cherish you, Poetry. You have my word on that," Monty said, kissing me softly on my lips.

Pulling away from his mouth, I rubbed his eyebrow and pecked him once more. "I'm not starting something I can't finish. Let's go see if breakfast is ready," I said, swinging my legs out of the bed."

"Poe, it's been over six weeks. I need to feel my pussy, baby." Monty whined.

"I know. How about we go fill the prescription for my birth control today? I'm not trying to be a mother with two babies in diapers, Monty. Plus, I don't want to hurt my head and end up back in the hospital because I've bumped it on the headboard."

"A'ight, I'm giving you a week. After that, no more excuses. Now, go brush your teeth because your parents are not going to love the tart smell of your mouth like I do," he said, laughing.

"Shut yo' ass up," I said, swinging at him with my fist before walking into the bathroom.

Deciding to take a quick shower after brushing my teeth, I washed my body twice and got out. When I walked back into the room, Monty sat on the bed waiting patiently. The towel I had wrapped around my body showed off my curvy figure. Aria did her mama good because I was thicker than before, but still not fat. My ass was even bigger and I was loving it.

"Ass so fat I need a lap dance," Monty sang as I walked to the dresser to get a bottle of coconut lotion.

"You need to quit being mannish," I said, sitting on the ottoman that was at the foot of the bed.

"Straight up, wifey. You thick as fuck! It's gonna be hard to keep my hands to myself. You know that, right? I think we can handle another baby right off back."

"Nigga, please. It ain't happening, Monty. My body will heal before I have another baby. Shit, we ain't having another one for at least three to four years. So, stop thinking about it," I huffed.

"Well we gon' practice for the meantime in between time."

After oiling my body, I got up and threw on a pair of leggings, a t-shirt, and a pair of cute socks. Aria was still sleeping soundly, so I turned the monitor toward her and headed for the door. Monty was right behind me, so I peeked over my shoulder catching him looking at my ass. I fucked with him by making my ass bounce with every step I took going down the stairs.

"You didn't put no draws on, Poe?" he asked.

"Nope," I responded making sure I popped the "p" hard.

"My dick is hard as hell, ma. Stop playing and go put on some underwear."

"It's not like I'm going outside. I'm in my house."

Continuing down the stairs, I turned to face Monty when I got to the last step. His eyes got big and he started laughing. "Go upstairs and change your shirt, Poe. Your nipples are leaking," I looked down and sure enough, the front of my shirt was wet right where my nipples were. I raced upstairs and Monty yelled behind me, "Put some draws on while you're up there, too."

I sprinted up the stairs to my bedroom, snatched the shirt over my head, and tossed it in the laundry hamper. I searched through the drawers because I didn't know where most of my clothes were. I located my underwear, a black nursing bra with pads, and a black t-shirt, as well.

Monty was my husband, but that moment embarrassed me. It made me self-conscious and I didn't really want to go down to the kitchen. After putting on the bra and shirt, I sat on the side of the bed with my head held down. Tears burned the back of my eyes, but I fought hard not to let them fall.

"Poe, why are you just sitting there?" Monty's voice filled the room. Turning to face the monitor, he was standing in front of the screen with a look of concern on his face. "Come down. Your food is getting cold." Wiping the tears that escaped from my eyes, I stood from the bed checking the front of my shirt. "There's nothing wrong with your shirt baby. You look good."

His phone started ringing and I grabbed it from the nightstand beside the monitor. "Answer it, Poe and bring it down with you. I love you," he said, walking away from the monitor.

The number that appeared was one I didn't recognize, so I let it go to voicemail, figuring it was a business call. As I walked toward the door, the phone rang again and the same number appeared.

"Hello," I said, answering the phone. There was a long pause on the other end that made me look at to see if the person was still there. "Hello," I repeated.

"Can I speak to Monty," a female asked nicely.

"Who's calling?"

"It doesn't matter who I am. I want to talk to Monty," she rudely replied.

"People in hell want ice water, but you don't always get what you want. So again, who is this?"

"An old friend. Is this the young bitch he's so in love with? Poetry? The one that's too young to do anything? The reason Monty was running to me every chance he got?

This bitch was throwing shit on thick and it didn't faze me one bit. She showed me maturity didn't have much to do with age.

This had to be the Mena chick Montez was talking about. Her ass was still salty as hell and big mad because he still chose me.

"The one and only, boo, but you can address me as Mrs. Williams from this point on. The same young bitch that you're speaking on, is now the number one stunna in his life. That's probably why you have to call him from different numbers to reach him. I can speak for my husband and say that he no longer needs you in his life.

Whatever the two of you had is over. I don't need you to go into detail about y'all history. It doesn't matter. What matters is the fact that he has a family that holds his attention more than a fling that didn't go beyond sex. Thanks for entertaining him and getting him ready for his forever with me and his daughter. We appreciate you."

"Married? Daughter? What the fuck!" she screamed.

"Goodbye, Mena. Life as you knew with Montez Williams is over. Enjoy the rest of your day, love," I replied, hanging up on her.

Mena continued to call Monty's phone and I ignored her each time. Grabbing my phone from the dresser, I left the room. I walked into the kitchen and handed Monty his phone and it rang as soon as I placed it in his hand.

"Don't answer that. We'll talk about it later," I said, taking a seat at the table. "Good morning, daddy."

"Good morning, baby. How are you feeling?"

"I'm fine. I'm ready to eat. What have y'all been down here talking about?" I asked.

"We've been talking to Monty about how proud we are of him for taking care of you and Aria," my mama said.

"I keep telling y'all I haven't done anything spectacular. What I've done is what I'm supposed to do as a husband and father. There's no way I will accept any praises for caring for my family." My husband was the best in my eyes and I was glad he was mine. "Who called my phone, Poe?" he asked, checking his call log.

Cutting the pancakes my mama made, I glanced up at Monty and responded, "Nobody important," as I added syrup. "I'm going

170

to need you to change your number though. I think your past is going to be a problem."

"You're talking in circles, babe. What happened?"

"Your mistake Mena called and thought throwing a little shade my way would upset me. She's the one that ended up with a little yoke on her face. I'm not the least bit concerned about a little girl in an adult body, but my life will not be disrupted with her bullshit," I stated truthfully. "Sorry for my language, but he wanted me to talk now."

"It's alright. Y'all address that situation amongst yourselves. Never discuss your marriage with an audience. Keep what happens in your home right there," my mama said. "The last thing you want is other people in your business.

"I'm not worried about any negativity. It's up to my husband to deal with his situation, not me. Another woman is not my concern. My health is my main focus," I said, eating my breakfast that consisted of pancakes, eggs, and turkey bacon.

My phone rang and Kaymee's face appeared on the screen. "Hey, sista! What's up?"

"I'm on my way to see you and my God baby. Poe, I did some shit I'm not proud of and I need to talk it out," she said.

"I'll be ready to listen when you get here. I'm eating as we speak."

"Okay, I'll be there in a minute."

Finishing my food, I picked up my plate and Monty was right there to cater to my needs. He walked the plates to the sink and his phone started ringing. Monty stared at it for a few seconds before answering.

"Yeah," Monty said, pausing while washing the dishes. He held the plate that he held in his hand, then placed it on the edge of the sink. "Stop right there! Whatever my wife said to you is the truth. I don't know why you hittin' my line anyway after the shit that went down. There's nothing for us to discuss, Mena."

I should've known it was her again. Mena stopped calling for about thirty minutes before trying again. I'm guessing she figured if she got him, the conversation would go in her favor. The bitch thought wrong.

"Yes, we are married, yes, we have a daughter and no there's no way I can talk to you on any level. This will be the last time you will be able to call me, Mena. Blocking you didn't work, so I have to take an extra step. You or anyone else will not come between my marriage. As a matter of fact, this conversation is over," Monty said, hanging up.

Aria's little cries filled the room and Monty dropped the dish towel to tend to her. "I got it, baby. Kaymee is on her way. Let her know I'm upstairs when she gets here. Mommy and daddy, I'll be back."

I was all smiles after hearing Monty set the record straight with Mena. *"This marriage thing was going to be alright with me,"* I thought to myself as I went to love on my baby.

***

"Heyyyy, Teetee's baby!" Kaymee screamed ten minutes after I went upstairs. Aria started crying because Kaymee startled her with that big ass mouth of hers. "I'm so sorry, Ari boo," she said, leaning down to kiss her forehead.

"Move your ass out the way so I can finish washing her ass. She shitted all up her back and thought the shit was funny. I don't think I will ever get used to the sight of baby feces. It looks horrible."

"You better get used to it, Poe. She will be doing it for a long time before she can handle that task by herself. Wait until it starts smelling. You're really gonna gag," Kaymee said, laughing. "What's wrong with Monty?"

"Why do you ask that?" I asked, wrapping Aria in a hooded towel.

"When I came in, I spoke and he waved his hand while talking on the phone. Are y'all feuding about something?"

"Nah, this bitch Mena called talking shit. I had to set her ass straight, then hung up on her. She called back and thought Monty was going to check me or something. It didn't work the way she thought. I hope he's smart enough not to be down there entertaining her with anymore conversation," I explained, walking into the bedroom.

"It sounded like he was talking to the phone company to be honest. It was the expression on his face that made me question things. I thought Monty blocked Mena's ass after we whooped her ass the last time."

"We jumped that girl, Kaymee? You know we don't get down like that."

"I wouldn't say she was jumped—wait! You don't remember any of this?" Kaymee asked.

"Unfortunately, no. Monty was telling me about his infidelities earlier and I guess we talked her up. There's so much I don't' remember, but it's all good."

"Well, to make a long story short, we whooped that trick. End of story. Monty is probably changing his number to eliminate any further bullshit."

"Whatever works for him. I'm not worried about her ass to be honest," I said, applying lotion to Aria's chest. "Why are you all happy and shit? I haven't seen you smile like that in a long time."

"I left with Los last night," she said, biting her bottom lip. "We went to the pool hall and I got into it with his ex and one of her friends."

"What! I know you weren't out there fighting, Kaymee."

"I didn't want to but when she swung on me, I tried to knock her muthafuckin' head off. Los and the owner of the pool hall didn't let it go too far. Anyway, we went back to his house and Dot called pissing me off. I drank too much and woke up naked in his bed. Poe, I can't tell you what happened last night, but this morning—" she stopped, talking mid-sentence and zoned out.

"Earth to Kaymee!" I said, snapping my fingers in her face. "Are you saying you let that man rub your booty?" I said, chuckling.

"Shid, bitch. Los did more than rubbed my ass! He did so much to my body and I'm scared to see him again. The shit he whispered in my ear had me cummin' long after he dropped me off. He asked if we could hang out today and I told him I was spending the day with you and Aria. Poe, I don't know if I can do this relationship thing again."

"Do you like him?" I asked, pulling a pink onesie over Aria's head that had "Daddy's Little Girl" on the front.

"I do and we have a good time when we hang out. I shouldn't have slept with him last night, Poe. I think it changed the dynamics of our friendship."

"Um, yeah it did. Now he knows what that lil' pussy feels like. Seriously though, I think Los is the complete opposite of lil' stupid dude though. Give it a chance and see where it goes. If it's not what you want, then be honest with him about it," I said as I put a diaper on the baby.

"The sex was all that and more! Dude didn't make me feel the way Los does. I don't know what to do," she said, sitting down. Chris Brown's "Undecided" came from her purse.

But I'm undecided, excited, ignited
And I don't wanna feel the way I do, but I like it
Look at all these sparks flying
But I'm still indecisive
And she want me to wife it
But I'm undecided

Pulling her phone out, she smiled and replied back to the text message. I watched her for a few before I continued dressing Aria. She looked cute in her pink outfit and I completed it with a pair of pink booties. Dressing her was like playing with a baby doll, but motherhood was far different from pretending as a child.

"What am I going to do?" Kaymee asked lowly.

"You're going to play it by ear and follow your heart. I can tell you're stuck between giving him a chance and walking away by the ringtone you assigned to his contact. Don't give up so quickly. You deserve happiness and Los just might be it," I said, picking up Aria. "Let's go spend some time with my parents. I believe they will be leaving soon since I'm doing better," I said, heading for the door.

174

Chapter 18

Drayton

Meeting MaKenzie at the airport was the best thing that happened to me in a while. We have spent countless days together in the few weeks since we've landed in Boston. Showing her around my town was my pleasure when she wasn't busy with work. It felt good to put a smile on her face after a stressful day.

I closed on my house a few days after I came back and she helped me decorate and pick out furniture. She suggested I hire a moving service. We went shopping and had everything delivered and didn't have to lift a finger. That's what the movers were for. My house was a home in a matter of hours.

Last night we were sitting back playing *Call of Duty* and I was surprised at how good MaKenzie was at the game. She started rubbing up my leg and one thing led to another. The sex session that took place to bless my house was one for the books. I wanted her in my life forever.

MaKenzie was gorgeous, so I had to throw her in Kaymee's face by sending a picture of the two of us in her inbox. When she saw the picture she replied, "cute" like it didn't make her feel some type of way. Deep down I knew she was jealous of the woman I had on my arm.

I had just gotten out of the shower to get dressed for my date with MaKenzie. She wanted to go to the club and out to eat and I was going to show her a good time. Her job assignment was almost over, so I wanted to spend as much time with her as possible. We agreed to meet at her hotel and I was eager as hell.

Going through the clothes in my closet, I chose a pair of denim jeans, and a black button-down shirt with my black loafers. Oiling body with shea butter, I slipped on my underwear and socks before I put on my outfit for the night. The waves in my hair made a nigga seasick because they were on point.

Taking my chain from the dresser and slipping it on my neck, I grabbed my wallet and phone before making my way to the front door. Entering the code into the alarm system, I locked the door and made my way to my car. After pushing the start button, I pulled my phone out and hit MaKenzie with a text.

Me: I'm heading your way. Meet me downstairs.

As I backed out of the driveway, an eerie feeling came over me. Shaking it off, I turned the radio on and Lil Wayne let me know I had no worries. He had bars back in the day but what happened from then to now is something he would have to figure out. MaKenzie hadn't responded to my text after ten minutes. Maybe she was still getting sexy for me.

Fifteen minutes later, I pulled into the parking lot of the Hyatt and cut the engine. Entering the hotel, I went to the elevator to go up to room 1523. When the elevator doors opened, a beautiful woman was standing there waiting to get on. She smiled and stepped to the side so I could get off.

"Good evening," I said, greeting her.

"Hello, handsome. Have a nice night," she replied, stepping onto the elevator pushing the button.

Walking down the hall, I stood in front of MaKenzie's door and knocked. There was no response and I didn't hear any movement inside the room. Knocking again, I waited a few seconds before taking my phone from my hip. I tapped on her name and the phone rang but went to voicemail.

I waited a few more seconds before I went back to the elevator. As I stepped off, the eerie feeling came back, but this time it was strong. Going to the front desk, I stood waiting patiently for her to finish the call.

"May I help you, sir?" she asked, placing the receiver on the base.

"Yes, can you send someone to room 1523? I'm here to pick up a friend that's staying in that room and she's not answering the door. I want to make sure she's alright because I didn't get an answer," I explained.

"Okay, let me see," she replied, tapping on the keyboard. "The occupant of that room checked out this morning. That would explain why you aren't getting an answer. The room is vacant," the clerk explained.

I was confused because we made plans before she left last night. Wondering why she didn't reach out to me about her departure, I thanked the clerk and left the hotel. Hitting MaKenzie's line as I walked to my ride, I got the same result. No answer. There was no other way for me to get in touch with her other than her phone and that wasn't getting me anywhere.

To take my mind off the possibility of getting played, I decided to hit the club by myself. A drink sounded really nice to take my mind off the bullshit that had just occurred. I felt like I was being watched as I got in my ride and that feeling came back full force. Glancing around the parking lot as I turned the key in the ignition, nothing was out of the ordinary, but the feeling didn't go away.

The desire to go out for a drink wasn't so appealing at that point. Navigating my car toward my crib, I kept checking the rearview mirror because something wasn't right. Merging onto the highway, I noticed a dark car behind me and the palm of my hands became sweaty instantly. Hitting my turn signal to get in the middle lane, the car pulled beside me and stayed there even though traffic was light.

The windows had dark tint and I couldn't see inside the vehicle. It bothered me. I wasn't about to let the muthafucka catch me that easily. Pressing the gas, I went from fifty-five to eighty quickly, but the car was on my ass. Before I knew it, whoever was driving was beside me again. The window started lowering and I knew I was about to get shot the fuck up.

I kept looking to my right, but all I could see was the top of a baseball cap. A nigga was nervous because I didn't know who would have a problem with me in Boston. I didn't fuck with these muthafuckas like that. I was trying to stay low from the shit that went down in Atlanta. But no one knew where I was. But anything could happen in this fucked up world we lived in.

A state trooper vehicle was hiding in the cut ahead and I was going to use that to my advantage. I pulled to the side of the highway and got out, going to my front wheel. The dark car kept going on the highway and the state trooper exited his car. Pretending to examine my wheel, the trooper approached me.

"Everything okay, sir?" he asked.

"Yeah. While I was driving, it felt as if my front wheel was wobbling on this side. I pulled over to make sure it wasn't threatening to come off while I drove. Nothing seems to be wrong with it though. Maybe I need a wheel ailment. I'll take it to the shop in the morning to be certain that everything is cool," I responded, standing up.

"That would be the smart thing to do. Better safe than sorry. Have a nice night and drive safely."

"You too," I said, getting back in my car, making sure to put on my seatbelt.

I waited until the trooper was back at his car before I pulled back onto the highway. I kept my eyes open for the vehicle that taunted me, but it was nowhere in sight. Driving the speed limit with caution for ten minutes in silence, I was nervous. My exit was coming up and getting home was all I wanted to do.

Relief came over me when I got off the highway and made it to my house without incident. Hurrying to unlock the door, I rushed in and leaned my back against it, breathing hard. I turned and looked at the alarm because it didn't beep when I entered and it wasn't lit up. The same eerie feeling came over me as I reached out to turn on the light.

"Hello, Dray. Did you miss me?" MaKenzie asked, sitting in in the arm chair that she had placed in the middle of the room facing the door.

She had on a black Adidas sweat suit, black Adidas sneakers, and a black Adidas hat. MaKenzie was dressed down in all black everything. Folks didn't just dress that way to break into someone's crib. I was a target.

"How did you get in my house?"

"Never answer a question with a question, love," she said, smirking.

178

"I'm not trying to hear that shit, MaKenzie. What the fuck are you doing in my house?" I was starting to get pissed off because she was playing with my mental and I didn't have time for the games. "Don't make me repeat myself."

"And if you do, what will happen, Dray? Not nothing. Why I'm in your house isn't important," she said with her hands in the pocket of her hoodie. "Why did you lie to me about what you do for a living? I did my homework and you are not a graduate of Morehouse—"

"I didn't lie to you! What the fuck you doing checking up on me? I've been nothing but good to you," I said, pushing off the door.

"Nigga, if you ever raise your voice at me again, shit will get real funky in this bitch. I need to know who I fuck with at all times, especially when things seem too good to be true." Not knowing where she was going with her little speech, I let her get shit off her chest. "See, for a nigga that just bought a home with no job—"

"I have a muthafuckin' job! I work for Boeing!" I walked toward her with my fist clenched.

She chuckled and said, "Pipe down homie. There's no need to get upset because you were caught in a lie. Oh, you can rest your hands because my name ain't Kaymee. You won't get away with putting your hands on me."

When she mentioned Kaymee I almost shitted myself. I allowed myself to get trapped and didn't see the shit coming. Staring her in the eyes, her gazed stayed on me but I didn't waver one bit. There was nothing she could do to me because she was the size of a sixteen-year-old and I was a grown ass man. It would take   nothing for me to restrain her.

As I crept toward her slowly, she got up out of the chair pulling her tool from her pocket and held it at her side. "See, Dray. I knew exactly who you were when I saw you at the airport. Not only did you put your hand on the wrong woman, you stole from the wrong nigga back in Atlanta. Did you really think you would get away with that shit?"

"That's grown men business. It has nothing to do with you, MaKenzie. If that's really your name."

"It has everything to do with me, nigga! For the record, I'm a straight forward bitch. I don't have to lie to make my life seem greater than it actually is. My name *is* MaKenzie, but you can call me Storm," she said, smiling.

When you fuck with the Goon Squad, you fuck with me. You were part of the squad for a short period of time and didn't get to meet all the players of the game. There's female goons in that muthafucka, too.

It wasn't too hard to get close to yo' ass, so that told me that you weren't fit to be one of us to begin with. Kaymee is family and you violated in the worse way. You should've been taught not to put yo' hands on a female early in life. Don't worry, you will definitely learn your lesson tonight. Now, where's my muthafuckin' money, Dray?"

"I don't owe you shit, bitch!" I screamed.

Pew, Pew.

She let two shots off that sounded like an air gun going off. I buckled and fell to the floor as the bullets shattered my left kneecap. "Aaaaahhh, shit!" I yelled out in pain.

"Disrespect is something I don't do well with, Dray. This should be a valuable lesson to not think about pussy after you've wrong somebody. It throws you off your game, but I'm glad you enjoyed the ride I sent you on."

"I'll give you the money and the pills! Just don't shoot me again, please. Everything is in the safe in the closet. The combination is 0711. Take whatever is there and leave." She had me crying like a bitch and I couldn't do shit about it. My knee felt like wet noodles under my hand because the bone was no longer intact.

"You are a pussy," she said, laughing. "There was no way you were cut out to be a Goon. If you were robbed back in Atlanta, Kaymee would've died fucking with you because the way you are acting now, you would've thrown her to the wolves. I can't stand a weak muthafucka. I'm gonna have fun getting rid of your punk ass," she said, walking toward me. My days of running were over, Jonathan sent a bitch to catch my ass slipping and I fucked up.

Meesha

Chapter 19

Jonathan

"Katrina!" I barked as I showered to go to the airport. Kaymee told me last week that Dot's counselor wanted her to participate in a meeting with her. There was no way I was going to allow her to go alone because Dot would try to beat her down mentally like she has done many times in the past.

"Why are you screaming my name like that, Jonathan?" Katrina asked from the doorway.

"There no towels in the linen closet. Where are they?"

"They're folded in the laundry room. You promised to put them away when I left yesterday to get my hair done, babe. I'll go downstairs and get them. Hold tight, big baby."

"Hurry please. I'm ready to get out of here," I called out to her.

"Don't rush me because you're running late. It's your fault because you wanted to eat breakfast in bed before getting up."

"And I enjoyed your cookies and milk too, baby. Now go get me a towel. You wasn't talking shit while holding my head, telling me to suck harder," I threw back at her, knowing that would shut her ass up.

I waited a few moments before I turned the water off and partially dried off with the hand towel. Sliding the shower door open, my beautiful woman was standing with a bath towel opened for me to step into. That was one of the reasons I loved her as much as I did. She always catered to my needs without being asked.

"Is Kaymee awake?" I asked, drying off.

"I um, called her to make sure she was awake and she will be meeting you at the airport."

"Baby, how is she meeting me at the airport and she hasn't even been here to pack?"

"She came by last night, packed her bag and left. She was with Los. I suppose he will take her to the airport."

"She better not produce no damn babies. Knowing them, they've been fucking like rabbits because she hasn't been here much."

"Jonathan, Kaymee is concentrating on her education. A baby is the last thing on her mind," Katrina said, rolling her eyes before walking out of the bathroom.

I wasn't trying to hear all of that. Walking into the bedroom, Katrina already had my clothes laid out on the bed, so I started to get dressed. The plane was set to depart at nine and it was already six thirty. I needed to be at the airport by seven to get through security without having to rush. It was something I hated doing.

Kaymee better beat me there because if she was late, we were going to miss the plane. She was late for everything when she really didn't want to participate. Dot was something she definitely didn't want to have anything to do with. But she was the one that agreed to this meeting. I'm going for moral support for my daughter.

As I tied my shoe and stood from the bed, I glanced around for my bag. "Come on, Jonathan. I'm not trying to be in this traffic while listening to you talk about being late," Katrina said from the doorway.

"Where is my bag?" I asked, looking around the room.

"Already in the car. I took care of that for you. Your wallet, keys, and phone are on the edge of the dresser. Grab them and let's go. Don't worry about your ticket. I've already sent it to your wallet on your phone."

"Thanks for always being two steps ahead of me, baby. I don't know what I would do without you."

"If you don't bring your ass, you will find out sooner than later. I'm ready to go back to bed and you dragging your feet," she complained, going down the stairs.

I should've made her ass wait until I came back instead of giving her that tongue massage this morning. She was pissed because she couldn't curl up and go the fuck to sleep afterwards. I wish she was going to Chicago with us, but she declined the offer since we were only going to be gone until the next night. We could've come back the same night, but Kaymee wanted to stay so she could enjoy the food and her city, so she says.

Traffic was flowing with ease, so it took no time to get to the airport. I gave Katrina a kiss before grabbing my bag from the backseat. There were many people going into the airport and I wanted to beat them to the security checkpoint.

"I'll call you when we land, baby. Drive carefully," I said, exiting the car.

As I stepped on the escalator, I took out my ID and pulled my boarding pass up on my phone. The line wasn't long and I was glad about that. Moving along in the line, I searched the area the best I could to see if Kaymee was there, but I didn't see her.

"Step forward, sir," the guard said, bringing my focus back to what was happening in front of me.

Placing my phone on the scanner and giving him my ID, I was allowed to enter. I pulled my wallet and keys out of my pocket and put them in a tray. Then took off my shoes and added them with the other items before putting my bag on the belt. I watched my belongings roll through the machine while waiting to be searched. Once on the other side, I gathered my things and made my way to B24 to wait.

Usually it's not that easy to get through security and I wasn't too happy about having to sit for an hour and a half doing nothing. My stomach reminded me that I didn't eat anything other than Katrina's kitty and I was hungry. So I went to the McDonald's and ordered two breakfast sandwiches, a hash brown, and orange juice. Not my ideal breakfast, but it was going to do for now.

While eating, my phone rang and it was the realtor who was helping me look for a spot for Monty's soul food joint. I wanted to see him succeed in life because he was working hard to finish school as well as providing for his family. Not to mention the things he had to do while Poetry recovered from her surgery and having the baby.

"What up, Sandy? Tell me something good."

"Good morning. You sound wide awake," Sandy said, laughing. "I found a beautiful spot in downtown Atlanta. It's on the corner of Marietta and Fairlie Street. I think it would be the best place for this restaurant. I will send pictures of the inside so you can visualize things from your perspective."

"Okay, that sounds good. Thank you, Sandy. I'll hit you up when I get to my destination and I'm able to look the photos over. Then I will arrange for us to meet up and we will go from there," I said, taking a bite of my sandwich.

"You're welcome. Talk to you soon."

I hung up from the realtor and dialed Monty's phone but hung up quickly. I forgot what time it was and he needed to sleep. If he wasn't out hustling, he was taking care of baby Aria while Poetry slept. He was almost finished with school and by the look of things, he and Kaymee would be graduating at the same time.

Finishing my quick breakfast that I wouldn't eat ever again, I tossed my bag on my shoulder and walked toward the gate. People were scattered about and I wanted to sit far away from them as possible. There was a row of seats vacated by the window, so I headed for them. Looking for an outlet to charge my phone, I put my earbuds in my ear and let Nipsey Hussle entertain me until they started boarding the plane.

I closed my eyes for a few and my phone vibrated in my hand. Glancing at the screen, it was Kaymee calling, "You better be in this airport," I said when I answered.

"I am. I'm looking for you at the gate."

Standing from my seat, I saw her standing in front of the counter that I was standing behind. "I'm behind the counter. Walk straight back." When I saw her coming my way, I ended the call and the music started playing again. Removing the earbud, I glared at her as she sashayed toward me in a pink jogging suit.

"Hey, daddy," she sang as she sat beside me. "How you doing?"

"Don't hey daddy me. I hope you are using protection when you're out all night with Los."

"Where that come from? Don't do that, daddy. I will not discuss what I do when I'm not under your roof. Los and I are trying to take things slow. It's not about sex at all. How do you think Dot is going to act when she sees you?" she asked, changing the subject.

"I don't know and don't care. I'm going for you, not her. We will touch on that subject again so don't think you got away with it. Another thing, I think we should go get your pizza and popcorn when we land because I need to get back to Katrina tonight."

"You said we could stay until tomorrow night! How are you gonna change up on me?" she said, pouting.

"Kaymee, you're too old to be acting like a spoiled brat. It's not like you have anyone in Chicago to visit. I really don't want to be in the city too long. Them niggas crazy as fuck now and I'm thinking about safety."

"We will be downtown. There's nothing happening on the Magnificent Mile, daddy."

"I'll see once we get there, but I'm not making any promises."

"We are now boarding for the A group for flight 3687 at gate B24," the intercom system announced for our flight. Both me and Kaymee stood and made our way to the line with phones in hand.

Being the first on the plane was a priority for me because I wanted to be seated and comfortable. As we walked through the tunnel, it was hot as hell and the pink folks were moving too slow for me. When we finally got on the plane, I went straight for the middle and threw my bag into the overhead department, waiting patiently for Kaymee to get down the aisle. I took her bag and threw it next to mine, but she sat by the window in the seats across from me and started texting on her phone.

"You not gon' sit with your old man?" I asked, sitting in the window seat.

"No, because both of us can't sit by the window. You can still see me from here," she said without looking up from her phone.

I left her alone and got comfortable in my seat until it was time for takeoff. The two hour flight went by quickly because I was asleep the entire time we were in the air. Kaymee shook me awake and I glanced out the window. We was in the Windy City. Stepping out of the airport, I led Kaymee to the truck I rented and helped her inside. I glanced at my watch and it was eleven thirty. We had to be at the center at four.

"This drive is about three hours away, so sit back and get comfortable. I'm well rested from my nap on the plane," I said to Kaymee as I pulled into traffic.

Getting out of the airport was a task, but when you're from Chicago, you know how to get out of any situation. Bypassing all the traffic, I took the street until I could hop on the expressway. From there, it was smooth sailing. The car was quiet for the first thirty minutes or so, with the exception of the sound of the wind blowing as I sped on the interstate.

"Daddy, can I ask you a question?" Kaymee asked, breaking the silence.

"You can talk to me about anything, baby girl. What's on your mind?"

She paused for a few minutes and fiddled with her phone. "Why didn't Dot love me?" she asked, turning to me.

"Kaymee, that's something you will have to ask her during this meeting. Speak your mind and try to get as many answers to the questions you have as possible. Don't be afraid because she can't hurt you anymore."

"The way she treated me all those years were the reason I took what Dray did to me as normal. I knew it was wrong, but at the same time, I thought that's what love really was. She fucked me up, daddy. Now here I have Los trying to do everything right and I've built this wall to stop him from getting to my heart.

Yes, he has issues with his ex, but he keeps it away from me at all costs. I've heard and seen him confront this woman and tell her it's over. Los has changed his number and eliminated all contact with her to prove he wanted to be with me. But I'm afraid to give in and be exclusive with him and I don't know what to do."

Hearing the hurt in my daughter's voice tugged at my heart. I didn't know she was mentally affected by the things that had happened to her to the extent that it stifled her. At that point, I knew Kaymee was an emotional wreck.

"I want you to know that you are not wrong for determining who is worthy enough to be in your life. If you feel that Los is capable of loving you the way you want to be loved, give him the opportunity to show you. Don't cheat him by judging him from your past experiences. You are young, Kaymee and there are going to be many more obstacles you'll have to overcome in life.

As far as Dray, he was a fuck nigga that didn't know what he had in a woman like you. He played off the things you told him about your past and used it to his advantage. A person like that is one that manipulates the mind of someone that's looking for love anyway they could get it. That someone was you, baby. If you would have told me about the things he had done early on, I would've told you to leave him alone. Then I would've killed him."

"That's the reason I didn't tell you or Monty about what he was doing to me. I didn't want either one of you to end up in jail for something I put up with. You served years in the prison system and I need you, of all people, in my life. Dray did what I allowed him to do and he ran with it. My heart is cold and it will take so much more than material things and sweet talking to melt the ice that surrounds my soul.

Maybe when this meeting is over, I will be able to give Los an honest chance to build with me. I want more than a boyfriend, daddy. I'm looking for my forever. I'm excelling in school and looking forward to starting my career. A man is a bonus in my life, it's not something that I need."

Hearing my baby speak like a mature woman made me proud. It was something she learned on her own through her heartaches and pain and it showed me she was ready to conquer anything that crossed her path. Kaymee just needed me there in case she wavered and I would have her back.

***

We pulled up to the facility at three forty-five because there was construction on the interstate that slowed us down. Turning off the car, I stepped out and stretched until my back popped. I leaned back inside and grabbed the water bottle from the cupholder and downed it. Kaymee got out on the passenger side, closing the door. She had a look of worry on her face, showing me she was nervous.

"You got this, baby girl. There's no need to worry," I said, walking up to her with my arms opened. She walked into the hug I offered and took a deep breath.

The door to the facility opened and a young black woman stepped outside and started down the stairs. "Hello, you must be Kaymee," she said, holding her hand out. "I'm Yvette."

"Yes, I'm Kaymee and this is my dad, Jonathan."

"Nice to meet you, Yvette," I said, shaking her hand.

"I wanted to come out and escort you guys inside personally. Dot hasn't been in the best of moods this week, so I hope everything changes when she sees the two of you," Yvette said with a broad smile on her face.

"Dot didn't want me to show up to this meeting. I don't think her mood will change because I'm in the building," I explained to her.

"This session is a start for her to move in a different direction than she has been going. It will work as long as we are able to get to the core of her problems. Are you willing to do what it takes to get your mother on the right path?"

"Yvette, I wouldn't have traveled damn near seven hundred miles if I didn't want to help. When it's all said and done, she's still my mother and I only get one in life. But I promise you this, if it doesn't work after I've given it my all, I'm done."

"I would never contact you again after this if things don't work out. The only way you will hear from me is if there's an emergency because you are the person on her paperwork. Other than that, you have my word. Let's go inside and get this session going," Yvette said, leading us into the building.

Serenity House looked like a luxury apartment building. It was clean and smelled good. As we traveled through the halls, I noticed there were many doors along the way, so they were heavily staffed. Passing the elevators, I wondered what the upstairs looked like. Hopefully, it was just as nice as the areas I've seen.

Yvette led us to a small conference like room that had arm chairs arranged in a circle. There was a table in the center that had bottles of water on it and a pitcher of ice and plastic disposable cups. Inspirational quotes were scattered along the walls in colorful frames, and pictures of poets, actors, actresses, and other famous people with positive quotes underneath. The atmosphere screamed comfort and I was sure things would go smoothly.

"I'll return in a few minutes. Grab some water and a snack from the table by the wall and we can begin shortly. I'm going upstairs to get Dot since she hasn't come down on her own," Yvette said as she headed for the door.

The table she mentioned was filled with chips, cookies, cheese, crackers, peanuts, and granola bars. I wasn't hungry, but it was good to know that I would have something to snack on while we drove back to the city. Kaymee was pacing back and forth, making my nerves twitch a little bit.

"Come have a sit, Kaaymee. Everything will be alright," I said to her.

Instead of sitting, she went to the window and stared outside. Kaymee stood there without speaking for about ten minutes. The door finally opened and in walked Yvette with Dot in tow.

"What the fuck are you doing here?" Dot lashed out the minute she saw me. "I was told only my bitch of a daughter was coming, not you!"

"Have a seat, Dot," Yvette spoke calmly.

"I'll sit down when this nigga tell me why he's here!" she screamed.

"I'm here for my daughter and to see what I can do to help you, Dot," I replied to her rant.

"Help me? After nineteen years, you all of a sudden want to help me now! I needed you the day I told you I was pregnant and you turned your back on me!"

"Yes, I want to help you. I've questioned myself since that day. I agreed to attend this meeting to talk things out. Dot, I want to see you do better with your life. It's time to let bygones be bygones."

"Stop for a minute, you guys. I believe this subject is where everything started and needs to be addressed, but I want you all to talk like the adults you are. Having an all-out screaming match is not going to solve the problem that's lingering in this room right now," Yvette stated, looking around the room. "Kaymee, come have a seat. You too, Dot."

Dot moved slowly toward the circle of chairs while staring daggers in Kaymee's face. She had so much hatred for our daughter in her body, she couldn't mask it if she wanted to. I've never seen a mother look at their child like Dot was doing at that moment. Yvette had to noticed it too because she scribbled something on her notepad.

Once everyone was seated, Yvette looked at me and cleared her throat. "Jonathan, explain why you left Dot when she disclosed to you that she was pregnant."

"Shit, we weren't in any position to take care of a kid. I voiced this to Dot at the time and suggested an abortion. She insisted on keeping the baby and threatened to tell my mother that she was pregnant. I beat Dot to the punch and told her myself. My mother cursed me out and called me stupid, then put me on the next plane to live with my grandparents.

I didn't want to leave, but I had no choice in the matter. I was at the hospital when Kaymee was born, but Dot refused to let me see her after she was discharged. I took care of my daughter, but the problem was the fact that I didn't want to be with her mother," I explained.

"We were a package deal! If you were going to be in my daughter's life, you were going to be in mine. Not one or the other, nigga!" Dot cut in.

"Wait a minute, Dot. I will give you a chance to speak," Yvette said, trying to defuse the outburst before it got out of hand. "Continue, Jonathan."

192

"When I went see Kaymee at her grandmother's house, Dot was never there. Miss Mae always allowed me to spend time with my daughter. The last time I saw Kaymee was when she was four years old. I caught a federal charge and served twelve years in the penitentiary.

I kept in contact with Miss Mae and provided for my daughter from behind bars. I never stopped taking care of my responsibility. When I got out of prison, I searched for Kaymee high and low with no luck. Dot knew how to contact me when I was locked up, but never reached out to tell me her mother had died. Instead, she took the money I sent and went on with her life."

"That money was owed to me, not my mother!" Dot shouted defensively.

"Correction, it was for Kaymee. To my understanding, she didn't get a dime of it either," I said, keeping my cool.

"She had a roof over her head, food in her stomach, and clothes on her back. I did what needed to be done for her."

"You provided all of that, but you were never home with me. I cooked my own meals and your friends bought my clothes until I was old enough to work and buy them myself. Not to mention, I had to pay rent in order to stay in your house. The money you were getting from my daddy, I knew nothing about until after I turned eighteen," Kaymee said, addressing her mother.

"All of that is in the past. I need to know why you punished me for the things you and Jonathan went through? The way I was treated, I didn't deserve any of that," she continued. "Why didn't you love me?" she said with tears in her eyes.

Dot sat back in the chair she was sitting in without uttering a vowel. It seemed as if she was going to ignore Kaymee's question altogether as she held her head down. Her eyes met Kaymee's and they were cold as ice. There were no signs of empathy for how her daughter felt. When she finally spoke, her voice was full of venom and every word was poisonous.

"You reminded me every day of the man that broke my heart. I didn't want nothing to do with you. That was the reason you were with your grandma so much. I couldn't stand to look at you and if I would've kept you with me, you wouldn't be sitting here today.

My life was destroyed when I pushed you out. I didn't have a job and my mama forced me to move on my own because of you! I lost the man that I loved, because of you! Dropping out of school, because of you! There was nothing I could do because of you, bitch!" Dot screamed, jumping to her feet.

"Dot—" I said her name, but Kaymee stopped me from talking.

"No, daddy. Let her say what she wants to say. She needs to get all of this anger out today," Kaymee said with her hand up.

"I could've been more than a baby's mama, but I was stuck taking care of a baby alone. While the man you idolize ran the streets without having to wake up one night to change a pamper or feed yo' ass. His life didn't stop until the pigs caught up with his ass and locked him in a cage! Before then, he was out enjoying life without worrying about anything." Dot went on.

"That's not true. I tried to be there for my daughter, but you wouldn't let me!" I replied.

"You were trying to be there for her, but what about me? You said you loved me, Jonathan! But that lil' bitch didn't make you want to stay! We made plans and all of that went out the window when I told you I was pregnant."

"We weren't ready, Dot! What part of that don't you understand? I gave you an option and you didn't take it, but I tried to help you with Kaymee. You were the one that prevented that from happening."

"I had to get ready with or without you, Jonathan. Now look at my life! I don't have one! My apartment, gone. Money, gone. My mama, gone. I don't talk to my brothers and sisters because after my mama died, I said fuck them. They didn't care enough about that girl to take her from me!" she cried.

"Take me for what? So you could party the way you did anyway? It wasn't their responsibility. I belonged to ya'll! You have so many excuses as to why you couldn't love me and I'm tired of hearing them. Your life is the way it is because of you!

194

Life don't happen to you. You happen to life. In order for you to get help, you have to want to help yourself! Stop making excuses for the things you have done. It's time for you to take responsibility for your actions.

I'm your child and I'm sitting here talking to you the way you should've done with me growing up. Instead of beating me down mentally, you should've been building me up. You tried to set me up to fail in this thing called life, but I beat the odds. The funny thing about it though, you're still trying to defeat me and all I want to do is help you.

Dot, you haven't called me by my name once since I've been in this room. It has been 'bitch', 'lil' bitch', 'that girl'. My name is Kaymee, dammit! Your daughter. The person that has stayed up many nights wondering why her own mother didn't love her. I asked you why didn't you love me and your response had everything to do with Jonathan and little to do with me.

I've never done you wrong. I've done so much that you should be proud of. Instead, you found ways to make me feel like I was worthless. It's a good thing I didn't let the negativity stop me from striving. Everything I've endured, I did on my own.

I don't think this session is going to help you, Dot. You are not ready for change because you don't see any wrongdoing on your part. You have blamed everyone but yourself. I wish you the best in life and I want you to know that I love and forgive you for everything you put me through."

Kaymee stood from her seat and walked out of the room. Yvette sat with a look of sadness on her face while Dot didn't have any expression at all. I stood and stared at Dot, hoping she would look at me, but she didn't.

"I'm sorry for all the hurt I put on your heart, Dot. You don't ever have to like me, but you should make things right with Kaymee. She needs her mother in her life. It's never too late to mend a broken heart," I said, tapping her on the shoulder. "Thank you for the invite, Yvette. Enjoy the rest of your evening," I said, leaving to catch up with Kaymee.

Meesha

Chapter 20

Dot

I was glad when that bitch and her daddy left. Both of them made me feel like a weak bitch in that room and I didn't like it. Yvette kept staring at me, so I got up to leave the room.

"Dot, sit down for a second," she said before I could get to the door.

"I don't want to talk anymore, Yvette. Let me process everything and I promise I'll talk to you. Right now, I just want to take a nap."

"Tomorrow I want you in my office at ten o'clock sharp. We will figure out a way for you to build a relationship with your daughter. Jonathan is right, your anger shouldn't be towards her. Deep down, you know that, too," Yvette said.

Leaving the room without responding to her, I walked down the hall to the living lounge. There was no one sitting in that area and I was glad about that. George, the security guard, strolled along a few minutes after I sat down. Since I'd been living in the facility, I had gain weight back in the right places.

"Hey, sweetness. How you doing today?" George asked, licking his lips.

"I'm fine. Meet me in the spot at ten pm. I need a favor," I said lowly.

"I'll be there if you giving me some of that tight pussy. You can have whatever you like," he said, walking away.

George and I had been fucking for a couple weeks and he fell for my trap. He had a big pipe and knew how to use it, but I had other things in mind other than getting a wet ass. I was about to put my plan in motion because I couldn't stay locked away another night. Ten minutes later, I was resting in my bed fast asleep.

When I woke up, it was eight-thirty and I was anxious to carry out my plan. I jumped in the shower, shaved my kitty, and washed thoroughly. George was getting the royal treatment because I wanted something from him. I've always used what I got to get what I want and it won't stop now.

I threw on a pair of lounge pants and a t-shirt with my Nikes the facility provided and left out of the room without my keys. The elevators were shut down after eight unless you are part of the staff with a key. So, I had to take the stairs to the basement.

George was standing by the door looking at his watch when I came out the stairwell. He opened the door and we walked out to the parking lot to his truck and got in the back. George laid the seats back and I immediately took my pants off. I laid back and allowed him to roam his hands over my body. Salivating at the mouth, he went directly for my kitty and I didn't stop him.

"Put that dick down my throat," I moaned as he wrapped his tongue around my clit.

He didn't think twice as he unbuckled his pants, turning so his head was between my legs and his dick was in my face. Guiding his long pole into my mouth, I sucked like my life depended on it. Saliva was running out the corners of my mouth because I wanted it to be sloppy.

"Damn, girl. Suck that shit!" he groaned, while pumping his rod deeper. My gag reflex was still on point and I knew his toes were curling in his work shoes.

I felt him palm my ass and lift it up to his mouth and his spit was running down my crack. He simultaneously went from my clit to my asshole like he was eating his last supper and I was enjoying every minute of it. Dipping his thumb into my ass, I yelped out loud and started grinding hard into his face. My chin was to my chest because he had damn near folded me into a ball. Sucking his dick wasn't an option the way my body was positioned.

"I'm cummin'!" I yelled out before I squirted down his throat. He lapped it up quicker than I could let it out.

"Shit, ma! That pussy was ready!" he said excitedly, getting on his knees. He reached into the armrest and pulled out a gold wrapper, tearing it open with his teeth. I turned my body around so he could have access to my kitty and started rubbing my fingers back and forth over my slit. "I'm about to fuck you good. I've been waiting on this pussy."

Lifting my legs over my head, he planted his pole at my opening and got lost in my wetness. The only sound that was heard was our skin slapping together. I felt his girth all in my guts and I couldn't hold back the moan that was caught in my throat.

"Mmmmm, yeah hit that shit, baby," I moaned, reaching between his legs.

"Oh shit, Dot! I'm about to explode!" he growled as his strokes got quicker. I wasn't mad because I was with him this time around. My stomach tightened and I took a deep breath, letting all my juices coat his pole.

"Aaaaaah, yeah!" I screamed as I slipped from the leather seat because it was drenched.

"Oooooooweeee! That shit is the bomb! I'm glad you chose me to give this pussy to," George said, getting his last strokes in. He rolled off me and leaned on the door panel as he took out his cigarettes. I didn't smoke, but I needed something.

Since the meeting earlier, the taste of crack was on my tongue and I needed it. George was enjoying his cigarette with his eyes closed as I noticed his key fob on the floor. Picking it up, I put it in my bra for safekeeping.

"Come on so you don't' get in trouble. I want to meet up again tomorrow because I need some more of that. Oh, what did you need from me? You know I got you," he said, fixing his clothes the best he could.

"I wanted to know if I could get a hundred dollars from you. My daughter didn't send me any money this week and I need it to hold me over. I'll repay you as soon as she sends me the money."

"I got you and don't worry about giving it back. That pussy is payment enough and you deserve all that I'm about to give you," he said, going into his wallet, pulling out three hundred dollars.

Acting shocked, I shook my head and tried to give two of the bills back. "This is too much, George. I don't need all this money."

"Take it, baby. Save it for a rainy day. There's more where that came from if you keep preforming like you just did. It's time to go back inside," he said, getting out the car and making sure the coast was clear before he helped me out.

Walking in front of me, George headed back to the building. I picked up a brick and hit him in the back of his head with it. I took his wallet out of his back pocket and took all the bills out, putting them in my pocket. Removing the key fob from my bra, I jumped in his truck and took off for the highway.

It was damn near one in the morning when I reached the city and I was happy as hell to be back on my own turf. I rode to the westside in search of crack. Them southside niggas wasn't about to get me again. There were a couple lil' niggas sitting on a porch and I saw one of them jog down the steps to serve a fiend. "Bingo," I said out loud as I parked and got out.

"What's up, cutie?" one of the guys asked lustfully.

"Let me get ten dimes," I said.

He didn't ask another question. He went in his stash and got what I wanted. Handing him the bill, I went back to the truck and pulled off. Going to an all-night diner, I acted like I was going to order and snatched a spoon from the counter and left. George had a lighter in his car and an opened bottle of water, so I was straight. The only thing I needed was a pipe.

I drove a few minutes and saw an old car that still had a steel antennae parked in a driveway. I got out the car and ripped the antennae off fast, then hopped back in the truck and pulled off. My last stop was to Walgreens to get some brillo. Even though I had money, I wasn't about to pay for that shit. I was in and out with what I needed in a matter of seconds.

As I was driving to the expressway, a police car was driving behind me with the lights on. I was scared shitless, so I pulled to the right and waited. Lucky for me, they were on a call somewhere else and I was free to go. I drove halfway to my destination and got out the truck with my items, leaving that bitch sitting there as I walked the rest of the way.

Entering a well-known crack house to druggies, I saw so many dope fiends inside nodding and high as hell. I was trying to be the same way. I found a vacant room and closed the door. I prepared my first hit and it was gone within minutes. I couldn't feel my face, but it didn't stop me from smoking.

I was dreaming about this high and I was getting it. The things Kaymee said to me kept running through my head and the heartache of Jonathan leaving me returned. My mama appeared in front of me when I looked up. Her mouth was moving, but I couldn't hear the words she spoke.

After taking a toke of the fresh rock I had placed into the pipe, my hand dropped to my side and the pipe fell out of it. My body started convulsing and my eyes rolled to the back of my head. Once again, I was overdosing but this time, it felt different. My soul was leaving my body as my eyes rolled to the back of my head. My heartbeat was rapid, but it started slowing down with every breath I tried to take. My last thought was "I love you, Kaymee." Then my light went out.

Meesha

Chapter 21

Kaymee

After the meeting with Dot, I didn't want to be in Chicago anymore. Daddy took me to get pizza and popcorn and he headed back to the airport. He never changed the flight, so we would be back in Atlanta at ten thirty. He kept asking me how I was feeling, but my response didn't change. Dot was never going to love me and I was ready to deal with it.

I slept the entire flight back and couldn't wait to get to Atlanta. Exiting the airport, I was expecting to see Katrina, but Los was there to pick us up. My daddy must've called him so he could get the real truth out of me. I wasn't in the mood to talk about what happened. I explained that to him several times.

"Hey, beautiful," Los said, gathering me in his arms as he planted a kiss on my temple. "You look tired."

"I am," I responded, getting in the backseat.

Listening to my music, I dosed off. A vision of Dot walking with a stream of light surrounding her appeared out of nowhere. The words "I love you Kaymee" filled my earbuds and I jolted in my seat. A feeling came over me that I couldn't explain and it scared me. The image appeared as if my mother was a spirit, but that was impossible because I had just left her at the center and she was fine.

I didn't say anything the rest of the ride and I didn't close my eyes again either. When Los pulled up to my dad's house, I got out and walked to the driver's side of the car. "Wait for me. I'll be right back," I said, rushing to the house.

Unlocking the door, I rushed upstairs, stopping in the doorway of my room. I looked down at the bag on my shoulder and laughed. There was no need for me to come inside when I still had an overnight bag packed from the trip. I walked down the stairs slowly and my dad was coming through the door.

"Are you going back out?" he asked.

"Yeah, I want to spend time with Carlos. I wanna give him a chance like you suggested. Getting everything off my chest to Dot, lifted a lot of weight off my shoulders. Life is too short to be bitter and I'm going to live my life to the fullest. I'll see you later, old man. I love you," I said, kissing his cheek.

"I love you too, baby girl. I'll always be here for you."

"I know you will, daddy," I said, leaving out the house.

Los was standing outside of his car waiting for me with the passenger door opened. I got inside and he shut the door before going to the other side to get in. He held my hand the entire ride to his house and I knew he felt me shaking. We entered his home and I went straight to his room and prepared for a shower.

I walked into his bathroom and Dot's voice kept echoing in my head. Stepping in the shower, I washed my body, then I let the water fall onto my back. Tears rolled down my cheeks because I wanted to hear my mother say the words I heard repeatedly in my head. The water was cold because I didn't realize how long I had been in the shower.

Turning the water off, I got out and dried my body. Not bothering to oil my skin, I pulled my nightshirt over my head and entered Los' bedroom. He was sitting up in his bed with his back against the headboard. I climbed in and laid my head on his chest.

"Talk to me, Kaymee," he said twirling one of my locs between his fingers.

"The meeting was a waste of time. My mother will never change. Her main concern was Jonathan and how he ruined her life and left her heartbroken. She went through a list reasons she didn't do anything because of me. I was at fault for the both of them bringing me into this fucked up world."

Thinking about what transpired with Dot at the center hurt me so bad that I started crying uncontrollably. Los held me close to his chest and let me cry it out. Dot's voice was echoing in my head repeating, "I love you, Kaymee." I covered my ears, trying to block out the words, but they only got louder.

"Kaymee, what is it?" Los asked. "There's something you're not telling me. I understand you want closure, but that's not what you're crying about. This is another type of cry that's hurting you deeply. Tell me what's wrong, baby," Los said, lifting my chin. I fought to catch my breath and my chest was burning. Struggling to speak, the words came out gibberish.

"Come on, ma. I can't understand what you're saying. Take your time and breathe so we can get through this together. You are not going to deal with this alone. I'm here for you as long as you need me to be," he said, rubbing my back.

Los got out of bed and left the room. He returned with a bottled water, twisting the top to open it. Putting it to my lips, I took two quick sips and pushed it away. My breathing was labored, but the tears continued to stain my cheeks.

"Are you okay?" he asked.

I shook my head no, wiping my nose on my nightshirt. "While you were driving from the airport, I dosed off. I saw my mother walking toward me with a ray of light surrounding her, Los. I've seen that before when my grandma died. I was six and still remember that day. She can't be dead because I just left her," I cried.

"You are probably putting too much into what that meant, Kaymee. Don't think the worse without knowing facts, baby. Call the center tomorrow and check on your mom. I'm quite sure she's resting, thinking about what happened today. When you talk to her, squash all the other shit and bond with your mother. Life is too short to hold grudges."

"I know! That's what I'm afraid of. Los, my mother has never called me by my name! In that dream, she said my name and told me she loved me. Dot has never uttered those words to me! Something's wrong!" I cried.

Rising from the bed, I went to the dresser and grabbed my phone. I pushed on my daddy's contact and listened to the phone ring while biting my nails, waiting for him to answer. Dot's voice continued to flow through my mind, making my anxiety rise.

"Baby girl, what's going on?" he asked when he picked up.

"Daddy, I think something is wrong with Dot," I said, crying.

"Hold on, what do you mean?"

"I dosed off in the car when we were coming from the airport and she came in my dream. She appeared angelic-like and she told me she loved me. Dot has never said that to me."

"Kaymee, you are thinking too much into this. I'm sure she's fine. You are in your feelings about what happened earlier and that's okay. Things will get better between the two of you. It will take time. Get some sleep and stop all that crying."

"Can you call the center and check on her? I don't want to hear what they will say if she's not alright," I asked hysterically.

"Send me the number and I'll call so you can get some sleep. They take her personal phone at night, right?"

"I think so, but I'm not sure. The number should be in your text messages. Call me back and let me know what they say. Even though the meeting didn't go the way I hoped, I still don't want anything to happen to her," I wailed.

"I'm on it now, Kaymee. We may have to wait until morning because it's late. But I'm gon' try tonight just for you. Sit tight," he said, hanging up.

I paced back and forth across the floor. Los followed me with his eyes before he decided to get up. He wrapped his arms around my waist and pulled me into him. I automatically started rocking side to side.

"Stop crying, ma. Everything is cool. Lay down, ease your mind, and tell me about you and your mom's relationship."

"There wasn't a relationship!" I sobbed as he led me to the bed. Los lifted me in his arms and crawled onto the bed, never letting me go. "She hated me and wished for my downfall in everything I worked hard to achieve.

She got mad whenever I excelled in something and it was often because I conquered them all. I don't want to talk about the bad things she did to me. I want her to be okay so we can make happy memories together," I cried.

I tried my best to stop crying because my head was pounding. Los' arms around me gave me a bit of comfort and I snuggled my head under his chin. My eyes fluttered shut as my phone rang. I raised my phone to my ear after swiping the bar to answer the call. It was Jonathan.

"What did they say?" I said into the phone.

"I didn't get an answer, baby girl. It's too late and I believe the phones are shut off at a certain time during the night. I'll try again in the morning. Yvette should be there by that time. I will check on Dot and soon as I find out anything, I'll call you. Go to sleep, Kaymee. Your mother is good. There's not much she can get into at that facility," he said calmly.

"Thank you for trying, daddy. I love you."

"I love you too. Stop worrying yourself over nothing, okay?"

"Okay. I'm about to take something for this headache so I can try to sleep."

"Yeah, do that and I'll talk with you soon."

Putting my phone on the nightstand, Los leaned over and opened the drawer on his side of the bed. "Here, take these. It's Tylenol," he said, handing me the pills with a bottled water.

I downed the medicine and laid back on the pillow, turning on my side. Los got out of bed and turned off the light before curling behind me. He held me close as I drifted off to sleep.

***

I was sleeping soundly when I felt Los rise up from the bed. I couldn't open my eyes, but I heard him leave the room and closed the door behind him. I snuggled back under the covers without opening my eyes.

"Kaymee, get up," Los said, coming back into the room.

"What's the matter?" I asked sleepily.

"We have to go over to Jonathan's house. Get up and get dressed," he said, pulling on a pair of joggers and a shirt.

Los was dressing very fast and nervousness kicked in. I sat up and rubbed my eyes to get them focused. "What's going on, Los?"

"Jonathan wants me to bring you to him. That's all he said when he called."

I snatched my phone off the nightstand, checking my call log. There weren't any missed calls from my daddy, so I was confused. Glancing at Los, I watched him lace his sneakers in a hurry.

"Why would he call you and not me?" I asked.

"Come on, Kaymee! He will talk to you when we get to the house. I don't know why he called me."

There was something Los wasn't saying, but I got out of bed and grabbed a pair of jeans and a shirt out of my overnight bag. Slipping on my shoes, I took my toothbrush into the bathroom to brush my teeth and wash my face. When I entered the bedroom, Los went in the bathroom to take care of his hygiene.

"Okay, let's go," he said, rushing out the room.

I picked up my phone and grabbed my purse, following behind him. I called my dad's number as I descended the stairs. He didn't answer and I was concerned, so I called Katrina's phone. She answered and I was relieved.

"Hey, ma. Where's my daddy? I called his phone but he didn't answer."

"He's in the yard and his phone is upstairs. Are you on your way over?" she asked.

There was something different about her voice, but I couldn't put my finger on it. "Yeah, we're leaving Los' house now. What does my dad want to talk to me about?"

"I'll let him discuss that with you. See you in a minute and tell Los to drive carefully."

"Okay, see you shortly," I said, walking out the front door.

I stood by the passenger's door and waited for Los to lock up the house. He looked good even though his beard was scruffy and his clothes were wrinkled. Running his tongue over his lips got me every time he did it. But the worried look on his place prevented me from lusting.

"What's the matter, Los? Just tell me," I said as he opened the door for me.

"I really don't know anything, Kaymee. I told you, Jonathan didn't go into detail," he said, closing the door and rushing to the other side of the car.

Los drove over the speed limit and he was weaving through traffic like there was an emergency. He spotted a police cruiser ahead and slowed down. We pulled into Jonathan's driveway fifteen minutes later and I hopped out. Using my key to gain entry, I called out to my dad.

"Daddy, where are you?" I yelled. Going to the back door, I opened it and there sat my daddy with a blunt in his hand. It was barely eleven o'clock in the morning and he was smoking with a glass of cognac on the table. "What's going on?" I said, walking up to him as he stared at me.

"Sit down, baby girl," he said solemnly as he lifted the glass to his lips. "I called the center this morning and Yvette said your mother left last night. She hit a guard with a brick when she convinced him to let her smoke a cigarette after hours. She stole his money and truck," he said, pausing.

Yvette received a call and before she could call you with the information she received, I called her first. Kaymee, what I'm about to say is hard for me, so I know it's gonna be even harder for you," he said, hitting the blunt. "Dot's body—"

"Nooooooo, don't say it! I told you something was wrong last night!" I screamed with tears falling from my eyes. Los hugged me from behind and I melted in his arms.

"Her body was found in an alley behind a garbage can. She died of a drug overdose. I'm sorry, baby," he said, standing to his feet.

"Daddy! I wanted her to love me! She can't be gone. We have to make it right!" I cried, hugging him around his waist. "She was gonna get herself together. I know she was. She just needed time!"

My heart shattered in a million pieces when I heard the words my daddy said to me. Dot treated me badly growing up, but it didn't take away from the fact that she was still my mother. I forgave her for everything she had ever said and done to me. At that moment, I wish I hadn't done so and maybe, just maybe she would still be alive.

***

I don't know how I got through the week because everything was foggy. We traveled back to Chicago and laid Dot to rest very nicely. None of her siblings showed up even though Jonathan tracked them down explaining everything. Her sister said she didn't care because Dot didn't show up to pay her last respects to my grandmother when she passed.

Burying my mother was a hard task for me. She looked at peace lying in the light pink casket that I chose for her. With everything Dot had put me through, my heart was still heavy. It made me smile knowing she used the last moments of her life to tell me she loved me.

I've been shown many things throughout life by many. The one thing I've learned that stood out more than others was Love Shouldn't Hurt, but it does.

Epilogue

1 year later
Kaymee

The past two years were full of good and bad. Life for me was finally stress-free and I was living happily. My dad and I developed a fantastic relationship and I loved him so much. He was the only parent I had left and I cherished every second that we had together.

Stepping off the plane as we returned from Barbados, Jonathan had planned the trip as a graduation gift and invited everyone to join us. Our extended family was everything to me and I enjoyed myself.

I was the first off and I stood back waiting patiently for the rest of the crew. Poetry and Monty exited first with baby Aria in his arms. They looked so happy that one would never know all the turmoil they endured to get where they were. My best friend had a glow to her that the sun kissed off of. It was due to the baby bump she possessed. Yes, her and my brother was expecting baby number two.

The memories that Poetry had of fighting for her life after giving birth to Aria, made her want to push forward in life without regrets. She had a home that she loved and a husband that worshipped the ground she walked on. Monty didn't let her give up on her dreams of becoming a nurse. Once she was able, Poetry went back to school and is expected to walk across the stage next year.

Monty got out of the game and fulfilled his dream of becoming an entrepreneur. Aria's Soul Food is one of the best soul food restaurants in Atlanta and Monty is hands on with his business. He is making his money the legit way, no longer dealing with the streets.

Jonathan and Katrina were next to get off the plane. They were married a couple months after Dot died and Katrina was officially ma to me. I wouldn't have picked anyone other than her to be my father's happily ever after. Their ceremony was elegant, beautiful, and royal worthy. So much love was put into the wedding and I was glad to be a part of it.

They went to the Dominican Republic for their honeymoon and now after almost twenty years, I'm going to be a big sister! Both of them have lost their minds waiting so long to produce a child, but I'm excited. The Goon Squad and their families made their way off the plane and it brought a smile to my face. My extended family always came through when it came to me.

I was waiting for one particular person to make his exit and when he did, my honey pot started tingling. Los looked good with his white khaki shorts, white wife beater, and white sneakers on his feet. The shades he wore over his eyes made him look like a GQ model. Our relationship had blossomed into something special once he gained my trust. I had to stop comparing apples to oranges in order to see the prize before me.

Los didn't try to buy my love. He earned every bit of it. There never was a time he didn't profess his love for me as well as show me every day. If I wasn't in his presence, I got a call or text that was filled with compliments and how much he missed me. He even finished the painting of me that he started. It came out great and can't wait for him to paint more.

Nikki hadn't bothered us anymore. She finally found her someone that was fucking her over like she did my boo. That bitch named Karma didn't play with these hoes out in these streets.

Dray hasn't been heard from since MaKenzie wined and dined him in Boston. No one is talking about the events that had taken place, but hopefully, she does a tell all about that shit. As long as he leaves me the fuck alone, he's good with me.

"You ready to blow this joint? We only have a couple hours before it's your time to shine," Los asked, wrapping his arms around me.

"I guess we need to roll because I need some of that thug lovin' outta of ya," I said, smirking.

"Aye, I don't want to hear that shit. I don't need to hear about my daughter getting nasty with a nigga," Jonathan said, walking up on the end of my statement.

"I know you ain't talking," I retorted. "I'm not the one that has a baby on the way, old man."

"Kaymee, you act like I'm fifty years old. Shid, my soldiers still marching and I'm proud of that shit. We are about to leave and I will see you at the center. My baby is about to be a college grad!" he yelled out loud.

"Hell yeah!"

"She did that!"

"I'm proud of you, Kaymee!"

"Spelman Alumni!"

Everyone was screaming some type of celebratory endearments and it made me feel so good. I just wished my mama was here to witness my accomplishments, but she was looking down on me smiling. We all piled into separate cars and headed in different directions to get ready for my graduation ceremony.

When I got home, yes, I moved in with Los. I undressed as I walked into the house, leaving a trail of clothing along the way. Entering the bedroom, I walked into the bathroom and looked in the mirror. Poetry spoke on how I was glowing and putting on weight the entire trip in Barbados. I didn't see what she meant until that moment.

My nose was wider and my face was pretty plump. Now that I was back home, I tried to think back on when I had my last period and I couldn't remember to save my life. I went into the Flo app on my phone and saw I hadn't documented anything in a couple months. Wrecking my brain for a good five minutes, I decided to take a test to be certain.

Relieving my bladder, I held the wand into the stream before I released all of it. I tore off a piece of tissue and set the application on the sink. While I waited, I turned on the shower and quickly hopped in. I ran the loofah over my body several times before getting out. My kitty was purring with the thought of my man sexing me.

"I looked at the test and to my surprise, there were two dark lines staring back at me. My eyes bulged wide and I covered my mouth with my hand. "How the fuck did this happen?" I asked myself lowly.

"Hurry up, baby! I need to drain the python!" Los hollered from the other side of the door interrupting my thoughts. I scanned the bathroom for a place to hide the test, but I couldn't find one that was good enough. "I'm coming in!" he said as the door opened.

Los didn't even look in my direction as he aimed his monster over the commode. I sighed with relief and fled the bathroom to hide the test in my underwear drawer. When I heard the water running in the sink, I jumped on the bed and got under the covers. Los loved for it to be cold as fuck in the house and I hated it.

"I thought you wanted me to fuck you to sleep, babe," he said, walking into the bedroom.

"That was the plan but after that shower, my body had other ideas. I'm sleepy." Learning I was pregnant took away my desire for sex immediately. I didn't know how Los would feel about becoming a dad and it scared me.

"Awww, well I'll give you a little something to make you fall asleep faster. You can only get about an hour and a half of sleep before you have to get up again," he said, crawling under the sheet from the foot of the bed.

Los lifted my leg up and kissed my inner thigh. My kitty started pulsating and he hadn't even got to her yet. Planting kisses on the top of my mound, he dove in head first, wrapping his tongue around my clit. I tried to lower my leg, but he wasn't having it. Los spread my legs wider and flung the sheet from his head without releasing the grip he had on my lady parts.

"Mmmm, shit," I moaned, rotating my hips into his mouth.

His tongue dipped into my tunnel like he was licking an ice cream cone. I felt my nectar oozing out with every motion. Grabbing the top of his head, I held him in place so he would continue to hit the same spot repeatedly. My stomach clinched and I knew I was about to bust a big one.

214

"Oh fuck! Right there, baby! Suck harder," I coached him on what I wanted. "Yes, Yes, Yes! Aaaaaahhhh!" I screamed out in ecstasy as I released all my love juice down his throat.

"Damn, bae. How many times do I have to tell you to warn a nigga? Yo' ass gone kill me one of these days," Los said, looking up at me with a shiny beard.

"You've been snacking on these cookies how long? You should already know when the tsunami's about to hit. Stop playing. I know you like that shit."

"I love it, but damn! It's hard for a nigga to breathe with a mouth full of fluid."

"Thank you for the tongue-lashing, baby. I got you later. Wake me in an hour," I said, rolling over.

An hour and fifteen minutes later, I was jolted out of my sleep by Los. "Mee, get up. It's time to get dressed so you can strut across that stage with yo' sexy ass."

My body was screaming one more hour, but I knew events like this couldn't be repeated. I swung my legs off the bed and stood up, stretching like a feline. The bathroom seemed so far away, but I managed get there with no problem. Taking another quick shower and freshening my mouth, I entered the bedroom with a towel wrapped around my body.

Los had my white pantsuit laid out on the bed ready for me to slip over my body. I oiled my body and slipped on the crystal-studded bra I was wearing under my suit jacket and pulled on the light linen pants. Pulling on the sea green Louboutin red bottoms Los purchased for me, I waltzed to the dresser to put on the matching accessories.

"Looking good, mama," he said, walking into the room with his sea green dress shirt and white slacks. My man looked so handsome when he cleaned up.

"You don't look so bad yourself, Mr. Pedraza," I said, adding my phone, keys, and ID to my sea green clutch. "We have to go. I have to be at the center in twenty minutes. I hope traffic isn't too bad."

"I'll get you there, baby. Don't worry," Los said, grabbing my cap and gown from the back of the door.

Following him out of the room, I remembered the pregnancy test and went back to get it. As I slipped it into my clutch, Los was calling for me to hurry up. I applied a light coat of lip gloss and hurried downstairs.

We made it to the center with five minutes to spare. I kissed him lightly on the lips and sprinted into the building while putting on my robe. The graduating class was lined up when I rounded the corner. I stepped right in line, putting my cap over my locs. Placing my Spelman sash around my neck, I was good to go for the ceremony.

The music started and we began to walk into the auditorium of the Georgia International Convention Center. I was nervous but excited at the same time. Once we were seated, the commencement started and it was boring as hell. My mind was really on the test I had in my pocketbook.

"Will Los want this baby? I just graduated college and now I'm pregnant! My career begins at Grady Hospital in two weeks, what will I do?" What will my daddy say? Will I be a good mother?" All these questions swarmed through my mind and I had to shake it off.

The Glee club had finally finished their song and the President of Spelman stepped to the podium. "Next we will hear from our valedictorian, Kaymee Morrison," she announced as I made my way to the stage. "This young woman beat all odds and walked into our building with success on her mine. Give Kaymee a round of applause, ladies and gentlemen." Everyone was on their feet and the sound was deafening.

Clearing my throat, I waited for the applause to die down before I spoke. "Congratulations to all of us today, we did it! We are moments away from being alumni's of this lovely institution and the feeling is great. Many of us fought to get here and fought harder to maintain the degree we've earned.

None of us are the same women that we were when we stepped through the doors of Spelman. We are unstoppable from this point on. We have been nurtured and prepared to conquer the world by the staff of Spelman College." Cheers from the graduates were wild.

"I'm a young girl from Chicago, Illinois that came to Georgia with a point to prove. Not to another person, but to myself. I was always told I would be another young black girl, living in the Cabrini Green projects with many babies," I said, chuckling. "I was valedictorian of my high school senior class and here I am, once again, valedictorian of Spelman College! My message to all of you today is don't let anyone, no matter who it may be, determine how your life turns out.

Take control of your destiny and succeed in every way you possibly can. I beat the odds and many of you did, too! So, in conclusion, congratulations and thanks to everyone that pushed us as black women to never quit!"

The standing ovation I received made me smile broadly. As I walked off the stage, Los was at the bottom of the stairs on bended knee, holding a ring box in his hand. The auditorium got quiet and all eyes were on us. "What are you doing?" I asked, approaching him slowly.

"I wanted to wait until afterwards, but your speech wouldn't allow me to do so. Kaymee, I've been patiently waiting on the perfect moment to ask you this question. You've been through so much and I was there a fraction of the way when you needed me. I'm here to let you know that you will never have to shed another tear behind bullshit.

Every woman needs a happy ending and I want yours to be with me. Would you give me the honor of being the best husband by becoming future Mrs. Pedraza?" Los asked.

I was stunned and couldn't find my voice, so I shook my head up and down instead, becoming a human bobblehead. My hand covered my mouth and happy tears clouded my vision. "Yes, I would love to become your wife," I screamed, throwing my arms around his neck. Los placed a beautiful ring on my finger and it was beautiful.

"She said yes!" the mayor of Georgia shouted into the mic. She was the guest speaker at the commencement and I interrupted her time on stage.

I forgot we were in the middle of the ceremony and felt embarrassed. Kissing his lips, I took a step back. "I have to get through this important moment of my life, but I would like for you to hold on to this for me," I said, handing him my clutch.

The rest of the ceremony was a blur. Los surprised the hell out of me with that proposal. It was time for me to accept the degree that I'd worked hard to achieve and I gushed with pride when my name was called.

"Kaymee Morrison," and the sounds of my family cheering me on were heard loud and clear.

"Yeah, baby girl! You did it!" Jonathan yelled.

"I'm proud of you, Kaymee. Great job," the President of the college said, hugging me.

"That's my best friend! That's my best friend!" Poetry yelled as I walked back to my seat.

Thirty minutes later, I was scanning the hall trying to find my people in the crowd. The first person I spotted was Poetry. She rushed toward me and threw her arms around my waist.

"I'm so proud of you, sis. You did that shit!"

"Nah, it took a village. We did it!" I whispered in her ear.

Breaking the hold Poetry had on me, I looked up and Los was walking toward me with a bouquet of roses in his hand. My daddy and the rest of the clan were behind him. Everyone crowded around me, congratulating me while shoving envelopes and flowers in my hands.

"Hand me my clutch, babe," I whispered in Los' ear." He gave it to me and I handed him the items in my hand. "You surprised me with that beautiful proposal and I love you for wanting to be in my life for the long haul," I said, unzipping the clutch. "I have something for you too and I hope it makes you as happy as it has made me."

Passing the test to him, I waited nervously for his reaction. Los stared at it for a couple seconds, then looked up and said,

"Thank you, God! Are you serious right now?" he asked excitedly. His reaction alone brought me to tears and I knew we would be alright as husband and wife.

"Yes, it's real. We are having a baby!" I confirmed.

"A what? Come again," my daddy said, looking over Los' shoulder.

"You heard right, daddy. Your baby girl is a graduate of Spelman, a Neonatal Nurse at Grady's, and a mother to be!" I beamed with pride. Los hugged me so tight, I didn't even hear what my daddy said in response. He wouldn't let me go and blessed the side of my face with tears of joy.

"I love you so much, Kaymee. I promise I will love you 'til the end of time."

"I love you back. We are about to show the world how to love without any hurt," I said, smacking him on the ass with a laugh.

The End

Submission Guideline

Submit the first three chapters of your completed manuscript to ldpsubmissions@gmail.com, subject line: Your book's title. The manuscript must be in a .doc file and sent as an attachment. Document should be in Times New Roman, double spaced and in size 12 font. Also, provide your synopsis and full contact information. If sending multiple submissions, they must each be in a separate email.

Have a story but no way to send it electronically? You can still submit to LDP/Ca$h Presents. Send in the first three chapters, written or typed, of your completed manuscript to:

LDP: Submissions Dept
Po Box 870494
Mesquite, Tx 75187

DO NOT send original manuscript. Must be a duplicate.

Provide your synopsis and a cover letter containing your full contact information.

Thanks for considering LDP and Ca$h Presents.

BOW DOWN TO MY GANGSTA
By **Ca$h**
TORN BETWEEN TWO
By **Coffee**
BLOOD STAINS OF A SHOTTA **III**
By **Jamaica**
STEADY MOBBIN **III**
By **Marcellus Allen**
BLOOD OF A BOSS **VI**
By **Askari**
LOYAL TO THE GAME **IV**
LIFE OF SIN III
By **T.J. & Jelissa**
A DOPEBOY'S PRAYER **II**
By **Eddie "Wolf" Lee**
IF LOVING YOU IS WRONG… **III**
LOVE ME EVEN WHEN IT HURTS **III**
By **Jelissa**
TRUE SAVAGE **VII**
By **Chris Green**
BLAST FOR ME **III**
DUFFLE BAG CARTEL III
By **Ghost**
ADDICTIED TO THE DRAMA **III**
By **Jamila Mathis**
A HUSTLER'S DECEIT 3
KILL ZONE **II**
BAE BELONGS TO ME III

Meesha

SOUL OF A MONSTER
By **Aryanna**
THE COST OF LOYALTY **III**
By **Kweli**
SHE FELL IN LOVE WITH A REAL ONE **II**
By **Tamara Butler**
RENEGADE BOYS **III**
By **Meesha**
CORRUPTED BY A GANGSTA **IV**
By **Destiny Skai**
A GANGSTER'S CODE **III**
By **J-Blunt**
KING OF NEW YORK V
RISE TO POWER III
COKE KINGS II
By **T.J. Edwards**
GORILLAZ IN THE BAY III
De'Kari
THE STREETS ARE CALLING II
Duquie Wilson
KINGPIN KILLAZ IV
STREET KINGS 2
PAID IN BLOOD 2
Hood Rich
SINS OF A HUSTLA II
ASAD
TRIGGADALE II
Elijah R. Freeman
MARRIED TO A BOSS III
By **Destiny Skai & Chris Green**

KINGS OF THE GAME III
Playa Ray

Available Now
RESTRAINING ORDER **I & II**
By **CA$H & Coffee**
LOVE KNOWS NO BOUNDARIES **I II & III**
By **Coffee**
RAISED AS A GOON I, II, III & IV
BRED BY THE SLUMS I, II, III
BLAST FOR ME I & II
ROTTEN TO THE CORE I III
A BRONX TALE I, II, III
DUFFEL BAG CARTEL I II
By **Ghost**
LAY IT DOWN **I & II**
LAST OF A DYING BREED
BLOOD STAINS OF A SHOTTA I & II
By **Jamaica**
LOYAL TO THE GAME
LOYAL TO THE GAME II
LOYAL TO THE GAME III
LIFE OF SIN I, II
By **TJ & Jelissa**
BLOODY COMMAS I & II
SKI MASK CARTEL I II & III
KING OF NEW YORK I II,III IV
RISE TO POWER I II
COKE KINGS

Meesha

By **T.J. Edwards**

IF LOVING HIM IS WRONG…I & II

LOVE ME EVEN WHEN IT HURTS I II

By **Jelissa**

WHEN THE STREETS CLAP BACK I & II III

By **Jibril Williams**

A DISTINGUISHED THUG STOLE MY HEART I II & III

LOVE SHOULDN'T HURT I II III IV

RENEGADE BOYS I & II

By **Meesha**

A GANGSTER'S CODE I &, II III

By **J-Blunt**

PUSH IT TO THE LIMIT

By **Bre' Hayes**

BLOOD OF A BOSS **I, II, III, IV, V**

By **Askari**

THE STREETS BLEED MURDER **I, II & III**

THE HEART OF A GANGSTA I II& III

By **Jerry Jackson**

CUM FOR ME

CUM FOR ME 2

CUM FOR ME 3

CUM FOR ME 4

An **LDP Erotica Collaboration**

BRIDE OF A HUSTLA **I II & II**

THE FETTI GIRLS **I, II& III**

CORRUPTED BY A GANGSTA I, II & III

By **Destiny Skai**

WHEN A GOOD GIRL GOES BAD

By **Adrienne**

224

GANGSTA SHYT **I II &III**
By **CATO**
THE ULTIMATE BETRAYAL
By **Phoenix**
BOSS'N UP **I , II & III**
By **Royal Nicole**
I LOVE YOU TO DEATH
By Destiny J
I RIDE FOR MY HITTA
I STILL RIDE FOR MY HITTA
By **Misty Holt**
LOVE & CHASIN' PAPER
By **Qay Crockett**
TO DIE IN VAIN
SINS OF A HUSTLA
By **ASAD**
BROOKLYN HUSTLAZ
By **Boogsy Morina**
BROOKLYN ON LOCK I & II
By **Sonovia**
GANGSTA CITY
By **Teddy Duke**
A DRUG KING AND HIS DIAMOND I & II III
A DOPEMAN'S RICHES
HER MAN, MINE'S TOO I, II
CASH MONEY HO'S
By Nicole Goosby
TRAPHOUSE KING **I II & III**
KINGPIN KILLAZ I II III
STREET KINGS

PAID IN BLOOD
By **Hood Rich**
LIPSTICK KILLAH **I, II, III**
CRIME OF PASSION I & II
By **Mimi**
STEADY MOBBN' **I, II, III**
By **Marcellus Allen**
WHO SHOT YA **I, II, III**
Renta
GORILLAZ IN THE BAY **I II**
DE'KARI
TRIGGADALE
Elijah R. Freeman
GOD BLESS THE TRAPPERS I, II, III
THESE SCANDALOUS STREETS I, II, III
FEAR MY GANGSTA I, II, III
THESE STREETS DON'T LOVE NOBODY I, II
BURY ME A G I, II, III, IV, V
A GANGSTA'S EMPIRE I, II, III
Tranay Adams
THE STREETS ARE CALLING
Duquie Wilson
MARRIED TO A BOSS… I II
By **Destiny Skai & Chris Green**
KINGS OF THE GAME I II
Playa Ray

BOOKS BY LDP'S CEO, CA$H

TRUST IN NO MAN

TRUST IN NO MAN 2

TRUST IN NO MAN 3

BONDED BY BLOOD

SHORTY GOT A THUG

THUGS CRY

THUGS CRY 2

THUGS CRY 3

TRUST NO BITCH

TRUST NO BITCH 2

TRUST NO BITCH 3

TIL MY CASKET DROPS

RESTRAINING ORDER

RESTRAINING ORDER 2

IN LOVE WITH A CONVICT

Coming Soon

BONDED BY BLOOD 2

BOW DOWN TO MY GANGSTA

Love Shouldn't Hurt 4